Bottle It Up

A Between the Pines Novel

Lisa Shelby

Also by Lisa Shelby

<u>Disregarded Heart</u>

A Grumpy / Sunshine, single dad contemporary romance.

The Between the Pines Series

Meet *The Crew* from Eastlyn in this series of standalone contemporary romance novels about found family.

<u>Raised On It</u>

<u>Bottle It Up</u>

Want to read Reece and Rachel's story? Sign-up for my newsletter and get their novella for FREE! <u>Click here for your copy of We Are Tonight!</u>

<u>Blackbird</u>

Standalone second chance contemporary romance.

The Gorgeous Duet

A steamy, suspenseful romance about breaking the rules and following your heart.

<u>Gorgeous: Book One</u>

<u>Gorgeous: Book Two</u>

The You & Me Series

Read this three-book series of sweet and sexy standalone novels filled with love, loss, secrets, and sass.

<u>You & Me: Part One</u>

<u>You & Me: Part Two</u>

<u>More</u>

<u>Something Just Like This</u>

Bottle It Up

(A Between the Pines Novel)

By
Lisa Shelby

Bottle It Up
(A Between the Pines Novel)

By

Lisa Shelby
Bottle It Up

Previously released as Dangerous Distraction.
Cover Design: Sarah Kil Creative Studio
Editor: Jenny @ Editing4Indies

S,

I know I don't need to say it, but I love you so much more.

~ L

*To Sam Hunt and everyone involved in creating the songs on,
Between the Pines - Acoustic Mixtape album,*

*Thank you for all the road trip sing-a-longs and for providing me
the vibe I needed to create Eastlyn.*

~ L

Chapter One

"Well, *Trespass* sounds like you're going to have another hit on your hands. I mean, Josh West and Kyle Day in the same film? Two of Hollywood's Sexiest Men Alive on screen together for the first time. You do know what a big deal this is to your fans around the world, don't you?"

"Well, I sure hope you're right, Candy. What I do know is we had a blast filming it. I just hope the fans are ready for a whole new level of action. I'm in it, and I still can't believe how great it looks on the big screen. And I really do hope folks will go out and see this in the theater because it's meant to be watched on the big screen. I promise they won't be disappointed."

"They may not be disappointed in the film, but if the rumors are true, I think many women out there may be disappointed to hear you're no longer single."

Here we go.

When Josh doesn't take the bait, Candy gets to the point. "So, are the rumors true?"

"Now, Candy. You know I don't like to talk about my personal life."

"Indulge me, Josh."

"What is it you'd like to know?"

There's a buzz around the room with the possibility that the network may be getting the scoop on Hollywood's most eligible bachelor. The cameraman next to me zooms in on Josh's flirty smile, ready for the shot to come back to him in his sexy worn leather jacket, black T-shirt, dark jeans, and rugged boot ensemble. Everything about him says sex on a stick. Even I can see it, and I love him like a brother. There's no denying his sex appeal.

"Well, your longtime friend, as you've called her in the past, seems to be wearing a very significant new piece of jewelry. Many would say she's more than a friend and someone who's actually pretty special in your life."

We have liftoff.

"Well, I have lots of friends, you know that." He winks, and one of the most respected national morning anchors blushes, no match for his charm. "But, yes, you are correct. There is someone special in my life, but that's really all I'm comfortable sharing."

Mission accomplished.

My existence has been confirmed, as well as the fact that I'm "someone special." But nothing more.

"And would you look at that? We're just getting to the good stuff, and we're out of time. Josh, it's been great having you back here on Wake Up America."

"It's always a pleasure, Candy. Thanks for having me."

Candy turns to the camera to sign off. "Thank you to the always endearing Josh West for being here today, and make sure you go to the theater this Friday to see Josh and Kyle Day in Trespass. Have a great day, America."

The room stays quiet for a silent count of three before a crew member announces, "And...we're clear."

I watch Josh do what he does best from my dark corner of the studio.

Act.

Thanking Candy and indulging her with a selfie, he acts like the superstar he is to the rest of the world. But deep down, he's still the small-town boy from Eastlyn, Oregon, who has been my best friend since grade school.

His fans around the planet think he belongs to them, and to a certain extent, he does. But a part of him will always belong to The Crew and me. When Josh is with his friends from home, you can see him breathe a little easier, stress a little less, and get just a little bit closer to being his true self. At least as close as he's ever going to get.

He's stopped again by members of the studio crew on his way to where I'm waiting behind the cameras, shooting me a look that says he's trying to get to me, and he's sorry.

His look in my direction piques the interest of others loitering around the sound stage, and I can feel several pairs of eyes and camera phones focused on me. I've learned to ignore the stares over the years. Unfortunately, it's something you have to do if you're going to spend time on the arm of Oscar-winning Josh West.

Finally free, he reaches me. "So, how'd I do?" he asks, even though he knows he did great.

He always does great.

"I don't think you need me to tell you how you did. I would say the blush on Candy's face made it pretty clear how you did."

He smiles that smile of his, and I see his eyes dart to the right for just a milli-second before he pushes a stray hair behind my ear and whispers, "Thank you," in my ear. At this exact moment, I hear the snapping of pictures being taken on more than one phone, and for the first time since this whole plan fell into place, I feel a little piece of myself slipping away.

This sweet, sexy moment was all for the cameras.

Nothing more.

I'm not surprised. This is exactly what I signed up for, but now that the ball has begun to roll, it's all feeling so real.

I shake off the hollow feeling and look into my best friend's eyes. His eyes say he's sorry, and he hates that we're doing this.

Is he having second thoughts?

After our fake moment has been well documented, we leave the studio with his publicist, Sibby, and his manager Jace. Once inside the black SUV waiting for us on the busy New York city street, we have a moment alone while Jace and Sibby talk on the sidewalk.

"This is more than you signed up for, isn't it?"

"What?" Yes. No. I don't know. "No, it's fine."

"Emmett, I know you better than you know yourself, and the reality of all of this is hitting you a bit more than you anticipated. I know it is. I saw you flinch when you heard the snap of that picture. Listen, I know you signed a contract, Emmy, but this is you and me. If this is too much, please let me know. We aren't in so deep that we can't end it now."

His face breaks my heart. I know internally he's warring with himself. He loves me. We've always been there for each other, and we always will be. There isn't anything I wouldn't do for him, and right now, he's afraid, desperate, and needs me.

"Nah, I'm fine, Josh. It's just going to take me a minute to adjust to this lifestyle. You'd think I'd be used to it after all of these years as your plus one, but I'm not sure I'll ever get used to people taking my picture."

He grabs my hand. "Thank you, Emmy. Love you." His words, are filled with sincerity, and I know I'm doing the right thing.

"Love you too, Joshy Washy."

The quiet of our moment ends with a rush of cold air and a flurry of activity when Sibby joins us in the back seat and Jace climbs in the front passenger seat with Reeves, the head of Josh's security team, who hops in the driver's seat and puts the car in motion.

"Listen, we have a small issue and need to have an emergency team meeting."

"Is everything okay?" Josh asks as his hand tightens around mine.

"Everything's fine, but with the official addition of Emmett into your life as your special someone, we need to rally the troops and make sure we're all on the same page," Sibby answers him without lifting her eyes from her phone. "Emmett on your arm with the addition of a ring on her finger means a lot more work for the rest of us, Josh. We're already stretched thin, and now we have another person to worry about. As if your life wasn't crazy enough."

"Sibby!" Josh interjects after her rude implication, but she cuts him off.

"I'm not being rude. I'm just being honest."

"You could be a little kinder and not make her feel like an inconvenience."

"Emmett, you know I think you're great, right?" she asks me, finally lifting her eyes off her phone. She doesn't fake a smile; she simply doesn't have the time for bullshit. I get it.

Sibby Spencer is the epitome of a no-nonsense woman who has earned the power she demands. She's the best at what she does, and this is why she works for Josh, as well as many other high-profile celebrities. She is also alarmingly beautiful, with her trademark platinum blond hair pulled into a tight chignon at the nape of her neck. Her pale complexion is always highlighted with the perfect smoky eye and matte red lipstick. And her wardrobe is something dreams are made of. Her perfection and directness have always intimidated me, and today is no different.

I smile in reply, wondering where this is going, when her attention turns to my fiancé. Man, that sounds so odd. No matter how many times I tell family and friends I'm engaged or pretend to be excited about the size of my ring. It still sounds so strange.

Probably because it's a lie.

It should feel strange.

"Listen, from a PR perspective; it's more work but also a part of the job. For Jace, it means he has another person to manage into your schedule. Tabitha will have another person to style, and we'll probably have to add a permanent hair and makeup crew just for Emmett, not to mention Reeves has another person to protect. I think the only person not affected is Paul. As your agent, the addition of Emmett shouldn't affect his job too much, but he still needs to be informed, and we all need to be on the same page. Besides, Emmett will need to get used to team meetings interrupting her life. You know that, Josh."

Whoa...I feel like I've moved to another planet and not just another state. Eastlyn, Oregon, may only be one state up from sunny Los Angeles, California, on the map, but the two towns couldn't be farther apart when it comes to lifestyle and pace of life. I've jumped on quite the roller coaster ride, and now that I'm strapped in, the wheels are turning, and we're headed to the top of the first big dip in the ride. But I'm all in. I couldn't get off even if I wanted to.

This ride is in motion, and I am most certainly not in control.

Chapter Two

"Hey, Emmy. You ready? Everyone's here."

Closing my book, I hold in my sigh so Josh doesn't notice my exasperation at stopping everything for another Josh-related meeting. Even if stopping everything means simply placing my bookmark in my book. It's not like it's a big inconvenience. My life here in LA is just as dull as it was in Eastlyn, even if it's busier than it's ever been.

I worked from home back in Oregon, and nothing has changed now that I'm here in sunny California. I work, read, and have the occasional fitting for fancy clothes I'll wear once because God forbid I be seen in the same dress twice. Except for the difference in the sizes on the tags, you would think my name was Kate, and I lived in a royal palace. It's absolutely ridiculous, but I've made sure to leave an entire section in my closet that is me—jeans, yoga pants, T-shirts, hoodies, and of course, comfortable shoes. That's my favorite part of the giant room, bigger than my entire bedroom at home—the comfy section.

Besides being fitted for one-time-use dresses, I answer questions on how I want the house decorated, and in the two short weeks since Josh confirmed he has someone special in his life, we've attended the New York premiere of Trespass. Thank goodness the movie had already been released internationally before I got to LA, so I didn't have to travel the globe for the sole purpose of appearing in pictures with him. Other than the premiere, we've had two charity events, one celebrity birthday party, and one dinner with an award-winning director who Josh is hoping to convince to direct his passion project.

We're busy, and I shouldn't be bored, but the reality is, I'm just here as decoration. Or maybe distraction would be a better way to describe my presence.

I pretty much work all day and then play dress-up at night. At most of the events we've attended, I'm barely spoken to and nearly as invisible as his bodyguard, Reeves, who goes everywhere with Josh. Some sort of business is constantly being discussed when those around us don't have their heads entirely up Josh's ass. Now, here we are in another meeting about how we can all make Josh's career stay on top or, better yet, skyrocket even further out into the universe, if that's even possible.

I'm just there for the photo op.

"Everyone's here? This wasn't on the schedule, you know?"

He shrugs. What can he say? It's not his doing. He's at Jace's and Sibby's mercy as much as I am.

"Did you go and get another fiancée that you haven't told me about?"

"Ha. Nope. One is more than enough." He extends his hand to help pull me off the plush white couch I have no business being near. I keep waiting for my first spill. "You never know what's up with these last-minute meetings. Glad I have you by my side for them these days, though."

He waits for me to pop an Altoid in my mouth but shakes his head no when I lift the tin to offer him one. I always have mints nearby; it's an addiction I've had since high school. Then, fresh breath taken care of, he wraps his arm around my shoulders and guides me through his colossal mansion. I hate to admit it, but I've gotten lost in here on more than one occasion.

"Happy to be here, Josh."

"So, you're reading another one of Mason's books?" he asks, referring to the book series our friend Miles's girlfriend wrote. She writes under the pen name of Nina Patrick, which sounds more mysterious than Mason O'Brien, her real name.

She's become a good friend, and I thought I would be a good friend in return and check out her work. Only now, I find myself addicted to her fictional world. I can't wait to finish so I can watch the TV series they adapted from her books. Her work is all about the feels but sexy as hell too. Between the pages is the only place I'll be getting any of these sexy feelings for the next couple of years.

"Yep, on book four. She's really good, Josh. It's too bad they already made a TV series because I could totally see you starring as the lead in the film version."

"Is that so?"

"Yep, the hero of these books is an arrogant pretty boy who leaves broken hearts in his wake until he finds the love of his life."

"Did you just call me an arrogant pretty boy?"

I wrap my arm around his waist and pull him closer. "I said you could play the part well. But if the personality traits fit..."

His arm around my shoulders quickly turns into a headlock, and his knuckles gently apply a noogie to the top of my head.

Some things never change.

"You better watch yourself, Emmy."

Opening my mouth to reply, I opt to remain silent when I see six pairs of prying eyes when we enter the dining room, and my words go running back inside my head. The other people in the room look very serious, and our immature antics feel very out of place.

Scanning the room, I recognize his manager Jace, publicist Sibby, and his agent Paul all sitting on Josh's plush white dining chairs in front of the dark table that screams masculine and modern. Reeves stands at the end of the table with two other men in dark suits similar to his. Reeves is tall and strong, but the man standing next to him is intimidating, to say the least.

Reeves's new team member has all of my attention: tall, barrel-chested, and devastatingly handsome in that "rugged, don't mess with me" way. But, unfortunately, everything about him says he's all business with no intention of making friends with anyone in the room.

Suddenly, team meetings have gotten a bit more interesting and inviting.

"Josh. Emmett. Please have a seat." Sibby motions to two empty chairs across from her, Jace and Paul.

Crap. Maybe serious guy is serious for a reason.

"What's going on, Sibby? Reeves, who are your friends?"

"Go ahead, Reeves." Sibby relinquishes the honors of explaining today's get-together.

"Mr. West, we've brought in additional protection for Miss Ford. I'd like to introduce you to Mr—"

"Just call me Hopper, sir." Serious guy interrupts Reeves, and surprisingly, Josh's head of security takes a step back and lets him take over. "Some threats have been made toward Miss Ford, and we're here to make sure she stays safe while you're away, and Reeves is accompanying you. This is Smith." He motions to the shaggy-haired blond also in a suit who Reeves is now standing next to. "He and I will stay here in Los Angeles with Miss Ford while you're away."

"What threats?" Josh asks the question stuck in my throat.

Reeves steps forward and slides a folder across the table toward Josh.

"What is this?" Josh asks, seemingly afraid to open the folder.

"Sir, an envelope was delivered today via the regular mail containing photos of Miss Ford, and they've caused us a bit of alarm. But it isn't anything we can't handle."

"What do you mean alarm? Here, let me see that." I huff, snatching the folder from Josh.

I throw the folder open with an attitude that swiftly fades to a whimper when I see the photos that have caused all the fuss. There are pictures of me, but they have been manipulated and show horrible things happening to me. Decapitation. Stabbing. My eyes ripped out and hanging from their sockets. You name it, and they've made it happen to me. There are no threatening words, just the primarily black and white paparazzi photos covered in blood red. And destruction.

"What the fuck? Who the hell would send something like this?" Josh asks yet another question I'd love the answer to.

Serious guy, Hopper, speaks again. "Sir, we're certain it's just a scare tactic from a jealous fan who hasn't taken too well to the new woman in your life." His eyes flick to mine ever so briefly, and even with the pictures laid out in front of me, I'd be lying if I said one look from him didn't make me so hot and bothered I nearly pick one of the pictures up to fan myself. "These are all photos taken by the paparazzi and have appeared in magazines, so we're pretty sure they aren't stalking Miss Ford to take the pictures. This is a good thing."

A good thing? Really? Are we finding the ray of light in this mess already?

"I want this asshole found now!" Josh bellows, pounding his fist into the cherry wood table. His rage sends a chill down my spine. I've never seen him like this.

"Hey, Josh. Calm down, man. We've got the best men on the job, and they'll keep Emmett safe. It's gonna be okay." Jace speaks up from across the table. He seems to be the only person who can make Josh see reason when he's worked up.

Sibby speaks directly to me and not to Josh. It's rather nice for a change. "You okay, Emmett?"

"Uh..." That's a very good question. "I think so, Sibby. Thank you for asking. I'm sure it's no big deal, and I appreciate the extra security, but I hate to be a burden."

"A burden?" Josh yells, looking at me as though I've lost my mind. "How are you a burden? It's not your fault that because you've agreed to be a part of my shitstorm of a life, there is some psycho out there doing this." He refers to the folder that he closes and slides back to Reeves. "This is not your fault, and I promise you, we'll do everything we can to keep you safe."

"Still..."

"No! Don't even go there, Emmett." He turns to the security team. "Tell us what to do, and we'll do it."

"There isn't much to do. We'll just need to make sure we go over both of your schedules to a T so we can plan. We'll also need a list of family and friends who should have clearance. Let's start with your schedules."

This is where Jace comes in. He knows precisely how Josh is going to spend every minute of every day for the next year or two. He has copies of Josh's itinerary for the film shoot he'll be leaving for in a few days and hands them out to everyone in attendance.

After we've gone over our schedules, all but the security team leaves, and I give them the names of my friends, family, and co-workers, so they have a list of approved people in my life.

Who would have ever thought I would be in a position to have to come up with a list like this? Or that I would be giving it to a team of bodyguards who are hotter than should be legal yet scary as all get-out. But mostly hot. It's so unfair when I have two years of celibacy ahead of me.

Reeves is your standard bodyguard. He has short dark hair and is attractive but not so handsome he stands out in a crowd. Smith looks like he rides big waves in his downtime with his sun-bleached waves curling around his neckline. They're both handsome, tall, and don't have an ounce of fat on them, but with Hopper in the room, I barely notice them.

When he was standing at the other end of the table, I was instantly attracted to him. But now, he's sitting in the chair next to me, going over the detailed list of people in my life, and I have an up-close and personal view.

It's as though I'm seeing him in HD.

His hair, which looked jet black from across the room, is subtly littered with bits of silver at his temples. His hair may be dark brown and not black, after all. There is a small scar above his eyebrow, one farther up on his forehead near his hairline, one on his chin, and one on his cheek that is round and barely there. I can't help but wonder if he can grow hair there if he were to grow a beard. However, all the scars have faded and are only noticeable due to our proximity.

It only takes a few minutes to give them the information they need, and much to my dismay, the room empties, leaving Josh and me alone at the dining room table.

"Fuck, Emmy. I am so sorry. I should have never asked you to come here."

"You didn't. I offered, remember?"

"If you had known this was going to happen, would you have volunteered to come here and play the part of my significant other?"

"It's only two years, Josh, and you've worked too hard to get where you are. Besides, it's not like you aren't giving me a great life. I mean, look at this place: the house, the clothes, the hobnobbing with the rich and famous. You haven't sold me into some sort of indentured slavery. There are worse situations I could be in. Best of all, I get to hang out with you more."

"But I have to leave. There's a psycho out there threatening you, and I'm supposed to leave you here for the next two months alone. This just doesn't feel right."

"It's your job, and I knew you would be gone a lot."

"Come with me, Emmy."

"You don't need me around. This is your chance to spend time with Jace. The world thinks you have a fiancée. Use the time in a faraway land to be with the one you love. Along with filming, you'll be in the middle of negotiations, so you don't need any distractions. It's the perfect reason for your manager to travel with you, and I have to go back home to Eastlyn for the store opening and Thanksgiving. Don't give me a second thought."

"Emmy, this feels so wrong."

"Well, it is what it is, and you're leaving me with a couple of big, strong studs. So I think I'll be just fine."

"How can you think about men at a time like this?" he asks incredulously.

"Gimme a break. Are you gonna sit there and try to tell me you didn't notice all the hotness in the room? And I'm not referring to you or Jace. You'd have to be blind not to notice."

Josh and Jace are quite the couple. Josh is tall and lean with his light brown hair and megawatt smile. Jace is several inches shorter than Josh but still fit and adorable with his olive complexion and chocolate waves tamed with a tight haircut.

"That big one, the boss man? I thought his biceps were gonna rip right through the arms of his suit," Josh admits quietly.

"Uh-huh. That's what I thought. It's a good thing he's staying home with me. Otherwise, he may cause some drama for you and Jace."

He looks at me sweetly. "Thank you, Em. I know what you're giving up to help me, and I'll never be able to thank you enough. Jace and I both appreciate you more than you know."

"Stop it. This is what friends do," I say, getting up from my chair, indicating I'm done and don't want to discuss it further.

"I'd say you're going above and beyond the terms and conditions of most friendships."

When we walk into the kitchen, Reeves and the bodyguard I'm calling Smith the Surfer in my head are in deep discussion. They both go mute when we enter, and I'm surprised to feel a pang of disappointment that the brawny, brooding one Josh called boss man is nowhere to be found. I miss him and all of his teeny tiny scars already.

Oh, this is bad.

Very, very bad.

Chapter Three

"Thank you, Hopper," I say just as formally as I have every other time I've spoken to the stone-cold, ice in his veins bodyguard.

It's been fourteen days since I first laid eyes on the stiff-backed man driving me to my yoga class today. Of those fourteen days, I have seen him ten. Yes, I know the number of days because on the weekends when he wasn't taking up residence at the kitchen island, I walked around with a pit of despair in my stomach.

It's not rational, but it's the truth.

On a couple of days, he's spent the afternoon in the security room, but just knowing he's in the house makes my day better.

We have yet to have an actual conversation. Not for my lack of trying. He doesn't seem interested in talking or me for that matter. Nonetheless, he is all I think about.

When we're out, he's always dressed to match my day's activity, and he is sure to be found standing with his feet shoulder-width apart, and his massive arms in front of him with his hands clasped. It's as though his life's goal is to become one with the wall or wherever he's standing so he can disappear. I know it's his job not to draw attention, but he doesn't appear to be much of a people person either.

Josh left a little over a week ago, and for the most part, I've stayed in and kept myself busy with work. I've gone on a couple of walks in the evening, but Smith was with me then. Smith isn't as bulky as Hopper, but he, too, is professional. Thank goodness, he's relaxed a little bit and will carry on a conversation with me since Josh left town. Hopper, not so much.

Today is my first outing with just Hopper and me alone in the car. And nothing has changed. He called me ma'am when he opened the back door for me, and then he got in the car and started driving.

No talking.

Just driving.

I took advantage of my ten seconds alone to watch him walk around the front of the sleek black Audi SUV. He's just so damn hot. And big. Not big like he does steroids, but big like he was born that way, and he lifts weights to accentuate what the good Lord gave him.

What I wouldn't give to catch him looking at me in the rearview mirror. But nope, it is evident that I am only his client. And his engaged client, at that. I know he knows the details of our situation and that the term *engaged* should be said with air quotes to those in the know, but we have never spoken about it.

Of course, we haven't. That would entail a conversation with my day shift babysitter. Smith, my night shift babysitter, is much more congenial, but he doesn't twist my insides into knots like Hopper does.

I try to remember if he had an accent the day he spoke at the meeting. Maybe that's why he rarely speaks. Maybe English isn't his first language? But unfortunately, there was so much going on in my head that day, and I can't remember. I do remember every detail of his face, but not whether or not he had a hint of an accent.

After ten minutes of awkward silence, he pulls the SUV up to the curb in front of the yoga studio where I'm meeting pop icon and now my friend, Nicolette Gwen. She's the only new friend I've made since becoming a part of Josh's life, and she's decided to take me under her wing for some odd reason. It doesn't get any bigger or better than Nicolette. Or, as I now call her, Nikki.

Hopper gets out of the SUV, and before he opens my back door, he lifts his sunglasses, places them on top of his head, and takes a look inside the studio. I guess he's making sure things are on the up and up. Once he deems the studio worthy, he heads to the car. Thank goodness because I was feeling awkward, wondering if I should let myself out or wait for him. I don't know how to handle this whole driver thing yet.

The door opens, and I step down onto the sidewalk, putting myself directly in front of my giant protector. I'm fairly tall for a woman at five feet nine inches, but I feel like one of Snow White's roommates standing next to him.

"Thank you," I say, looking him in the eyes for the first time in such close proximity. His eyes, which I can now confirm, are a hazel mixture of golds and greens, have locked on mine and knocked all the air from my lungs. My heart is pounding, and as labored as my breath is, you'd think I had already done an hour's worth of yoga.

"Ma'am," he says, his face giving nothing away, but his eyes are searching for something in mine.

Whoa.

Still, he only speaks a single word, but I feel it deep down inside.

I know our gaze only locks for a second or two, but it feels as though we've been standing on the sidewalk staring at each other for a lifetime.

He's the one to break the spell when he shuts my door and starts walking toward the entrance to the yoga studio. He's dressed casually today in jeans and a plain white T-shirt. His olive skin stands outs, and up this close, I can see that his barely-there haircut has recently been shorn to perfection.

Catching our reflection in the window, I look small next to him. I'm no waif. I have curves, and there is undoubtedly a bit of a bubble to the butt filling my yoga pants, but I look tiny with his reflection next to mine. Tiny is certainly not a word that has ever been used to describe me, but I feel comfortable in my own skin and have never felt the need to change anything about myself. Well, maybe my hair. I do change that regularly. At the moment, it's an auburn red and up in a ponytail.

Hopper reaches for the door, and I see him notice me watching us in the window.

Crap!

How embarrassing is that?

Of course, he doesn't utter a word or give any hint of emotion. Instead, he simply opens the door for me to walk through.

I'm just about to the front desk to check-in when the door that just clicked closed reopens, and Nikki announces her arrival.

"There she is! The girl Hollywood is buzzing about." Her arms are open wide, and her smile is infectious. "Get over here and give me a hug. I haven't seen you since Vegas. Texts are not enough!"

"It's great to see you. Thanks so much for getting me out of the house," I say while being wrapped up in a great big bear hug from the tiny blond waif of a woman.

"Darlin', if you bring eye candy like this with you, I'll be sure to get you out of the house more often," she whispers in my ear, and I giggle in return, unable to control the itty-bitty twinge of jealousy that bites at me unexpectedly. I mean, who would look at me when there's an icon in nothing but a sports bra and yoga shorts standing next to me? Not sure it's possible, but she looks even better in person.

Her bodyguard is here as well, but he's not nearly as attractive as Hopper, and he's already up at the front desk chatting with the receptionist.

Doing what I assume is the polite thing, I introduce her to Hopper. He extends a hand to Nikki, and once again, that little green monster tries to reach the surface. I've never even gotten to shake his hand, which hardly seems fair. Not one little bit.

Nikki happily takes his hand and says, "You can relax, you know. I rent the place out for one-on-one training. Nobody's here but the four of us and the trainer. Well, and I guess the receptionist. There isn't anybody here to kill. Just stay up here with Mark, and I promise to take good care of her."

He nods, but his eyes lock on mine to ask if I'm okay with this. I nod back, letting him know it's cool. After holding my gaze one quick second, he moves toward the door and leans against the wall next to it. Back straight. Hands clasped in front of him.

Nikki walks arm and arm with me to the back room, where the trainer waits for us. "Good God, woman. He's as sexy as he is serious. Hubba, hubba."

"I agree, but he doesn't have much of a personality."

"Don't take it personally. Those are the rules. He's just trying to keep it professional. As much time as we spend with our staff, especially our personal protection, we would all be having torrid affairs with them, and the paparazzi would have a field day. He knows what he's doing. Trust him and follow his lead."

"You're right. I know you are. This is all just a huge adjustment for me. I miss driving myself around, and I hate the opening and closing of the car door. I just don't know what to do. Let myself out? Wait for him? Ugh, I have no clue what I'm doing."

"Ask him later what he prefers when it comes to letting yourself out of the car. Otherwise, try to take your mind off the hot giant in reception and focus on your mind, body, and soul." She tries to stay serious, but she bursts out laughing within two seconds. "Ha! Who am I kidding? There's no getting that tall drink of water out of your head."

"You're bad; you know that?"

"I do, but that's why we're friends, right?"

"Ladies, are we ready?" With her dark curls piled on top of her hair and not one stitch of makeup, our perfect-looking yogi is the picture of Zen when she asks very kindly, telling us to shut our traps and get into position.

Hopper was outside waiting for me next to the Audi when the class had finished. Unfortunately, his sunglasses were back on, covering his hazel eyes again. Now, I'm sitting in the back of the car, and he's jumping into the driver's seat.

He starts down the road, and I pick up my phone to occupy myself during what I am sure is about to be another silent ride when I'm startled by the sound of his voice.

"Ma'am, we're going to have to take the long way home." I look up and find him looking back at me in the rearview mirror. If only he didn't have his shades on. But at least I can confirm there is no accent. It appears English is his native tongue, after all.

"Is everything okay?" I ask, trying to prolong the conversation.

"Everything is fine, ma'am. Shouldn't be too long," he replies but picks up his phone and makes a call.

From what I can gather from his side of a couple of different phone calls, Smith is in a matching Audi, and he is letting him, and another driver know where we are so we can sync up and then separate and confuse someone who may be following us.

Why do I get the feeling things aren't really fine?

"Excuse me, but is everything really okay?"

"Yes, ma'am. There were just some pictures posted online of you and Miss Gwen entering the yoga studio, which means your whereabouts are known. It's best to add some confusion to the situation if someone is following us."

"I guess this is what I should expect if I hang out with Nikki. I mean, she is the biggest pop star alive right now."

"Ma'am, the headline was about you, not Miss Gwen."

"Why in the world would anyone care where I go to work out?"

"To the world, you are the woman who stole the heart of Josh West. People care."

"Well, they need to get a life because that's just sad."

I swear his eyes crinkle behind his glasses from a smile, but I'll never know for sure.

We ride along in our usual silence once again, and even though I hear Nikki's advice in my ears about keeping it professional, I figure it can't hurt to ask some basic questions. I can keep it professional. Work-related. Besides, he spoke to me while looking at me in the rearview mirror. I would say we're making progress.

"So, how long have you been in this line of work?" I ask, feigning confidence.

"Nine years." He replies with a clipped tone that says, where is this going?

"How did you get into the bodyguard business?"

There is a beat of silence that has me internally pleading with him not to shut me down, and I'm barely able to hold back a squeal when he answers.

"Made some connections in the military."

"Do you like what you do?"

"Yes, ma'am."

"The schedule doesn't get to you?"

"No, ma'am."

Enough with the ma'ams!

"Where are you from?"

"Back East," he bites.

His answers are clipped and given through a clenched jaw. I don't think he is enjoying my rousing round of twenty questions.

"Would you rather I not ask about your personal life?" I ask, trying to be respectful of his privacy.

Silence.

It's no wonder I feel so alone. I can't even make friends with the people paid to be around me.

Sighing loud enough that I'm sure he heard it, I cross my arms and throw an internal tantrum. I'm not sure what's wrong with me or why I have this need to get to know my protector. I mean, geesh, I was only trying to do what people do. Make simple conversation and get to know the person I spend more time with than I do anyone else.

Yes, I know he's trying to keep things professional, blah, blah, blah, but I was just asking him about himself. I didn't ask him to crawl into the back seat and do me.

Not that it hasn't crossed my mind.

I am human, after all.

I know it was just one moment, but those few seconds on

the sidewalk when his golden eyes held mine are hard to shake. There was no relaxing during class because the cadence of my heart never slowed down, no matter how desperately I tried to find my inner peace.

His phone rings, thankfully tearing me from my pitiful pouting.

"Hopper," he answers sternly.

Silence.

"You there already?"

Silence.

"Thanks. See you in five."

And then more silence.

Hello! What's going on? Talk to me!!!!

"We headed back to the house?" I finally ask, irritated when he continues to leave me in the dark.

"Yes, ma'am."

Was that so hard?

"You know you don't have to call me ma'am. Please feel free to call me Emmett."

"I'll keep that in mind, ma'am."

Ugh. He is so annoying.

Once we reach the house, the car is barely in park when I hop out of the back seat before he can get my door for me. I'm a grown-ass woman, and I can open my own damn door. Thank you very much.

I march across the driveway as quickly as I can in a pair of flip-flops, but I can feel him right behind me. Of course, his long legs catch up to me, and he gets to the front door before I do. He opens the door, and I make sure not to look in his direction. Afraid of what another look into his eyes might do to me.

Without a word, I march to my room, strip down, and get in the shower before the water has a chance to heat up. Letting the lukewarm water cascade over my face, I try to rationalize my behavior.

Am I just bored?

Lonely?

Horny?

All of the above?

Or maybe I'm simply projecting my emotions onto Hopper when I'm really upset by the fact that I'm starting to regret my arrangement with Josh.

Thirty minutes later, I've washed away my temperamental mood, thrown on an oversized sweater and knee-length yoga pants—my usual work from home attire—and am meandering through the halls of Josh's beautiful home. Not just any home, but a home that has adorned the pages of Architectural Digest. I may have gotten lost in here in the past, but I know my way to the kitchen.

As soon as I see Hopper sitting at his reserved perch at the kitchen island, I regret not blow-drying my hair or putting on mascara. Engrossed, like always, he doesn't even look up from his computer when I enter the room.

What is he doing on that computer anyway? You'd think he was running a Fortune 500 company with all the time he spends with his face aglow by the screen in front of him, rustling through the never-ending files he pulls from his bag. But it is how damn good he looks in those thick black-rimmed glasses he wears when he's running his secret empire that are going to be my downfall.

Doing my best to ignore him, I join Greta, Josh's; well, I'm not sure what her actual title is. I think of her as the house manager. Yes, she cooks, but she runs things too. If there is an issue with the landscapers, Greta handles it. If there is a delivery or a meeting to organize, Greta handles it. If something needs to be fixed, Greta handles it. So in my mind, she manages this place, hence house manager. However, house CEO may be a better title. She may be small, five feet one and a hundred and ten pounds if she's lucky, but she is fierce. She must be in her mid-fifties, but there isn't a gray hair on her brunette head, and she doesn't look a day over forty.

"What can I get you, Miss Ford?"

"Nothing, Greta. I promise not to get in your way. I'm just gonna make myself lunch."

"Well, let me know what you want, and I can get that for you."

"I'm sure you can, but I would like to make my lunch today."

The irritation from earlier that I thought I had washed away starts to twist in my stomach again.

"Miss Ford, you know it is my job to make you whatever you like. I can do your laundry and make your bed. I'm afraid to imagine what Mr. West would think if he found out you won't let me do any of this for you." She's looking at me with pleading eyes, clearly upset.

"Greta, Mr. West would be fine to hear that I'm taking care of myself, just as I have always done. I am a thirty-one-year-old woman who would like to make my own lunch. I don't want anyone else doing my laundry. Why should you have to touch my dirty underwear?"

"But Miss—" Greta tries to interrupt me, but something about today is eating at me, and I am done with all of the hired help who are here to help me. I mean, for fuck's sake, I'm surprised she isn't offering to hold my hand while I pee.

"Greta, I'm sorry that I'm not the fiancée you hoped for, but I'm what you've got. I like to cook. I like to do laundry. And I like the ritual of making my bed in the mornings. It's nothing personal, and when Josh is home, you can cater to his every whim, but that's just not me. Please know I'm not trying to upset you, I'm just trying to adjust to this new life of mine the best way I can. And taking care of myself keeps me sane."

I can see the compassion in her eyes. She heard me, and she understands. It's almost like a silent understanding woman to woman.

"Of course, Miss Ford. But do let me know if you need anything."

"I'll be sure to do that. So, what can I make the three of us? Does anything sound good?" I ask, opening the gray refrigerator doors that match the cupboards and blend into the rest of the gray and black kitchen.

When I close the fridge door and turn around, Greta is staring at me, unsure what to say, and I do believe I see Hopper trying to smother a grin. When he lifts his eyes from his laptop, I catch his glance. His eyes are dancing with humor, and I know if I were closer, I'd see the golds and greens of his irises sparkling like they were a couple of hours ago on that sidewalk.

Once again, the moment is short-lived, and with a silent chuckle his gaze is back on the screen in front of him.

Chapter Four

I need to get out of this house and squash this horrible case of cabin fever I have. And what better way to do that than to check out a bookstore and maybe even drive myself there. I've been dying to check out The Last Bookstore since I got to Los Angeles, and today is the day.

Dressed and ready to go, I have one small problem. I don't know where Josh keeps his car keys. I know Hopper can take me wherever I want to go, but I miss driving and want to drive myself.

After searching for a good fifteen minutes for car keys, I give up. Then, trying to play it cool, I nonchalantly approach Hopper and say, "I'm gonna go out for a bit, but I can't find car keys anywhere."

"I'll drive you, ma'am," he says, removing his glasses as he rises from his stool at the kitchen island.

"You do know I've had my driver's license for quite some time now?" I retort from the other end of the island. "I was driving a tractor before I was sixteen, so I think I can handle it. And please call me Emmett."

He just stares at me. No facial expression. Nothing.

Could he be any more frustrating?

"I don't need you to drive me. I can drive one of Josh's cars."

"Ma...Ms. Ford, I'm sorry, but I can't let you do that."

"Ms. Ford is my mother. My name is Emmett. Now, what do you mean you can't let me do that? Do you mean you can't or you won't?"

He takes a couple of steps closer, the eye contact intense.

His protective bodyguard persona is a bit much, but it sure looks good on him.

"Miss...it's not safe," he shares reluctantly.

Whoa.

"Really? It's that serious?"

"It is," he confirms solemnly.

"Fine. Hope you like bookstores," I bite out with a hint of venom. Not sure why. It isn't his fault.

"Give me five minutes, and I'll take you wherever you'd like to go."

I pick at a bowl of grapes as he closes his laptop and gathers his paperwork, putting it all in a dark brown leather messenger bag. He disappears for a minute or so, and when he returns, he simply motions with his arm in the direction of the front door. Apparently, he's ready to go. I pop one last grape in my mouth and follow his lead, not minding walking behind him to the car.

Watching him walk is one of my favorite pastimes. His taut back muscles flex under his T-shirt while his thighs strain the denim of his jeans to their limits. But his jeans...I don't even know how you describe such perfection. I grew up in small town America where everyone wore jeans every day, and I've still never seen a pair fit quite like Hopper's.

The man can fill out a pair of jeans.

Aside from telling him where I wanted to go when we first got in the car, the ride is quiet as always. I have got to remember to put a pair of earbuds in my purse because the awkwardness from the lack of conversation is suffocating. I'm a people person, and tired of everyone in the house treating me like their employer instead of a capable human being. I need to have a little chat with Josh because this isn't me, and I need him to make his staff feel a bit more at ease around me.

Finally, The Last Bookstore is in sight, and I'm not sure how it's possible, but Hopper pulls up to a parking spot practically in front of the store doors. This is downtown LA, and I had read that parking in this area was tough to come by. I guess it's just another one of the perks that come along with my new life.

We both hop out, and I'm glad to see he has to feed the meter like the rest of us ordinary folk. Waiting next to the car, I stare up at the neon sign in the window and admire the building. Our little bookstore isn't going to be anything like this, but I still can't wait to check it out and see what ideas I can steal.

"Ready when you are, Miss Ford."

I open my mouth to tell him for the hundredth time that my name is Emmett, but I'm too excited to be out of the house. No need to ruin my mood. So, I ignore him and enter the door he's opened for me.

The store is grand, and although it's full of books, it feels more like a huge art installation rather than a bookstore. I'm used to our trips to Portland and our visits to Powell's Books. Powell's has three floors crammed with new and used books to purchase. Of course, there are books for sale here, but they are also used as art pieces.

With so much to look at, I don't even shop the first half-hour or so. Instead, I wander through the store with Hopper keeping a comfortable distance behind me, I casually stroll, touching the spines of the classics and cracking open used books that smell and feel different than brand new books. There is something about a book that has been passed through the hands of generations, providing an escape to reader after reader that adds a mystic quality to it that new books can't capture.

When I walk under an archway built of books with lights illuminating the stacks of bound words above me, I'm taken in by the quirky beauty of the space while a wave of melancholy washes over me for the briefest of moments. However, I shake it off and make my way to the romance section, where I find four full shelves of Nina Patrick books. Wow, I knew Mason was a big-time author, but I'm shocked to see how much space she takes up.

I stop and take a selfie with all her book babies behind me and post it on social media, tagging her, so she knows I'm thinking about her and showing my support. I also text her a picture of me with the last two books in the series with a sad face because my journey with her amazing characters is almost over.

Once I have Mason's books in my hands, I go a little crazy, suddenly needing to fill my arms with hours of escape. Brand new best sellers and classics. Some I've read, and some I haven't. Even if I don't read them all, they can always go on the shelves of the bookstore Mason, and I are opening back home.

Just One More Chapter will be open in a matter of weeks.

I'm going to be a business owner. In my hometown. If only I were home to enjoy it to the fullest. Mason and I text, call and email several times a day, and I've been a part of every decision and have done all of the ordering, but it's not the same as being there to do the work.

I'm loaded down with literature and am about to drop what's in my arms when Hopper appears out of nowhere.

"Here. Give me some of those. You look like you've got a little more than you can handle."

"Yeah, I've gone a little overboard, haven't I?"

"Not for me to say, Miss Ford."

Professional as always. And what exactly does he mean by that?

"Well, I know carrying books isn't exactly in your job description, but I really appreciate your arms."

What in the world did I just say?

"I mean, I thank you for having arms big enough to hold all of these books."

Oh, my God. I'm an idiot. I have to turn away from him, so he doesn't see the blush I feel heating my face.

"It's not a problem, Miss Ford," he says with a smile in his voice.

"Well, I think that's enough for one day. We should probably get out of here before I buy the whole place. Your arms are big, but they aren't that big."

I stop walking and hide my face in my hands. Why do I keep talking about his arms? I take a deep breath and pull myself together, knowing he's standing right behind me.

He follows me to the checkout line, and we stand in silence while I wait for my turn. I still haven't turned around to look at him. Mature, I know.

Things don't usually embarrass me, and I don't know why I'm behaving like an idiot around Hopper. I'm the girl who changes her hair color every few months. I'm the girl who has no problem being the only one out on the dance floor line dancing at The Verdict. I don't mind attention. I run a department of thirty at work. Maybe it's because I'm out of my element? It's easy to be tough when I only talk to my co-workers through emails, IM's, and phone calls. And Eastlyn is home, and there's nowhere I feel more comfortable.

I think I've let LA get the best of me, and it's time to find the me I like much better than this quiet, do what I'm told version of myself. Hopefully, filling my new LA shelves with my new books will help.

We finally make it to the counter, and the clerk looks at me like I'm some kind of lunatic.

"Wow, getting a jump on your holiday shopping or opening your own bookstore?"

"I guess a little bit of both."

The clerk looks skeptical.

"No, really, we're opening a shop back home. I know there is a much more affordable way to get inventory on the shelves, but when in Rome and all that."

"That's cool. Congratulations."

"Thanks." I grin ridiculously. "It is cool, isn't it?"

He just smiles and rings me up. I pay for my book haul, trying not to choke on the total. Oh well, I can afford it, but I did go a little crazy.

Hopper grabs two of the three canvas bags of bags and leads us out of the store. When we get to the car, he puts the bags in the back while I get in and then jumps in the front and pulls into weekday traffic.

"Sorry, I probably didn't pick the best time of day to visit downtown."

"It's no problem at all, Miss Ford."

"Of course it's not," I say under my breath.

"Excuse me, ma'am?"

"I just said, of course it's not a problem."

"Is there a problem with driving you not being a problem?"

"No, not at all. It's just that everyone is so accommodating. I'm still adjusting to a lifestyle of being catered to, is all. Having a staff at my beck and call is new, and I'm not sure if I like it. I'll figure it out, though."

He doesn't reply, but he adjusts the rearview mirror, and I do believe he might just be looking at me from under those sunglasses of his.

A couple of minutes pass, and I'm cursing myself for not having earbuds on me when he startles me by speaking.

"So, what did you think of the bookstore?"

Oh, what the timbre of his voice does to my heart.

"It was really cool. A bit more art installation than bookstore, but I enjoyed it. I wish I hadn't gone so crazy on the books because I didn't even get to glance at the music section. I don't have a record player, but something about looking through old records can cause me to lose track of time just like books do."

"Did I hear you tell the clerk you're opening your own bookstore back in your hometown?"

Hopper instigating conversation has me feeling all a flutter while also feeling more like myself than I have in weeks. It's amazing what a little human interaction will do for a girl.

"You sure did. I can't wait. I'm sure you've heard me mention my friends Mason and Miles, or at least you've seen their names on my little list of approved contacts at the very least. I still can't believe such a list exists."

"I have, and that little list is for your safety, Miss Ford. Now tell me more about your store."

"For the record, I know it's for my safety, but I'm allowed to be a bit annoyed with the situation, don't ya think?"

I see one of his eyebrows lift above the rim of his shades, but he doesn't reply. So I carry on.

"Well, Mason is a bestselling author. She writes under the name Nina Patrick. Maybe you've heard of her? There's a TV series based on her 'Manhattan Diaries' books?" He shakes his head. "Anyway, she noticed the one thing missing in our town was a local bookstore. We have a library, but there is something about a local bookstore that's so much better than a library. So, we were talking one night over drinks right before I left, and we came up with the idea of opening one ourselves. We'll have theme nights that will include drink nights, of course, and host book clubs. I think it's gonna be a lot of fun. We're calling it Just One More Chapter."

"Sounds like a great idea. May I ask how you're going to run it from Los Angeles?"

"Well, we've gone in fifty/fifty, and now that Mason is Miles's fiancée, she'll be there to oversee things at the start, but we have some great local friends who will work there and run things. Our friend Amelia is a school teacher, and she'll help in the summers when some of the other employees want to take time off. Surprisingly, we've got it all worked out. I'm pretty excited."

"New and used books?" he asks from the front seat.

"Yep. No vinyl records like The Last Bookstore, unfortunately."

"Sounds like you're a big music lover?"

"You could say that."

"What do you listen to?"

"The question should really be, what don't I listen to? I just love good music. How about you?"

"What about me?"

Please tell me he isn't going to get professional with me again. We were doing so well.

"Are you a music fan?"

"Sure."

"And what do you like to listen to?"

He waits for a beat, and I think he's done talking, but he surprises me again. "I like just about everything, but my true love is 90s hip-hop if I'm honest."

Not sure how, but I manage to hold my laughter inside. And I do believe I see him smiling in the mirror. He knows his answer wasn't what I was expecting. But what he doesn't know is that I'm picturing him driving in a convertible Impala, smoking a joint with Nate Dogg singing in the background as he slowly rolls through Josh's snobby neighborhood.

"Not what I thought you would say, but I like your style, Hopper."

"Why, thank you, Miss Ford."

My panties are beginning to melt right off my body when my phone rings, halting our easy banter. But, because it's work, I have to take it.

While my boss drones on about budgets, I search my purse and silently curse when I don't find what I'm looking for inside. But much to my surprise, I hear the sound of mints shaking against tin as Hopper passes me what I was looking for.

My call doesn't end until we reach the gates to Josh's place. I can't help but wonder if I shouldn't get used to this new chatty side of Hopper.

Of course, he grabs all three bags from the back of the car, and this time, I get to open the front door for him.

As he passes me in the entryway, he pauses when he asks, "Where shall I take these?"

It's a simple question, but he's so close, and even though his sunglasses are still covering his eyes, I know he's looking me in the eye. The moment lingers, and a hint of that same chemistry from the other day on the sidewalk sparks between us, leaving me breathless.

Somehow, I manage to find enough air in my lungs to reply. "My office would be great." Unfortunately, my answer causes him to break our connection when he walks down the hallway to my office.

He isn't my personal valet, and it feels awkward to have him carry my things. Even though he says he doesn't mind, I do. But alas, I've given up trying to stop him from carrying items or opening doors for me. I guess he does spend most of his day sitting around waiting for something to happen. Maybe it's a good distraction from whatever he's doing on that laptop of his. I bet he can't wait to get out of here every night when Smith takes over.

They each work seven to seven. Hopper seven in the morning until seven at night.

Seven o'clock.

My least favorite time of the day.

The house always feels eerily silent from the absent tapping of his fingers on his keyboard.

Smith is fine, but he's not Hopper.

"On the desk?" he asks, filling the middle of the room like only he can while holding my bags of books out as if they were filled with feathers instead of tens of pounds of books.

Dear Lord, he is a big man.

"On the desk would be great, thank you."

He places the books on the massive white desk Josh had built for me. The entire room was custom-made for me. The walls are gray and lined with white bookshelves that have more décor than books on them at the moment, but today's shopping trip should help to change this. There is a light blue and silver shag rug in the middle of the room, and beautiful watercolor paintings adorn the walls. I tell myself they are just cheap prints put on canvas and ordered from Homegoods, but I have a feeling they cost a pretty penny.

Spinning the tin of Altoids between my fingers like I have a habit of doing, I remember these aren't mine. "Oh, here you go. Thanks, you're a lifesaver. It's a bit of an addiction."

"Keep them, Miss Ford. I kept them in the car for you when I noticed they're one of your favorites. I'll be sure the car is always stocked just in case."

Whoa. He knows my favorite mint. What the...?

"Can I do anything else for you, Miss Ford?" he asks.

Placing his sunglasses on top of his head now that his hands are free, he gives me a full view of his golden eyes.

If I didn't know better, I would say he's stalling for time. Like he doesn't want to leave the room just yet. I'm pretty sure I know better, though, and I make sure to look away quickly to avoid another one-sided moment from happening.

"Hopper, you don't have to help me with household tasks like putting books on shelves," I say, moving in next to him at the desk to start emptying the bags.

"I don't mind at all, and it is all a part of the job, ma-"

"Don't even think about it," I interrupt, pointing a finger at him to stop him before he gets the whole word out.

He smiles the biggest smile I've seen from him yet.

It. Is. Breathtaking.

For all his brawn, he is one beautiful man. More beautiful than any watercolor on the walls of this room, that's for sure.

Still smiling, he starts over, correcting himself. "It's all a part of the job, Miss Ford." He takes a couple of books out of the bag in front of him, helping me stack them on the desk nonchalantly, adding, "Besides, I've done much worse."

"Is that so?" I say, abandoning my bag of books.

He lifts an eyebrow and gives me a sideways glance that says, wouldn't you like to know.

Yes, I would! I really would! But I know he can't share information about his other clients with me. No matter how desperately I'm dying to know all the details.

"Hmm...my imagination is running wild."

"Well, I wish I could say that your imagination is wilder than reality, but when it comes to the rich and famous, I'm afraid your imagination wouldn't even come close."

"Now, you're just being mean. I bet you have some stories to tell, but I know you can't say anything. Besides, I wouldn't want you sharing stories about me with anyone else."

"Miss Ford, you are by far the easiest client I have ever worked for."

All the books are on the desk, so I start stacking them on various shelves, and he steps aside but doesn't leave the room.

"You mean the most boring, right?"

"I didn't say that."

The elephant in the room makes it hard to breathe, and I can't help but bring it up. Knowing he's signed a nondisclosure agreement means I can speak freely with him, but it doesn't make it any easier.

"I can't imagine what you must think of me?" I say with my back to him.

"It's not my job to have an opinion."

He speaks kindly, but his reply feels judgmental, which, in turn, has me feeling defensive.

"I'm not with him for fame and fortune, you know?" I spin around, looking him in the eyes to make sure he knows the person I truly am. It may not be his job to have an opinion, but for some crazy reason, his opinion matters.

To me, anyway.

"Again, there's no judging on my part. That is also not part of the job."

I've finally found something that isn't a part of his job, and it is infuriating! His lack of judgment sounds more like the opposite, and I can't let it go.

"I'm helping out my friend. My best friend. I have my own money. I may not have a private jet, but I am not out spending his money on bags of books. I can afford this all on my own! It's only two years, and not only did he need me, but I needed a change."

He puts his hands in his pockets! His reply is to put his hands in his freaking pockets and stare at me.

Hopper, being Hopper, doesn't say a thing and stands there waiting for me to continue. Me, being me, I do just that.

"I love Josh, and I hate that he has to hide who he really is. I wish he could just tell the world, not that anyone should have to make an announcement about their personal life, but I hope one day he can show his true self to the world because he's a pretty great guy. In the meantime, I'm here to help. I know we aren't confirming anything with the press and instead letting them assume there is an engagement."

I feel sick hearing myself say all of this out loud for the first time.

"But even though we haven't confirmed an engagement publicly, I am wearing a rather large diamond ring on *that* finger, and I'm always his plus one, so we aren't lying to the press, but let's face it, as much as we tell ourselves we're implying and not lying, we're lying. It feels wrong on so many levels, Hopper, and I am starting to hate myself. But he's worked hard to get where he is, and I'd do anything to protect my friend."

After all of my word vomit, all I get is a nod of his head before he turns and leaves the room. Note to self...don't have an emotional breakdown with your bodyguard because he clearly doesn't get paid to judge, have an opinion, or care.

Standing alone in my office, I can't help but wonder to myself if all of that was to convince Hopper I'm doing the right thing or to convince myself?

Maybe he left the room without comment because he already knows the answer to that question.

Chapter Five

"Audrey, I understand. I really do. But, it doesn't mean I'm not going to pout. I just miss you and Parker so damn much."

Greta enters the room but pays me no mind. She's used to me wearing earbuds and talking for work all day. Me talking to an empty room is the norm. She may be used to me talking to an empty room, but it doesn't prevent her from throwing her usual side-eye in my direction when she sees what I'm up to. She refuses to get over me doing my laundry, and at the moment, I'm folding a basket of clothes. Hence, the side-eye.

"Married life. It's all give and take. This year, Thanksgiving with my family, and next year, we'll be back in Eastlyn. The timing of the store opening is just too close to the holiday. You know we'd be there if we could be. Please tell me you know that."

"Of course I do, and I don't want you to give it another thought. You'll be there in spirit."

"Thank you. Please know we're so proud of you and Emmett. I can't believe there's never been a bookstore in Eastlyn. It's a great idea. It's just unbelievable how fast it came to fruition."

"I know; we got so freaking lucky. Burns Hardware moved out a year ago, and the place was just sitting there waiting for somebody to save it. We finished the paperwork two weeks ago, and Miles and Emmett have been putting it all together. I can't wait to get home and help."

"Don't feel bad, you know Miles loves this kind of stuff, and besides, he's Miles. He has people who can help. All he has to do is ask, and that whole town will be there to pitch in."

"I know, but I hate missing out on all the work that goes into it. Besides the serious case of FOMO, I miss home."

"You doing okay, Emmy?"

"Yep, doing great," I lie. "This place is amazing. You'll have to come visit after the holidays."

"We'd love that, but listen, I have to run into a meeting. I hope it all goes well, and we'll be thinking about you."

"Thanks. Hug that hubby of yours for me. Safe travels, girl."

"You have a great trip back home. Happy Thanksgiving, and congrats again! I'll call you when we get back."

We end the call, and the moment I say goodbye, Greta is on me like a helicopter that's been waiting to land.

"Miss Ford, why do you insist on torturing me like this? No offense, but you don't know what you're doing. Please let me take care of your laundry."

Swinging around, I'm about to give Greta a piece of my mind. Hopper is at his usual perch at the kitchen island, and the shake of his shoulders would lead me to believe he finds Greta's observation amusing.

How long has he been sitting there anyway?

Not that I mind the visual of him in his tight oatmeal Henley. How does he even find clothes to fit him? Good grief.

"Oh, so you're on her side, are you?"

He starts to answer, but I stop him.

"I know, it's *not your job* to take sides," I say with an exaggerated eye roll.

His chuckles disappear, as does the smile on his beautiful lips when he puts his glasses back on and turns his attention back to his computer.

Excellent job, Emmett.

You had to ruin the moment.

"Sorry, that was rude." He looks up from the glowing screen in front of him.

He nods, as per usual.

I've learned this to mean he understands and hears me, but it's not his job to get involved.

"Miss Ford, you're about to leave to go see your friends, and they're going to think you've been living out of your car if you keep folding your clothes like that!" Greta yells, snatching my Eastlyn Eagles T-shirt out of my hand.

"Greta, just because I fold differently than you doesn't mean it's wrong."

She lifts an eyebrow to say she disagrees.

"Fine, I'll go finish this in my room, so you don't have to watch the disgraceful treatment of my clothes."

"Or you can let me do it for you," she says with her hands on her hips, not giving up on her quest to save my clothes from my mistreatment of them. "I can help you pack if you like?"

"You are tenacious. I'll give you that."

"Just doing my job, Miss Ford."

Standing directly in front of me, hands still on her hips, I swear she's planning how she'll tackle me if I try to leave the room with my laundry.

"Oh, my goodness! Please call me Emmett? The formalities around here make me feel like I'm staying at a hotel. I know you're both paid to be here, and neither of you intends to be my new BFF, but I'd really like things to be a little less formal, if you don't mind?" Putting my hands together as though I'm praying, I finish my plea. "I beg you both. Please call me Emmett."

Hopper lifts his eyes from his laptop, his face expressionless. Greta just stares at me, hands still on her hips.

Their replies leave me throwing my hands in the air, defeated.

"Whatever, I tried."

Needing to get out of the room and away from the two of them, I throw my clothes in the basket and start to leave the room but stop myself. Balancing my laundry basket on my hip, I address the male fitness model at the kitchen island. "So, Hopper, will you be traveling back with me, or will Smith be coming with me?"

"Smith and another associate have already left for Eastlyn, and I'll be traveling with you on the plane tomorrow."

"Why are they going a day early?"

"They just want to clear the bookstore and your house and ensure things are secure before you get there."

"Oh."

Seems a bit dramatic, doesn't it?

"Bookstore?" Greta asks. I'm not sure if she's being kind and trying to lighten the mood or if she's really interested, but I'll take the distraction.

"Oh, um, yes. My friend Mason and I are opening a little bookstore in my hometown. She's a pretty big author. Maybe you've heard of her? She writes under the pen name, Nina Patrick."

That was all it took to tear down that professional exterior Greta had firmly in place. Apparently, she's Mason's number one fan, and we spend the next thirty minutes playing Manhattan Diaries trivia. Sadly, I think Greta may have me beat. I swear I learn just as much about Mason from Greta as

Greta does from me. The best part is that she calls me Emmett at the end of the conversation instead of Miss Ford.

Looks like all it takes is being friends with a famous romance author and not being fake engaged to a Hollywood star to get her attention.

* * *

This morning when I woke up, my bags were packed, by me, not Greta, and I had them waiting by my bedroom door. I couldn't get dressed fast enough. I was ready and waiting in the living room with my bags at my feet like a six-year-old on their way to Disneyland for the first time.

Hopper stayed at the house last night, which meant I didn't get much shut-eye knowing that he was downstairs. When he was finally ready to go, I followed him out to a waiting Town Car, where an older gentleman in a black suit was standing next to the back door with his hands clasped in front of him.

It felt odd having someone new drive me. I know it's only been a month and a half since Hopper was added to the team, but having someone other than him or sometimes Smith drive me since Josh has been gone is not my norm. Of course, I never would have thought having a driver would feel normal at all.

I was disappointed Hopper sat up front with the man he introduced as Williams, but did I expect him to sit in back with me? It certainly isn't his job to do that.

Sitting behind Hopper and not being able to glance at his sunglass-covered eyes in the rearview mirror felt odd, but not nearly as bizarre as pulling onto the tarmac where a private jet was parked and waiting.

Just for me.

As soon as the plane came into view, the high I'd been riding all morning in anticipation of getting home to Eastlyn, evaporated into thin air.

Now, here I sit on a private jet transporting just myself and my bodyguard. It would be one thing if there were others on the flight with us, but with the other two bodyguards already in Eastlyn and Sibby not arriving until the day of the opening, not that I fully understand the need for her to be there, it's just Hopper and me.

The stoic man of few words is sitting across from me, staring out the window deep in thought, his silence already frying my nerves and the plane's wheels have just left the ground.

"This feels like a bit much, doesn't it? I mean, we could have flown commercial. It's embarrassing to be using this kind of resource to fly two people one state away."

"It's safer this way," he says to the window.

His short answer is followed by more silence.

I pop an Altoid in my mouth and push the tin across the little table separating us.

"No thanks."

I shrug and put the mints back in my bag.

Once the plane levels out, I unbuckle my seat belt and walk up to the front of the aircraft to talk to our flight attendant, Kyle, and see if he has any suggestions on passing the time. Unfortunately, all he has is a deck of cards, but right about now, I'll take it.

Sitting back down, Hopper looks up at me. "Everything okay?"

"Yep, found a deck of cards. Wanna play?"

As per usual, he doesn't say anything.

"Oh, come on. I'm not asking you to play strip poker or anything. We can keep it simple. Go Fish? Slap Jack? War? You pick."

"War."

I'm so surprised he agreed to play. I'm not sure I heard him correctly. "I'm sorry, what was that?"

"War. But I warn you, I'm pretty good."

Holy shit. I'm about to play War with Hopper.

"Is that really something to brag about? It's not exactly a game of skill. It's all luck."

"Well, I guess I'm lucky when it comes to card games then. I rarely lose."

"We'll see."

I take my time shuffling the cards on the table that separates us and then split up the deck, so we each have half.

My stack of cards keeps getting bigger as we play the game while his dwindles away. It's been killing me not to make smart-ass comments as I take his cards, but when we both lay down threes, I can't take it anymore.

"Okay, big man, now would be the time for you to try to get back in the game because the cards don't lie, and right now, they are saying your luck may have run out."

"Why don't you just lay down your cards, and we'll see what they have to say."

"Sensitive much?"

"Nope. I just know how this game works, and it's far from over, Miss Ford."

"Listen, if I win this war, you have to call me Emmett. Deal?"

"Just lay down your cards, Miss Ford."

We each lay down our first card, and as silly as it is, you can feel the tension mounting as we each flip over our next card. Mine is a queen, and his a king, but I'm so off-kilter from our easy banter that I instinctively reach for the cards as if I've won. But because I haven't, my hand lands on his as he pulls away his loot.

"Excuse me, ma'am, but these are my cards. King beats

queen last time I played this game." He quips but doesn't make any effort to pull his hand back.

"Oh crap, you're right. Sorry about that."

I pull away but not before heat rolls over my body from head to toe from our momentary connection.

"What were you saying about the cards not lying?" he says, clearly unfazed and not experiencing the same euphoria our touch provided me.

"One winning hand does not win the game, my friend."

"It's a start." He lays down his next card, a ten, which beats my four. "Would you look at that? That's two in a row. See, lady luck is still on my side; she just doesn't feel the need to rush things."

"Is that so?" I say, laying down a five and beating his two. "Seems she's not quite sure whose side she's on."

I continue to win the next couple of hands when we both lay down tens. Neither of us speaks as we go to war. He wins again. Damn!

He wins the next war, and the next one, and all but two of the following hands. He's back to being quiet, but the smug look on his face says it all.

Told you so.

When we go to war one last time, I'm one card short of finishing the hand.

"Oh, did you run out of cards, Miss Ford?"

I stick my tongue out at him, unable to stop the immature reaction.

"Wow, a sore loser. I had you pegged all wrong." I roll my eyes, and his chest lifts in a low chuckle I can only imagine since I can't hear it over the roar of the engine.

"How about we just go with what you have. Let's just flip the second card and call it good."

"How charitable of you."

"I do what I can," he says, shrugging his broad shoulders. "Now, flip your card."

"So bossy."

I flip over my last card, and of course, it's a two, which means his measly four wins the game just as he predicted.

"Miss Ford, it seems I've won."

"So, it does." His smug smile turns playful, and just like that, losing feels like winning. "I was really hoping I'd win. This Miss Ford stuff is so annoying. You're stuck spending most of your time with me, so you'd think we could at least call each other by our first names."

Ignoring my last statement, he shockingly keeps talking. "So, you're terrible at cards, may need a 12-step program for your addiction to mints, love books, and you work for one of the biggest communication companies in the world, but I have no idea what you actually do."

Is he making small talk?

Did he just list off things he knows about me?

Are my eyes bugging out of my head?

Wait. I didn't think it was his job to care?

Am I hallucinating?

"Correction, I am good at cards, but I thought I would let you win, so your giant ego didn't take a hit." He smiles, and my heart flutters. "As for my job, well, I manage all of the travel for the company. We have offices and business relations worldwide, and my team plans all domestic and international travel. Flights, hotels, car services, meetings, and whatever else is needed. We have team members all around the world."

"Do you like what you do?"

That's a good question.

"Well, if I'm being honest...I miss the actual travel planning I used to do. It was fun putting all the trips together. But, management isn't all bad. I'm making a good living, and I get to work from home, so no complaints, really."

"Are you going to continue working?"

"What do you mean?"

"Well, I would think that Josh West's wife in corporate America could be a little distracting in meetings."

"I hadn't thought about that, but I guess you do have a point."

"You hadn't thought of that yet?"

"I can't say that I had. I mean, most of my co-workers know he's my best friend. They've seen me on his arm in magazines for years now."

"There's a big difference between being a plus one and a fiancée or wife."

"True."

"And what about your family and friends back home? Do they know this isn't real?"

"No," I admit sheepishly.

"Why haven't you told them?"

"Sibby thought it was best not to put anyone in a place of having to lie to the press or to accidentally let the truth slip out if they were ever asked."

"How do you think everyone will feel when they find out?"

"I know my close friends will understand in the end, but I'd be lying if I didn't admit I'm worried about what the older folks in our town will say. My hope, is that we have a long engagement that will, of course, never end in a wedding, and we can just say it didn't work out, and we were better as friends. If my grandma doesn't have to know we lied, that would be ideal."

Suddenly, I can't breathe. The seat belt strapping me to the chair feels like a metaphor for my life. I feel trapped. I fumble with the belt, desperately needing to be free from its constraints.

Once it falls to my sides, I jump out of my seat and pace the small aisle way.

Oh, God. I'm freaking out. Forty thousand feet in the air with Hopper as my witness, I decide to let what I've done set it. Leave it to me to pick the perfect moment for a panic attack.

"To be honest, I didn't think it all through," I say, stopping my manic pacing in front of our seats but with my hands fisting in my hair like a madwoman. "He needed me, and I needed to get out of the same small town as my ex, if you even want to call him that. Except for when I went away for college, I haven't lived anywhere except Eastlyn. It's ironic that I help people travel for a living, and I've never left North America. So, I guess I just needed a change."

"Makes sense."

"And now, with the bookstore opening, I have the change I might have been looking for, but I'm not even there to enjoy it. I feel like I'm entering a new chapter in my life, pun intended."

His chuckle shuts me up, and I realize I'm not alone. He may be smiling at my pun, but the look in his eyes is like looking in a mirror. He thinks I've made a mistake, no matter how well-intentioned my decision was.

Stinging tears pool in my eyes, and my voice quivers when I ask what we're both thinking.

"Hopper, what have I done?" I keep talking, not letting him answer. "I didn't think about the aftermath. I didn't think this through at all, did I?"

"Mr. West cares about you, and I'm sure he and his team will do all they can to make sure the next couple of years and the aftermath that follows are as pain-free as possible."

"Please stop with the Mr. and Miss stuff. He's Josh. I'm Emmett."

He nods.

"Hopper, what's your name?"

He looks up at me with his head tilted, confused.

"I'll call you Hopper if you prefer it, but it feels strange not knowing your first name."

He clears his throat. "Max."

Why was that so hard for him? And why does knowing his first name lessen my hysterics?

"Hi, Max," I say, reaching out to shake his hand while saying his name repeatedly in my head until the warmth of his hand taking mine distracts me.

Oh, my. There's that feeling again.

Please don't let go of my hand, Max.

"Nice to meet you, Emmett," he says with a subtle smile, not releasing my hand right away.

Holding my gaze and my hand, he doesn't let go until the pilot interrupts us, letting us know we're almost to Pendleton.

He lets go of my grip and leans back in his seat. I take my seat across from him, his focus still on me.

"Anything I need to know before we get there? Any annoying neighbors? Do we need to have a code word in case you need rescuing?"

Oh, Max. I can think of a million different ways you could rescue me.

"Nah."

"What about this ex of yours?"

"Oh, he won't speak directly to me. If he's at The Verdict, our local bar, he might make things a little uncomfortable. Of course, if he gets drunk, there's a chance he'll call me a bitch or give me stink eye all night, but I doubt we'll have to worry about him."

"Does he always give you a hard time?" Max growls. His jaw twitching.

"He's nothing I can't handle. Besides, I'm used to it. I only go out with my core group of friends. I always have backup. He knows better."

"How long has this been going on?"

"I don't know? Five or six years? Listen, when you have a relationship, no matter how long or short, with someone in a small town, and you break up, it's always gonna be rough. And when one person feels more for the other person, it's even tougher on that person. He's just hurt, is all."

The furrow of his brow says he doesn't like my answer, but the bump from the plane's wheels touching down on the runway brings our conversation to a halt, but not the ticking in his jaw.

Chapter Six

To say it's uncomfortable pulling into my own driveway being driven in a blacked-out SUV by my bodyguard doesn't even begin to cover it. Not to mention the SUV's twin is waiting on the street in front of the house. It's uncomfortable in LA, but here in Eastlyn, it couldn't feel more out of place.

I insisted on sitting in the front passenger seat. It felt like the only way for me to take a tiny bit of control of what feels almost like an out-of-body situation, and I was shocked when Hopper didn't put up a fight. I wouldn't say things between us changed dramatically on the plane, but something seems to have shifted ever so slightly.

For me, the knowledge of his first name changed something. I'm not sure why knowing his first name makes things feel different, but it does. I'm also not sure why I haven't called him by his name just yet. He didn't tell me I couldn't call him Max, but he didn't say he wanted me to either. For now, I'll let the knowledge of it roll around in my head and do my best not to use his first or last name if I can help it.

Once the car is in park, I can't get out of the damn thing fast enough. I run to the back to get my bags, and he's already there, as are Smith and a new guy. The new guy is older, shorter, rounder...let's just say maybe it would have been better if he had been assigned as my principal handler. I might not be so distracted or feel whatever it is I feel when my current handler is around.

"They've got our bags. So we can go ahead and go in."

"Okay, but first, I'd like to meet our new addition. Hi, I'm Emmett."

"Miss Ford, this is Cleveland."

Taking my offered hand, he gives me a fatherly smile. "Nice to meet you, Cleveland."

"Shall we?" Max asks, annoyed for some reason.

"Geesh, don't you have any manners?"

As we cross the driveway, uneasiness washes over me. I can't imagine what it must look like to my neighbors to see me walking around with three large men. Max is in front of me, and I thought the other two were behind me, but Smith is gone, and it's only Cleveland there when we reach my sweet little doormat that says "Be Happy" in the bottom right corner. Seeing it puts a smile on my face and some breath in my lungs. Who knew a welcome mat could have such a calming effect?

"Smith went around back, and I will go in first. Please wait here with Cleveland."

"You're kidding, right?"

His face says, "do you even need to ask" for a brief second before he turns on his heels and walks away to clear my tiny little house.

Cleveland closes the door behind us, leaving us to stand awkwardly in the entry to my living room, my bags in his hands.

"So, I am assuming Cleveland is your last name?"

"Yes, ma'am."

Cleveland seems sweet. He isn't strung quite as tight as the rest of the team. And for the brief time I've known him, there has been a slight smile on his face. He's confident. I like him already.

"Please ignore your co-workers and call me Emmett, if you like."

"Yes, ma'am."

Ugh.

The house is a small 1960s era ranch-style home, so it doesn't take long before Max is back, giving me the all-clear.

He stands to the side, letting me continue into my own home.

How kind of him.

Walking into my living room, I have two men following behind me and one standing at my back door.

How did this become my life?

"I'll be back with the last of the bags."

"Thank you, Smith."

I throw my purse on the beautiful farm-style kitchen table I purchased with my first bonus after my promotion into management. Big and bold, even if it only seats six with the leaf in it, white legs, and a weathered light blue top. It still makes me smile.

Out of habit, I open the fridge to see what's there. Not much.

"Gentlemen, would you like some ketchup, mustard, baking soda, or tap water?"

"Trying to cut back on my condiment intake, but thank you for asking," Max jokes, bringing back some of the natural ease we had on the plane.

The ease that had him placing his hand on the small of my back as we walked through the plane door onto the stairs that led us to the tarmac and our waiting vehicle. I thought about those two seconds the entire drive home.

Smith returns with the bags, and it hits me that I don't have room for all of them.

"Guys, I am so sorry. I only have two spare bedrooms, but I can make up the couch. You'll have to draw straws, though. I don't want to decide who gets stuck out here."

"Smith and Cleveland just came out to prepare for your arrival and will be taking some time off after your event. They'll be heading home for Thanksgiving."

"Prepare for my arrival? Good grief, what are you guys, the Secret Service? I'm not the president or a member of the royal family. I think we may be going a little overboard with all of this, don't you think?"

"It's protocol."

"Whatever you say. I'm going to go unpack, but I am happy to hear you two will get to be home for the holiday."

Once I'm alone in my bedroom, I throw myself on my bed, already exhausted from the anxiety of the lies I know I will have to tell while I'm home. After years of burning vanilla candles and applying vanilla lotion each night before bed, the scent of my personal space grounds me while the shades of blue decorating the room and the softness of my old comforter cocoon me. The space is small, but it's mine.

Josh's house in the Hollywood Hills still doesn't feel like home, but there is one positive about being in Los Angeles. It doesn't include the people closest to me, which means I'm not lying to the people I love on a daily basis. At least not to their faces. That is the one and only thing I like about being in Los Angeles. Well, that and Max.

Max is one of my constant, yet usually silent, companions in California, and having him here in my small home feels more personal. Intimate. Seeing his imposing frame in the middle of my living room a few minutes ago made the house feel tiny. He takes up a tremendous amount of space and most of the oxygen as well. I know this because I have difficulty getting in more than is essential for life when I'm in close quarters with him.

My mind is spending far too much time on a man with whom I'll never have more than a professional relationship, and I don't have time for daydreaming. I'm home for a reason, and there is a lot to do. Not to mention, I haven't even called the girls yet.

Forcing myself off the bed, I miss more than I should, considering I've had this mattress my entire adult life, I should probably replace it. At Josh's place, I live in the lap of luxury and sleep on a bed that costs—I don't even want to know what it costs. But I'll take this tiny bedroom with no primary ensuite any day.

Shit.

I'm going to have to share a bathroom with Max. My mind spins with all the different reasons I could accidentally walk in on him when he's in the shower. Or maybe even better, just after I hear the water stop and he's drying off.

Stop!

Get a grip, Emmett!

You do not get to fantasize about your bodyguard. You are not only his client but you're supposed to be engaged!

The reality that I'm not going to have sex for two years finally sank in after Max placed his hand on my low back. That was all it took. A touch.

Max is always there and therefore, the one you're hot for.

It's not real, so get over it!

Right, okay. Internal chastising is over, so let's get moving.

While I unpack, I call Amelia and Mason to let them know I'm here and that I'll see them at Just One More Chapter in a couple of hours.

Unpacked, the girls called, and I have no real reason to hide in my room anymore. It's time to go do what I do. Be awkward around Max. I've perfected this daily occurrence. Not sure why things feel that much more awkward just because I'm home.

Thank goodness I need to head to the store for groceries. I'll need the alone time to clear my head. Knowing I'll get a break from him, I pull open my bedroom door and brave the hallway.

I may not have a kitchen island, but I do have a kitchen table, and not surprisingly, this is where he has set up shop. Laptop open and glasses on, he's working away when I round the corner into the kitchen. Damn, those glasses! They make me all warm and fuzzy inside and not in the oh, what a cute puppy kind of way.

Why does he have to be so freaking hot? And big? No matter what room he's in, he takes up all the space.

Taking my car keys off the hook on the kitchen wall, I try to be as nonchalant as I can in the hopes I'll get to make this trip to the store alone.

"Hey, I'm gonna head to the store to pick up a few things, so we have something besides condiments to eat. I should only be gone about thirty minutes." He makes to stand like he's coming with me. "Nope, I got this, Hopper. Eastlyn is my home, my people. I'm safe here."

"I'll drive. No need for your keys."

"No. You'll only draw attention."

"Miss Ford, I'm sorry, but this is the way it has to be."

"Ugh, fine, but I'm sitting in the front again. In fact, let's just plan on that while we're here in Eastlyn. No chauffeuring me around. It's embarrassing."

The drive to the store is too quiet for my liking. Even though it's only a few minutes away, it's too much for me to take. So I plug the aux cord into my phone and hit play. When he smiles and taps his finger on the steering wheel, I know I've chosen the right 90s hip-hop song.

Dr. Dre and Snoop Dog get us to the store without the

usual stuffiness that engulfs us in California. Between the formalities and the smog, breathing a full breath is hard to do some days.

Eastlyn has a couple of small corner stores, but Hooley's Supermarket is our only full-service grocery store. Owned by the Hooley family and passed down for generations, it's an Eastlyn landmark. Everyone knows everyone here, so when I walk in with the equivalent of the Jolly Green Giant trailing me, we certainly get some funny looks. The women who say hello give my shadow wide-eyed looks that ask if he's real. And the men look him up and down, skeptical of the new stranger in town.

I introduce him as Max and simply say he works for Josh and leave it at that. Back in produce, I'm bagging up all the fixins for a kick-ass salad, a little more than usual since I have to feed Max too when I realize I don't know what he likes.

"You like salad?"

"Sure. Who doesn't?"

"Well, a man your size has to eat more than salad. Any special requests? I'm not too shabby in the kitchen."

"Don't worry about me; I can make do with anything."

"Oh, come on. There has to be something I can make you or that we can get to have around the house for you."

"I mean, if they have protein shakes, some frozen berries, kale, and anything else I can throw in the blender or juicer, I can always make myself some green juice smoothies in the morning."

"Why does that not surprise me?"

"What? You asked. I answered."

"Yes, you did. I'm just not used to the men in my life being so easy."

"I'm a simple man. It doesn't take much to make me happy, I guess."

"I have a feeling you are far from simple, but yes, in the grocery department, you seem to be."

"I try."

"Hopper?" I say stopping his progress down the aisle with the cart.

"Miss Ford?"

"When do you ever get a moment to yourself? Your entire life is based around my schedule and where I need to go. Where and when I want to eat. There has to be a part of you that resents me just a little bit. I mean, you're going to miss Thanksgiving with your family. They must hate me."

"Well, it is my job. I knew what I was signing up for."

How does he always seem to answer a question without ever really answering the question? I have no idea how he feels about much of anything. I know the facts but have no idea how he feels.

"You don't even get all of your weekends to yourself. If I have something going on for some reason, you have to be there, even if it's your day off. So, when *do* you get time off?"

"I'll take a couple of days once we're back in LA," he says, putting a Hermiston watermelon in the cart.

"You know we're famous for those in these parts."

"So, I've heard. Figured I should try one for myself."

"Well, it's a little out of season, that's why they're so small, but it will still be the best watermelon you've ever tasted."

"I can't wait," he says with a wink.

Be still my beating heart.

* * *

Once the groceries were put away and we each ate our made-to-order deli sandwiches, I was too excited to wait around the house, so we left for the bookstore a little early.

My chin nearly hit the ground when we pulled up. Seeing the store awning with Just One More Chapter adorned on it and our beautiful logo come to life in the front window had my eyes welling up with tears. Walking in to find Miles and Mason already there and hard at work was all I needed to push the tears down my cheeks.

"Well, look who's here! Get over here, girl!" Miles has me off my feet in one of his awesome bear hugs before I'm two feet in the door. "Sure is good to see you, Emmy. I know it hasn't been that long, but it feels like forever. So much has happened," he says, putting me back on my feet.

"You're telling me? I leave town for a couple of months, and the next thing I know, you're getting hitched!"

Mason flashes her hand between us, and there's the proof. Our small-town playboy is off the market, and he couldn't be happier about it. The moment Miles laid eyes on her, he was a goner. He knew in that instant. Just the thought of it makes me all mushy inside.

"Wow, it's even prettier in person. Well done, Montgomery."

"I wouldn't have cared if it was a ring out of a Cracker Jack box, but this one is pretty nice." The beauty, who could be the model for our logo, sighs herself. Her honey-blond hair is up in a high ponytail, and with her glasses on, all she needs is a steaming cup and a book in front of her, and she's the girl on our window.

As they do, Miles and Mason get lost in each other's eyes for a noticeable beat, and I let them have it. Finally, she snaps out of it, quickly wrapping her arms around me.

"I'm so glad you're here! Now that you're actually standing here with me, it all feels real." She pulls back and mouths, who's that?

So lost in the moment, I had forgotten about Max.

"Oh, um...guys, this is Max Hopper. He works for Josh. Max Hopper, this is Miles and Mason, and yes, they're on the list."

Shocker, Max nods his hello and leaves it at that, standing near the door with his hands in front of him as per usual.

"Nice to meet you, Max. What exactly do you do for Josh?" Miles asks, arms crossed over his puffed-up chest.

Always the protector.

"Max is my um...bodyguard."

"Personal protection associate," Max says quietly from behind me.

Huh? That's new.

"Okay, I guess I mean personal protection associate."

Mason takes in a breath. "Why do you need a personal protection associate?"

"That's a very good question, Emmett." Miles is speaking to me, but he hasn't moved an inch and is still staring at Max. "Why do you need a bodyguard?"

"Well, there have been some threats since things with Josh, and I have become a bit more public. It's no big deal, though."

This gets his attention, unfortunately for me, not the kind of attention I want.

"And why didn't you tell us about these threats. You're on the phone with Mason every day."

His tan face turns a crimson color. I don't see on him too often.

"Because, as I said, it's no big deal. Josh is just being over-protective."

Usually annoyed by Max's stoic silence, tonight, I'm glad he's a man of few words. There's no need for him to share the gory details.

"Listen, it's nothing for you to worry about. Just consider us lucky to have an extra pair of hands. You don't mind helping us set up, do you?"

As I ask the question and he shakes his head to say he doesn't mind, I realize this isn't a part of the gig. He isn't here to unload boxes and lift heavy things. I'm sure it's on his *It's Not My Job* list.

"Emmy."

"Miles."

"You really aren't going to tell me what's going on?"

"Nothing is going on. Now, where do you want me, Mason?"

"You know I can call Josh and ask him myself."

"Good luck with that. He's pretty busy filming."

"Well, since it seems as though you aren't going to give me the full story, I'll just have to bug him until he answers. And he will answer me."

"Cool, sounds like a plan." I reply, walking around Miles over to Max, who appears to be holding up the wall next to the entrance pretty well. I'm sorry, I mouth to him.

The corners of his mouth lift, and he gives me a barely noticeable wink telling me it's okay while setting me on fire. "Put me to work. I'm sure there are some heavy boxes for me to lift."

That's two winks!

One more, and I may just mount him right here and now.

"Sure are, and I wouldn't mind the help," Miles pipes in. "We've got dozens more boxes out back if you wanna help me bring them in?"

"Lead the way," Max says, and they disappear through the back of the store.

"Oh, my gosh, Mason! Everything looks so great! Show me everything! Did the leather chairs come in? How about the bookmarks? Did I order enough, or are the shelves going to look empty? Please give me a quick tour, and I promise I'll get to work. Your video tours are great, but I'm here, and I want to touch it all!"

Laughing, Mason lifts an eyebrow that is on the same level as my mom when she thinks I'm lying to her.

"What?" I sound confused because I am.

"What do you mean, what? Your bodyguard, of course."

"What about him?"

"You have seen him, haven't you?"

"Yes. What are you getting at?" Oh man, I sure hope it isn't obvious I have a crush on him.

"He's a bit distracting."

"Nah, I barely notice he's there," I lie right to her face.

"Whatever you say, Emmett. Come on, let me show you the reading nook. The chairs work perfectly."

I'm so grateful she doesn't say anything else about Max. As far as everyone is concerned, I'm engaged, and I don't need anyone getting the wrong impression.

Mason takes me on a quick walkthrough of the store, and while we're in the back office looking at all the swag I ordered, the guys keep passing by, each of them carrying heavy box after heavy box.

Once all the boxes are inside, I start unloading books onto one of our many shelves of what we hope will be an extensive romance section. We vowed that our store wouldn't be like so many others that have one tiny shelf of romance tucked into a back corner of the store. Instead, we will put our romance section out front, loud and proud!

The bell above the door chimes, and I hear the sweet voice of my favorite petite redhead behind me. "Emmy, I have a surprise for you!"

"Melly, I don't need a surprise; all I need is..." There's no stopping the scream I release before finishing my statement.

"Surprise!" Amelia squeals jumping up and down, proud as punch.

"Oh, my God! You should be ashamed of yourself, Audrey Calhoun! You've been lying to me for weeks!"

"I know, but it was worth the surprise," she says in my ear now that I have my arms around her.

"What am I, chopped liver?"

"Parker, you knew the first time you brought her home, we liked her better than you. We were all pretty up front about that," I tease, but he knows how much he means to me.

"Shut up and give me a hug."

"I know I just saw you in Vegas less than six months ago, but it feels like years ago. How's married life treating you?"

Parker is an original member of The Crew, and his wife Audrey might as well be. She's been one of us since Reece met her in college and introduced her to Parker.

"Life is as great as it was before she put a ring on it. As long as I have that woman right there, all is right in the world."

"Since when did all the guys in The Crew get so dang mushy?" Amelia jokes, wrapping her arm around Miles's waist so short her head doesn't come anywhere near his shoulder.

"Melly, I know you're still hanging out with Andrew, but you're gonna have a man swoon over you like this one day, this I know."

She just rolls her eyes, thinking he's crazy. She's the mom of the group, the one who makes sure we're all doing okay, and we take care of her right back, but it sure would be nice to see her find her person. Yes, she's dating Andrew, and he considers her his girlfriend, but he's not the one. I hear her eye roll loud and clear, though. I feel the same way, only where she feels pity that she hasn't found the one. I have to fake being in love even though I've never felt more alone.

"Too bad Reece and Rachel weren't home, then we'd have

everyone here," I say to the group tucked into Parker's side, only my head is able to rest on his shoulder.

"Um, sweetie...what about Josh?" Amelia says with a knowing pity in her eyes.

Shit, you forgot about your fiancé. Nicely done, you moron.

"Well, he's going to FaceTime us, so, he'll kind of be here. We'll at least get to see him and talk to him. I think I'm just so used to him traveling that having him live on video is practically like date night."

Abort! Abort! Stop trying to convince them you didn't forget about him when you clearly did.

"Babe, promise me you'll let me know if our date nights feel the same to you as Face Timing. Because if that's the case, then I'm doing something wrong."

"Miles." Mason furrows her brow at what she sees as her fiancé's rudeness, but he's just Miles being Miles. Telling it like it is.

"Enough about date night. We're here to help! So, put us to work." Amelia gives me another look as she bulldozes the awkward moment and sees right through me.

She knows. She freaking knows. Of course, she does.

Amelia is the quiet observer of the group. The most empathetic person I've ever known. She can read people and always knows just what everyone needs before we know it ourselves. But still, I can't believe she's already figured it out.

I don't know why I'm surprised. She and I always wondered about Josh's sexuality growing up. Not because we cared but because we hated that he thought he couldn't be himself around us, especially those of us in The Crew. Deep down, she knows this is all a ruse. I wouldn't be surprised if they all know, but we haven't gotten anything but support so far. I hate lying to them, but if it saves them from knowing and having also to lie for us, then so be it. I don't want to put them in that position, and Josh isn't here to share his truth, and I'm certainly not about to do it for him when he's gone to such lengths to protect it.

A couple of hours later, we've just about finished all that can be done for the night and devoured several pizzas from Chuck's down the street. Miles and Parker are in the back office, and Max leaves to take the pizza boxes out to the dumpster. The moment he's out of earshot, the girls act like a bunch of tweens whispering while gushing over how hot my personal protection is.

"Amelia, you could climb him like a tree. He's huge; he wouldn't even notice teeny tiny you. Go ahead, give it a try so we can all live vicariously through you."

"Audrey, you're terrible!" Amelia gasps. "But you're right. He's pretty cute if you're into the strong, silent, I could kill you with my pinky finger type."

Our little gaggle of girls falls silent when the main topic of conversation enters the room with Miles and Parker behind him.

"Ladies, we're gonna leave you to catch up while the two of us head down to The Verdict. Text when you're done for the night, or meet us down there." Miles says the last part to Mason, kissing her on the cheek sweetly. "Take good care of them, Hopper. You may want to join us at the end of the night for a beer; I have a feeling you're gonna need one after getting stuck here with all this girl talk. Sorry, buddy."

"Thanks, but I think I can handle it."

Uncharacteristically, Max flashes a sugary sweet grin in our direction, and I swear the air whooshes right out of the store.

Once the guys are gone, our third bottle of champagne is popped, and glasses are filled. The four of us are doing a great job breaking in the new leather chairs back in the reading corner.

"So, Emmy, have you guys set a date yet?" Audrey asks innocently, but her question has my stomach twisting in knots.

"No date yet. The next year or two are pretty well planned out for Josh already. After that, I have a feeling it will be a couple of years before we have time to do it right."

There's a sadness in Amelia's eyes. She knows it's all a big sham, but she's a good friend and doesn't say a word.

"Well, as much as I can't wait to attend your wedding, I can't really give you too much crap about a long engagement. We were engaged over eight years before we finally did the deed. It will happen when the time is right."

"No doubt, Audrey. I didn't think you and Parker were ever gonna walk down the aisle." Amelia once again moves the conversation off me.

"Things were good the way they were. We didn't need a piece of paper, you know?" We all nod our understanding. "But I have to admit I love calling him my husband. Mason and Emmett, you'll both see. Nothing has ever felt so right."

I catch Max's sympathetic eye. Yet again, glad he's a man of few words. His eyes say it all. He knows I hate lying to my friends. But, he also knows this is what I signed up for—like literally, signed a contract and a nondisclosure agreement. This is the consequence of my decision.

Would I have done it if I had known it would feel like this? I haven't even seen my family, and I already feel sick about it now that it's public.

"Speaking of, how about the other engaged couple? Have you and Miles picked a date, Mason? I need another reason to come back to Eastlyn; please tell me you two aren't waiting two years?"

Max's phone lights up, and he steps farther away to take it. Curious about everything about him, I am dying to know who it is. Is it Smith, Cleveland, or, God forbid, his girlfriend?

"Have you met Miles? There's no way he could wait that long. We both wanted to just do it, but he said there was no way he was doing anything this big while Reece and Rachel were in Africa. We've talked about the anniversary of the day we met, so if that works out, you'll be back here in early July!"

We toast to impending nuptials, passing the champagne bottle around and refilling our glasses. Before long, we're laughing until we cry, and the decibels are getting higher and higher.

Later in the evening, Amelia catches Max shaking his head and then sticking his finger in his ear. He's not sitting right near us but near enough. He's out in one of the aisleways. I know it's not only to give us privacy but also because he can see the front and back exits from where he's placed himself. I bet he's bored without his laptop to keep him busy.

"We get pretty loud, don't we?" Amelia screams over the rest of us when she catches him with his finger in his ear.

"I barely noticed, ma'am."

"Ma'am? Did he just call me, ma'am?" she asks, swaying on the edge of her chair.

"It's annoying, isn't it?" I say, sticking my tongue out at him and earning myself one of his rare smiles.

I do my best to ignore what his smile does to me and the way my stomach drops. When Amelia continues talking to him all of the girls zip their lips and turn in their seats to pay attention to the barrel-chested man who's endured plenty already after listening to us for the last hour and then some.

"So, Max, can I call you Max? How annoying is Emmy?" she asks without letting him answer how he feels about her using his first name.

"Miss Ford isn't annoying at all, ma'am. One of the easiest clients I've ever worked with."

I was about to tell her to leave him alone, not expecting to find his answer as enjoyable as it was. But, it turns out, I rather liked his answer, and if the way she's now sitting with her feet under her like we're at a slumber party is any indication, she has much more to ask.

Nah, I don't think I'll stop her. He's a tough guy. He can handle little ole Melly.

"Wow, they must be paying you well because I know that can't be true. But, I'll give you my number, and if you ever need to call and vent, I'll lend you an understanding ear."

"Melly, be nice!" I chastise her.

"Thank you for your concern, but I'm sure I'll be fine." He chuckles at the same time.

"Shh...Max and I are talking, Emmett. A, B conversation. C your way out of it."

"How many refills have you had, Amelia? And what grade are we in again? I haven't heard that one since middle school."

"Audrey, did I stutter? Max and I are talking."

Audrey and Mason look at me, and the three of us burst into a fit of laughter. I have no idea what's gotten into our sweet little Melly, but it sure is entertaining.

"Ignore them," she continues over our howls. "How long have you been in this line of work?"

"Going on nine years now."

"Are you good at your job?"

"I sure as hell hope so, or I shouldn't be here."

"What did you do before this?"

"I spent six and a half years in the Marine Corps, went to school, and got my business degree, and here I am."

"How do you stay in shape if you're always with Miss Ford?"

Oh my goodness, she is so embarrassing.

"He's not with me every minute of every day. There are other guys who take turns babysitting me. Max is only with me during the day or when Josh and I have an event to attend."

It hadn't hit me before I heard myself say it out loud.

Why is that? Why is he always with me at events, even when it's a night off?

"Are you single?"

He nods.

So, not his girlfriend on the phone. Whew.

"Looking?"

No nod. No answer.

"How tall are you?"

"Six four."

"What do you do on your days off?"

"Well, I spend time with my dog and my..."

"You have a dog?" I hear myself asking, shocked I didn't know this.

He nods.

"What's your dog's name?" I hear myself asking.

"Molly." He's smiling from ear to ear and shaking his head at my excitement. "Her name is Molly. She's a French Bulldog."

"No way! You better start bringing her to work with you! How could you keep her away from me?"

"It didn't seem professional to bring my pet to work, ma'am. Besides, I'm not sure Mr. West would appreciate it."

"Well, Mr. West is never home, so I don't think he gets a say. But, I would love to have her at the house. Oh, please tell me you'll bring her over when we get back? Please, that big old house could use some life in it."

I know I'm begging, but I feel so alone back in Los Angeles. A furry friend may be just what I need.

"Sure, Miss Ford. I'll bring her by."

He stands from his chair, and his attention leaves the four of us. He takes a step back a moment later, blending into the wall behind him.

I hear Miles before I see him. "All right, all right. You can stop talking about us now." He rounds the corner with Parker behind him. "Ladies, you know I love you, but I'm tired, and I need this beautiful woman to take me home and put me to bed."

Mason doesn't argue with him. Once he entered the room, all she wanted was him. Their need for one another is equally matched, and I, for one, wouldn't want to get in the way of it.

The store empties with Amelia leaving with Parker and Audrey. Then it's just my personal protection associate and me. Finally, I'm left to close up the store with the weight of my deceit heavy on my heart.

Max and I don't exchange words on the short drive back to my place. When we get home, I make a beeline for my room, collapsing on my bed.

I hate this.

This isn't me.

I don't lie to the people who mean the most to me in the world, and I don't break down in a puddle of tears and shame. But since that's what's happening right now, I guess I do. Or maybe it's the champagne?

Hell, I don't even know the person looking back at me in the mirror these days.

A light knock scares me half to death. That knock can only be from one person. He's the only other person in the house and the last person I want to see me like this.

When I don't answer, he speaks through the door. "Miss Ford? I just wanted to check in before calling it a night. Did you need anything before I turn in?"

I sit up on the edge of the bed and try to speak, but between the sobs, I'm trying my best to keep silent, no response comes through.

"Miss Ford?" He knocks again, only louder this time. "Miss Ford, you okay?"

Hoping he'll just walk away, I focus on settling my breathing instead of answering.

"Miss Ford, I'm coming in."

The door opens with an urgent swoosh, but shame prevents me from looking at him.

The bed dips next to me without a word, and a strong arm is around me, pulling me into his side. My instinct is to wrap my arms around his waist, but I resist, knowing he isn't holding me for the right reasons.

He's taking pity on me.

Because I'm pathetic.

Time doesn't exist. I have no idea how long we sit, with only the sound of my whimpering and sniffling filling the room. Once my breathing has leveled out and my blubbering turns into me staring vacantly at the floor, the warmth from his arm around me leaves my shoulders, and he rubs two slow circles on my back. When he moves his arm away from me, it leaves me no choice but to pull away from the security of his side.

When I finally look at him, his eyes search mine with an intensity that once again relieves my lungs of the air that had been there mere seconds ago, only this time for a completely different reason.

Is he going to kiss me?

Oh, Max. Please kiss me, even if only out of pity.

As if hearing my internal pleading and realizing we're crossing a line we both know shouldn't be crossed, he says, "Good night, Miss Ford."

Standing without another word or looking in my direction, he leaves me on my bed, closing the door behind him.

Chapter Seven

"Poodle, there you are! Come give your Grammy some love."

My beloved grandmother holds her arms open from her favorite recliner, and I can't get to her fast enough.

I hate having to come to a senior living facility to see her, but luckily, everyone loves her here as much as I do, and they take great care of her. It's not ideal, but it's what she wanted. Always clear she didn't want to live with family after Gramps passed. She didn't want to be a burden or slow down anyone's lie.

"Oh, Grammy, it's so good to see you. I've missed you!"

She feels frail in my arms, yet her hold, as always, gives me strength.

"Let me look at you, Poodle."

Grabbing the chair in the corner I pull it next to hers, letting her take her inspection of me and wait for her to ask me if I've been eating and when I'm going back to my natural hair color.

"Oh, Poodle. Don't they feed you in Los Angeles?"

She never lets me down.

"They do feed me, but they also have yoga classes."

"Yoga? Sounds sexy."

Again, an expected comment that makes Grammy well... Grammy. If only Max weren't standing outside the open door keeping watch, because you know, senior living homes in Pendleton, Oregon, are a hub for abductions.

"Well, if you consider sweating your face off with your hair stuck to the side of your head sexy, then yep, yoga is sexy. But, speaking of sexy, I have something for you."

"It better not be too sexy; I'm an old lady."

"I think it's just the right sexy for you. Here you go. The last two books in Mason's series."

Grammy and I have been reading Mason's books together. My grandmother is what I like to call spicy with her witty, slightly off-color comments and her shelves of Harlequins lining an entire wall of her room. She refuses to give any of them up and has it in her will that they'll all go to me when the dreaded day comes that she leaves us. And I'm sure I won't be able to give a single one of them up either.

"Thank you, Emmy. I can't wait to see what happens. Your friend sure has a way with the heart, doesn't she?"

"Yes, she does. I'm going to bring her out here with me over the holiday. She can't wait to meet you."

"That would be wonderful, darlin'. I sure am sorry I won't be able to make your big grand opening tomorrow. But, be sure to take lots of pictures and make me one of those video things you do and give me a tour when you get a chance."

"I wish you could be there too, but it will be busy, and I wouldn't get much time with you anyway. I promise pictures and videos, though."

My heart cracks with the knowledge that she's not well enough to be there tomorrow or later in the week for Thanksgiving dinner. The realization that she's unable to attend family functions means we may not have much time left with her, and that is not something I can even contemplate.

"Poodle, I'm so proud of you. You are beautiful, kind, smart, successful, and now a business owner on top of everything else. I hope that Josh of yours realizes how lucky he is."

I was hoping Josh wouldn't come up, but here we are.

"He does, Grammy."

That's not a lie. He appreciates me; I know he does.

I also know Max can hear our conversation, and I'm not so sure he would agree. But, then again, it's not his job to have an opinion.

* * *

"Emmett, enough small talk. Talk to me."

"I am talking to you. We've been talking for close to ten minutes now."

"Emmett Louise Ford, you know what I'm talking about. Why are you doing this?"

We're at the local diner called The Jury Room, and Max is sitting in the booth next to ours. He's behind Amelia, but I have full view of him. He's been giving us privacy, sipping on his coffee, keeping his eyes trained out the window as if we aren't even here. He's good at giving me my space. He hasn't mentioned my breakdown or what he may have overheard at Grammy's. Instead, he's his stoic self. Minding his own business. But with Amelia's question lingering in the air, his eyes have found me.

"Doing what?"

I've never been able to hide anything from her. So I don't know why I'm prolonging her interrogation.

"Emmett. Stop it. Why are you marrying Josh?"

I focus on Amelia, unable to face the man, with no opinion one booth over.

"Amelia, I don't know how you always know, but you do."

"Sweetie, I love you and Josh both. But I think we all know you two shouldn't be getting married. So, why are you?"

"Melly, you know we always had our pact. Well, I'm thirty-one, and he turned thirty six months ago. Everyone always knew the deal. If we were both single at thirty, we'd get married."

"Sweetie, we all say things when we're kids. I said I was going to move to New York and be a Rockette. We can all see that didn't come to fruition. I blame my height or lack thereof, but back to you and your ridiculous reasoning."

"I know, Melly. You're right, but I saw my friend in need and didn't consider the ramifications. I didn't want him to lose everything because of some silly rumors if there was a way I could fix it."

My whispered answer has her hissing back under her breath.

"He pays people to fix things like this for him. That's not your job."

"I know, trust me, I know that now more than ever. If I could go back in time, I would. But it's too late. I signed a contract, and now, on top of lying to everyone, including Grammy, I mean, who lies to Grammy, there are these stupid threats, and we have no idea where they're coming from. But they know things, Amelia. They know where I'm going to be and if you saw the threats they've sent." I shiver when the flash of the pictures of my decapitated head flashes through my memory. "Josh thinks it's someone on his staff, can you believe that? All I wanted to do was make things better, and all I've done is create more issues for him. I'm just making things worse."

Her freckled face reddens with anger. She may be small, but when she's upset, she is mighty.

"Don't go there. This is on Josh for agreeing to this crazy idea and especially for making you sign your life away. I am glad he's making sure you're plenty safe, though." She jerks her ginger head toward Max.

"Oh, I am. It's all a bit overboard if you ask me."

"Emmy, what if you meet someone? Are you supposed to just isolate yourself and miss an opportunity at love if it comes your way?"

Without thinking, my eyes shoot to Max, and I feel it in my bones. I have met that someone. He holds my gaze. This has been our norm since the plane. Eye contact that is held, but nothing is said. No emotion shown.

"Well, with my track record, I'll meet someone, and it will be one-sided. So, it won't matter anyway. Besides, it's only for two years."

"Two years! He made you sign a contract saying you would be his fake fiancée for two years, meaning you can't date anyone else that entire time?"

"Amelia, keep your voice down. Josh didn't make me do it; his people did. He gave me the chance to back out, and I didn't take it. So, this is on me, not Josh."

"So, no sex for two years?"

"Oh, God. When you put it that way...what have I done?" I chuckle, doing my best to lighten the mood.

Luckily for me, she laughs too, and I can only hope our conversation is taking a turn. I hate discussing this with Max in earshot. It's so embarrassing.

"Em, seriously, though. You deserve happiness as much as Josh does. Do you think this will last two years?"

"I signed a contract."

"Who cares! This is Josh. He can tell his people to rip it up. This is bullshit, Emmett!"

"I don't have to actually marry him."

"And that makes this okay?"

At a loss for words, all I can do is shrug.

"Em, this is a mess."

"I know," I say, chancing a glance at Max.

To an outsider, his face holds no emotion, but I can see the empathy in his eyes.

Chapter Eight

"Emmett, I love that you're the girl who changes her hair color on a whim, and you're brave enough to make crazy choices, but damn girl, it's nice to see you with your natural color. You're even more beautiful like this."

"Thanks, Miles, it does feel good. We'll see how long it lasts. You know I get bored."

Miles' opinion matters, but it was the hitch in Max's breath when I walked out of Tell Me About It, our local beauty shop, that confirmed I had made the right decision to go back to my natural color. Dark brown.

As I was leaving Grammy's today, she grabbed my face and said, "Don't forget who you are, Emmy. I know you love Josh, but don't lose yourself in his world. Keep a hold of that little brown-haired girl who used to wear wildflowers in her hair. You can change your outside to look any way you want, darlin', as long as you don't forget that little girl and all of her dreams still waiting to come true who lives inside you."

Her words struck a chord. I was texting Cara to see if she had any openings as soon as I was in the car.

When Cara spun my chair around, I fought to hold back

tears. It was the first time in months I recognized the woman looking back at me. It felt good.

"I agree with Miles; you look damn good, girl." Parker kisses me on the temple.

"Okay, okay. I get it. You didn't like the red. Noted."

"There's only room for one redhead in this group, lady. I was going to give you another month, and then we were going to have words," Amelia jokes.

"Leave the Night On" by Sam Hunt starts playing, and all discussion of my hair color is forgotten. This song describes our town to a T and became one that our Crew gravitated to. Audrey, Amelia, and I break into song like we're the only ones in the bar. Being new to the group, Mason cuddles up with Miles and enjoys the show.

Taking a bow at the end of the song, I take a discrete glance at the big man not so discreetly sitting at the bar. Strangers don't blend in at The Verdict, and this stranger also doesn't miss that I've snuck a peek at him. His nearly imperceptible nod isn't needed when his eyes burn through me the way his do. I'm too chicken to nod back, averting my eyes quickly, focusing on my friends.

The moment only lasted a couple of seconds. But, Max simply nodding to let me know he was there, watching, doing his job sent me into an internal joy spiral and has me obsessing over the fact that his eyes were already on me when I looked up.

How long had he been watching?

My phone rings that funny ring that says Josh is on the other line and wants to video chat and my thoughts about Max are momentarily interrupted. I pick up, and his handsome face fills the screen.

"Hey, mister! Guess where I am?"

Holding the phone out in front of me so he can see the rest of The Crew, Miles yells, "What's up, Hollywood?"

"Aw, man, are you all at The V without me? Holy shit, are Parker and Audrey there too? I cannot believe I'm missing this! I wish I were there instead of freezing my balls off up here in Montreal." He pouts.

"We wish you were here too," Parker shouts over my head.

After everyone says their hellos and has given Josh a significant amount of crap, I sneak off into a corner booth so I can hear him better. He updates me on filming being behind schedule and the fact that the crew will have to work through the holiday. Jace went home for Thanksgiving, so he's bored on his downtime. His bodyguard, Reeves, is the only one on his team still there with him, and he sounds lonely.

"Maybe I can come visit after Thanksgiving?" I offer in the hopes of lifting his spirits.

"You know you're always welcome, but Jace will be back Friday, and he'll snap me out of my funk."

My heart plummets. I may not be his real fiancée, but he's still my best friend, even if he doesn't seem to need me in that capacity anymore.

More doubt creeps into my psyche, but I push it aside when I feel Max's stare from across the room. I pretend I'm looking around the room for someone so he doesn't catch me again, because you know, I'm smooth like that, but when my fake room scan catches him watching me, I lose all my cool.

The corners of my mouth lift, and I smile at him.

As per usual, he nods. Not smiling back.

Cue the mortified blush heating my face.

"What's goin' on there, Emmy?"

"What? Oh, nothing. Why?"

"I see that blush."

"You're imagining things."

"Whatever. I'll let you go and have fun. Call me later, okay?"

"I will, and you try not to miss Jace too much."

"I'll do my best. Love you, Emmy."

"Love you."

As I make my way to the little girl's room, there's no way I can avoid Max. I give him a shy grin plastering my happy face on, but don't stop to chat.

Finding myself alone in the bathroom, my disappointment with Josh not wanting me to visit turns to anger when brown hair catches my eye. Josh didn't even comment on my hair. Not that I need compliments from him, but the entire call was, as always, about him. It's always about him, including the next two years of my life.

Enough. It's not Josh's fault. You agreed to this, knowing him better than anyone, and you still offered to help. Now, go have fun.

The Crew is out on the dance floor, and I head right to them, avoiding the hazel eyes at the bar.

Ten songs later, when a slow melody begins to play, Amelia, our resident dancing queen, and I leave all the lovebirds to slow dance and steal some kisses.

"Hey, we're gonna get another round. Can I get you anything?" I ask Max on my way to place an order.

He lifts his glass of water. "No, I'm fine."

"You bored?"

"Nope, all good. Don't worry about me, Miss Ford."

All it takes is hearing him call me Miss Ford, and I move along.

Yes, I know. You're just doing your job.

"You guys need another round?" Beau, the best bartender in Eastern Oregon, asks when he sees us headed his way.

Before I can answer, my ex, Brandon, cuts me off.

"C'mon, Beau. I was up here waiting to order before her. If I had a pair of tits, would you have taken my order first?"

"Brandon, don't start," Beau warns.

"What is it, Emmy? You think because you're marrying that fuck head, you can roll back into town, and everyone is just gonna bend over and take it up the ass because you want a drink? Fuck off."

"Hey, Beau, will you just send those over to the table when they're ready?" I yell over Brandon, who has clearly already had plenty tonight.

"Sure thing, Em."

Amelia links her arm with mine, turning me away from my asshole of an ex-boyfriend still going off at the bar. Before we get two steps away, Max is up off his stool, ready to take care of things, but I give him a thumbs-up letting him know I'm okay.

Everything would have been fine if Brandon had been smart enough to just let it go.

"Really, you're too good to speak to a lowlife like me?" Then, grabbing my wrist, he pulls on me to stop me from walking away.

The next thirty seconds go by in blurry slow motion.

Max grabs Brandon by the back of the neck, and his hand releases me instantly. My bodyguard gives Beau a look over his shoulder, and he points at the hallway just past the bar. No words exchanged. Like Max and Beau had already planned for this, as Brandon is manhandled down the hall.

As they disappear, my pulse throbs in my ears, and I'm not quite sure what happened.

"C'mon, honey. Let's go sit down."

"What the hell was that all about?" Miles asks, when the loved-up couples meet us at the booth.

"Brandon was being Brandon. And then Max happened. You guys, it was amazing! Max grabbed him by the neck and took him out back just like that!" Amelia explains with a snap of her fingers.

"Miss Ford, are you ready to go?"

All eyes focus over my shoulder. Then, cautiously, I turn toward his deep and always serious voice only to find a storm brewing in Max's eyes, and his twitching jaw muscle working overtime. I've never seen him this way before, and even if I wasn't ready to leave just yet, I am now.

"Yep, just one sec."

"Whoa," Amelia mouths.

"Hey all, I have to get up early tomorrow, so I'm gonna head out. Mason, I'll see you at the store at noon to prep for our big day." Not prolonging the goodbyes, I turn on my heel with a wave.

Much to my surprise, Max places his hand on the small of my back, guiding me to the exit while my stomach cartwheels all over itself. When he moves his hand to open the door for me, I release a deep breath I hadn't realized I had been holding since the moment his fingertips touched me.

The bite of the cool night air sends a chill up my spine, only to be blanketed with the heat of his hand on the small of my back once again.

My thoughts are scattered by the massive swing in his demeanor, leaving me even more rattled after he carefully assists me into the passenger seat. It's not the first time I've sat in the front seat with him, but this time, it's because he wants me in the front seat. This much is very clear.

I only get the time it takes for him to get around the front of the car for my brain to struggle to figure out why he's so upset. His job isn't to have an opinion about how I live my life, but it is certainly his job to protect me. You would think getting to deal with Brandon would add a little excitement to his usually dull day. Sitting at my kitchen island day after day must bore him to death, so what in the world has gotten into him?

If I thought the walk from the bar to the car was out of character for him, the vibe that follows him into the car has me thrown for a loop. Shutting the door, he pushes the button to start the car and waits for a beat before putting the vehicle in drive. The streetlight outside illuminates a face full of contemplation as though he's warring with himself.

Giving him his space, I focus my attention out the passenger side window, trying to clear my head. The car has just pulled away from the curb when his fingertips brush the back of my hand, seeking permission without words. Turning my hand over, I unfurl my clenched fist, letting him slip his fingers through mine. When I feel the heat of his palm pressed against mine, it sends the cadence of my heart into overdrive.

Worried I'll ruin the moment, I continue watching my hometown glide by as we drive down the streets I grew up on. Felt safe on. Dreamed on. Now, driving down these same streets, I realize how vulnerable I was before I had Max's hand in mine. His touch stabilizes me somehow, calming the same nerves his touch excites.

There's a strange juxtaposition of emotions bubbling up in my chest. Calm and excitement. There's also a sense of relief that I may not be alone in my feelings. Yet the prospect that he could feel more for me is terrifying, given the situation.

When we turn onto my street, my anxiety spikes, knowing not only will he have to let go of my hand in a moment but also because we'll soon be alone in the house.

Walking from the driveway to the house, I shiver visibly. Not from the late November breeze whipping through my hair and not even from his hand guiding me once again. No, I'm shaking from the inside out, anticipating what's to come once we cross the threshold.

Closing the door behind us, he locks up, leaving us both standing in my tiny living room. His eyes search mine, but for what? I have no idea.

"You okay?" I finally have to ask him.

"Fine." And just like that, whatever had taken hold of him back at the bar is gone. His eyes no longer search mine. His back straightens, his professional demeanor back in place. "Do you need anything else, Miss Ford?"

"No, thank you. I'm fine."

With a nod, he walks away, his fists flexing at his side as he strides down the dark hallway. The only sound is the click of his bedroom door closing shortly after he's out of sight.

I lied. I'm not fine. I'm far from fine. I'm confused, and just as his fists would indicate, I'm frustrated, just like Max.

Chapter Nine

The steam from my shower isn't enough to quell the smell of hickory-smoked bacon lingering through the house. The scent is almost as good as the actual bacon tasted smothered in the warm maple syrup that had seeped off the stack of fluffy pancakes. Pancakes that had been waiting for me when I woke up this morning.

Wiping the condensation off the bathroom mirror, I see a face I can barely believe is my own. It's not just the new hair; it's the flush of my skin, the light in my eyes, the apples of my cheeks more prominent than ever. I pinch myself to ensure I'm not still in bed under my covers dreaming.

When I shuffled to the kitchen this morning, excited about the coffee I could smell from my bedroom, I was stunned to find the kitchen in utter disarray. The counters were covered in flour and eggshells, and there were utensils everywhere, but who cares when Max is standing in the middle of it all in a T-shirt, gym shorts, and bare feet.

Bare feet.

I don't care how strong the cup of joe. Seeing him dressed

down like that stirred me awake more than any coffee ever could.

Good morning, was all he said with a glass of orange juice held out to me. As he pulled my chair out, he added a steaming cup of caffeine elixir to my table setting. I didn't think I would be able to eat a bite. My stomach was too mixed up with the flurry of butterflies frantically crashing into one another in their excitement.

His demeanor was cool and calm, as if he cooked breakfast for me in bare feet every day. He asked me how many pancakes I wanted when he set down a plate of bacon and a gravy boat of warmed maple syrup.

He warmed the syrup!

And Lord have mercy; when he sucked some of the sticky goodness off his thumb, my heartbeat went into overdrive. After everything was in front of me, he told me to leave my dishes on the table, and he would take care of them after I was done. Then he left the room, not eating with me. He just left the room, and a few minutes later, I heard the shower turn on.

He knew what I needed this morning, and he gave it to me. He was sweet, quiet, casual, and because he knows I am often too distracted to eat breakfast—he's heard Greta lecture me about this many times—he made sure I didn't forget.

I'm a nervous wreck knowing I'll have to speak publicly today, especially since it's apparently a big enough deal that Sibby, Josh's PR rep, is flying in for the event and then flying right back out. I'm not exactly sure what kind of damage I'll do to Josh's reputation by speaking in front of a few people in my hometown outside of our tiny little bookstore, but if she wants to take two commercial flights to get to our tiny hometown then so be it.

Max was there when I got the news that Sibby would be attending today, and unfortunately for him, he was the person I vented to after I hung up. He didn't reply, just listened—because it's not his job to do otherwise.

Now, the day is here, and it's not the nerves about the store opening consuming me; it's the intense feelings about the man I hear doing dishes down the hall while I get ready.

I wonder if his feet are still bare?

The shaking of my hand is making the application of mascara a daunting task. If I'm not careful, I may take an eye out and spend the opening at St. Anthony's. That idea doesn't sound too bad. It would get me out of this whole speaking thing. As nervous as I am, I'm thrilled to be opening this store in my hometown. I really do think it's just what our sweet little town needs.

Finally, my hair and makeup are done. I'm dressed in black high-waisted wide-leg slacks, an emerald green blouse, black blazer, and matching emerald heels. I know I look a little fancy for Eastlyn, but I want to portray a professional image as a new business owner. I add a couple of small accessories, grab my purse, inhale a deep breath, and leave the comfort of my room.

I need to take a lot more deep cleansing breaths these days. I blame it on my personal protection associate down the hall.

Rounding the corner into the kitchen, I expect to see Max still cleaning, but if it weren't for the scent in the air, you wouldn't even know he had been here. Everything is sparkling clean.

The man responsible is standing outside in the brisk morning air staring into the distance, and unfortunately, he's fully dressed. It's only in the upper forties today, yet he's sans coat and just in his dark jeans and a gray button-down shirt with the sleeves rolled up, exposing the muscles of his forearms. His hands are in his front pockets, and his face is aimed toward the sky, almost as if he were praying. When his torso lifts and falls from a deep breath, I can't help but wonder what strength from above he may be searching for?

Not wanting to interrupt his quiet time or get caught watching him out the kitchen window, I start to sneak away when I hear his phone ring. He answers, and I head to the hall closet to get my coat, grateful he didn't catch me spying.

I reach for my heavy winter coat, but with the whoosh of the sliding back door opening and closing, I instantly heat, knowing Max is back in the house. Just like that, I'm too warm and opt for a lighter option. I let out a scream when I push the door shut to find Max standing a few feet away.

"Sorry if I scared you, Miss Ford."

"No, it's fine. I'm just a little bit lost in my thoughts right now. But seriously, how does a big guy like you walk around without making a sound? It just doesn't seem possible."

His eyes are shining—lit with amusement—which makes me happy. Even if just for a moment.

"Just got the call that the store is clear, and we can head over whenever you're ready."

"What do you mean the store is clear?"

"Well, the other guys have been there all morning, ensuring that things are safe for your arrival."

"I've said it before, and I'll say it again. I think you guys are going just a smidge overboard, don't ya think?"

"Whenever you're ready."

Ugh. He is so frustrating.

"I'm ready."

He opens the door for me, and as he stops to lock up, I make sure I don't step on any cracks on my way to the car. Today is not the day to tempt fate by ignoring a crazy superstition.

He catches up to me by the time I reach the blacked-out SUV. It still looks odd sitting in my driveway.

As he leans in front of me to get my door, his free hand

lands gently on my low back like it did last night. Is this barely-there touch part of the job?

Is it a protective move, or is it more?

Maybe it's just good manners?

Or maybe I'm crazy?

I settle into my seat and reach for my seat belt when I notice he's still holding my door open.

"You look great, Miss Ford. You have nothing to worry about. It's going to go well."

"Thank you," I manage to get out through the shock of his unexpected compliment.

He doesn't dish out any more compliments when he gets in the car, keeping both hands on the wheel. No repeat of the handholding from last night. But he does open the center console to show me where my mints are stored.

"Just in case."

"Thanks."

His kind gestures know no limit today, and as much as I try to tell myself, it doesn't mean anything; I can't help that with each of his gestures a tiny piece of me hopes it might mean more than it does.

Too soon, he's pulling up in front of the shop where Sibby is talking to two men I don't recognize.

"I need a second, if you don't mind?"

He puts the car in park, not saying a word. He does turn in his seat to look at me. I, on the other hand, continue to look straight ahead at Main Street. He's waiting for me to tell him why I'm nervous. Knowing I'll speak when I'm ready, he doesn't push. He just waits.

He knows me better than many people who have known me most of my life.

"I'm nervous."

"Why?"

"I don't know. I mean, the real attention will be on Mason. She's the famous author who moved to a small town for love and decided to open a bookstore. People are looking forward to hearing her speak, not me, and I know this. I wish I could blame the fact that Sibby is here, making this a much bigger deal than it needs to be, but I think having her here is a giant reminder that I'm standing in front of my hometown pretending to be Josh's fiancée. Lying to everyone." I finally look at him. "Max, I'm a liar."

"Miss Ford, Sibby is here as a precaution. In case you're asked about your engagement. She is just trying to stay ahead of things. But I'm sure she'll realize there was no reason for her to be here because there will be nothing for her to spin. Also, I think you'll find you are mistaken. People are here for you just as much as they are for Miss O'Brien. You're their hometown girl done good. Don't sell yourself short. You're kind of awesome."

I look in the back seat and over my shoulder to see who he might be talking to because he couldn't have just told me I was awesome.

"Yes, I'm talking to you. You're a kick-ass woman, and today is going to be great. The thing is, you have to get out of the car to see for yourself and prove me right."

My tongue sticks out at him in a sassy reply.

He chuckles. "C'mon, let's go."

With that, he's out of the car. I watch him dumbfounded as he walks around the front of the vehicle. Sometimes when I watch him round the car, I wonder if he's real. So big, broad, and beautiful in his own unique brooding way. But right now, I'm pretty sure he's a figment of my imagination.

Before both of my feet are out of the car, Sibby meets me on the sidewalk with a whirling dervish of information. I know she likes to keep moving, so I do just that, and she follows me.

"Morning, Emmett. Everything is set. People magazine sent a photographer, and there are a couple of other paps here. It should be pretty low-key, but the right people are here covering things."

The ring of the bell chimes as we cross the threshold, causing the other two bodyguards to walk out from the back office.

"What do you mean a couple of other paps, and why is People magazine here?"

"Did you think I would fly out here and not make it worth it? This is great publicity for Josh. He may not be opening the store, but his fiancée is, and you're an extension of him. Doing something good for the community you two grew up in is almost as good as Josh doing it himself. Having Nina Patrick as your business partner is a bonus."

"Why didn't I know about this?" I say to Sibby but glare at Max.

"No offense, Emmett, but Josh is my client, not you. He's aware, and I assumed he would have filled you in."

"From now on, I'd like to be kept in the loop. My team needs to be aware of all aspects of events like this. We need to clear any media you bring along," Max growls, storming to the back of the store and huddling up in conversation with the other two bodyguards. I mean, personal protection associates.

I'm relieved he didn't keep this from me. He's just as pissed as I am.

"Geez, he sure is uptight." She disparages him, but her eyes give him a full inspection, and I want to pull her bleach blond chignon right off her head. "Besides, the other two security guys already cleared the paps. I wouldn't bring anyone I didn't know or who I didn't think would serve you well."

"Well, in the future, I'd like to know what's going on, if you don't mind."

Thankfully, I spot Miles and Mason across the street with Mason's three besties from New York. I take the opportunity to walk back outside, happily leaving Sibby inside to meet them on the sidewalk.

Mason's friends seem great, but I'm so distracted by thoughts of bare feet, pancakes, compliments, and words of encouragement that I'm not giving them my full attention. I do hear Mason say we should get inside to finish setting up, and I'm just about to follow them all inside the store when my parents stop me.

"Emmet Ford, get over here and give your dad a hug."

When I turn on my heels, my dad is waiting with open arms while my mother beams, clutching her pearls—literally, clutching her pearls.

"Oh, I'm so glad you're here. Sorry I haven't been by yet."

"We know you've been busy, even if you did make time for Grammy."

He releases me, and I bend down to hug my petite mom, who stands at least six inches shorter than me. I'm the spitting image of my mother, except for the fact that I tower over her. I get my height from my dad. He's a strapping six foot four, just like another certain someone in my life.

"Ignore your father; we know you've been busy."

"So, what do you think?" I say, turning the three of us toward the front window display at the exact moment Max walks out of the store, leaving us all staring right at him as he finds a spot on the sidewalk to discreetly stand watch.

"Who's the scary man?" Mom whispers.

Getting his attention isn't hard when I wave Max over.

"Mom. Dad. This is Max; he works for Josh and travels with me. He keeps me safe."

"You have a bodyguard, and you didn't tell us? Why do you need a bodyguard?"

My dad's tone says he's not happy with this situation, and he wants an explanation, but Max steps forward, extending his hand.

"Sir, it's nice to meet you. I'm just here as a precaution. You can never be too careful."

"Will you be here with Emmett for the holiday?" My mom asks.

"Yes, ma'am. I'll be staying in Eastlyn the entire time she's home."

"Well, I'll be sure to set an extra plate at the table for Thanksgiving."

"Ma'am, that won't be..."

"It's settled."

I wrap my arm around my mom. I love her giving heart so much.

"Thank you, ma'am, but..."

"Max, I know we don't know each other, but it's settled."

He looks at me with pleading eyes.

"Don't fight it, Max. Nothing can be done once she's set her mind to something."

I expect him to smile, but instead, his brow furrows even deeper, and somehow, he grows even more serious than usual.

"Thank you for the invitation, Mrs. Ford. I look forward to it."

"Make sure you bring your appetite." Then, turning her attention to me, she's beaming again. "Now, show me your store."

"You're gonna love it, Mom."

Mom, Dad and I have just wrapped up their tour of the store when Amelia, Parker, and Audrey arrive to help us put up the grand opening signs outside and inside the store. Before I know it, the shop is packed with family and friends, and it's time to push everyone outside for the ribbon cutting and speeches.

Surprisingly, the crowd outside floods into Main Street, and it seems we've closed down the main artery in Eastlyn.

It's time, and I'm up first. Luckily, Lou, Miles's dog, is adorned in one of our Just One More Chapter T-shirts and an adorable bow tie. All the attention is on him while the local kids take selfies with him.

Max is standing discreetly behind me, and while everyone is distracted by Lou, I turn to him. "I changed my mind. Why don't we bail while the dog has everyone's attention?"

"I think it's a little too late for that." He chuckles, giving me a wink that, as per usual, stops my heart, distracting me from my trepidation. "Now, go open your store, Miss Ford."

Chapter Ten

"Emmett, I think you're a natural," Sibby says, sitting next to me in the back seat. Of course, without looking up from her phone.

After acting all tough when we first got home and insisting I sit in the front seat while we were here, I caved, and now I'm in the back because it felt like the proper thing to do with Sibby riding with us.

Yep, I'm really tough.

"I wouldn't go that far, but thanks. Of course, it helps that I knew everyone there, except for your friends with the cameras. Was that really necessary?"

Her fingers finally stop moving, and she looks up from her device.

"Trust me; you're going to love the spread in People. Even if it's just a page or two, it will be great. Just be sure that you don't let too loose when you're out with your friends tonight. The team from the magazine may still be lingering around to get shots of Josh West's hometown. Not to mention the new hometown of Nina, I mean Mason. They're gonna want to see what could get her to give up her penthouse Manhattan apartment for small-town Oregon."

"I'll do my very best not to tarnish Josh's good name. And just so you know, Mason doesn't need to give up anything. It's not like that with the two of them. She may have moved to East-lyn, but she's keeping her apartment. So it's not like she's moving here, and they'll never go back to New York. Besides, it's not so bad here."

"Great." She dismisses me. "Now, after you're home from Thanksgiving, I have some outings scheduled for you. We need to make sure we keep you out there while Josh is away."

"What sort of outings?"

"We just need to make sure you make your mark on the charity scene. And before you say it, yes, people will want you there even if it's not on Josh's arm. And a few more yoga dates with Nicolette Gwen would be nice."

"I'm sorry, but my friendship with Nikki isn't about getting publicity. Are you the one who tipped off the paparazzi last time?"

"No, but I thank whoever did."

"Sibby, if that's going to happen every time I meet with Nikki, I'll just stop going. I don't want my picture in the paper if I didn't pose for it. It's one thing to be a part of a photo op with Josh, but to have those leeches waiting for me every time I leave the house may mean I turn into a hermit."

"Emmett, today was a big day. We'll talk once you're back in LA. For now, let's just enjoy the moment."

"Whatever."

I barrel out of the car, ignoring Sibby and her conde-scending comments about how adorable my little house is as she follows me. I have one thing on my mind. Getting changed into something more comfortable and meeting The Crew for drinks before I head to my parents' for dinner.

Max beats me to the front door, and with Sibby stopped in the middle of the driveway, distracted by something on her phone, he leans down when he opens the door and whispers in my ear.

"You should be proud of yourself. You did great today. Just like I told you you would."

My feet are frozen to the spot, staring at him and wondering just where in the world he came from. But, once again, he's gifting me the encouragement I need after my frustrating conversation with Sibby. He gives me one of his classic nods, and I'm starting to think his nods are like their own kind of sign language.

The tapping of Sibby's heels coming up the walkway moves me along, rushing inside. Once inside, she's over the top about how cute my place is, and all it does is get under my skin. Half the time, she's looking at her phone, and it couldn't be clearer that she's faking it because she knows I wasn't happy about our conversation in the car.

"Hey, I'm gonna go change and..."

Max's pocket pings and both he and Sibby look down at their phones. Sibby's face pales, and Max's hardens, and somehow his jaw ticks, and his nostrils flare all at once.

"What?"

Sibby looks at Max. "I'm calling 911."

"No!" he barks. "That's what they want. I'll take care of it."

"Miss Ford, wait right here, please."

"What do you mean wait right here?"

Storming past me and down the hall, he checks the bathroom and all three bedrooms.

"Miss Ford, go ahead and change, and please pack a bag," he orders, disappearing into the spare room he's staying in.

"What do you mean pack a bag? It's only Tuesday; we aren't leaving until Sunday."

"Pack for a week just to be safe. Be sure to bring some winter clothes." He's calm. Matter of fact. Throwing his things in his bag and dialing his phone.

"Smith, you got it too?"

He pauses, listening to Smith on the other end.

"Yep, I'll text you our travel details shortly. You and Cleveland okay to hang back to see what you can find here in Eastlyn?"

What the hell do they all know that I don't?

"I'll be in touch."

"What's going on, Max?"

"If you could go pack, I'll work on getting our flights arranged."

"Where are we going?" I ask louder. Firmer.

"Somewhere safe." His eyes are full of sincerity, and I know I should do what he's asking, but why won't he tell me what's going on?"

"Somewhere safe? What are you talking about?"

"Miss Ford, please just do as I ask."

"You aren't asking; you're telling, Max!" I scream at him.

"Emmett, Max is right. Do what he says, sweetie." Sibby puts her hands on my shoulders, guiding me to my room.

"But I'm supposed to meet up with everyone for drinks and then my parents for dinner."

"Text them from the car, honey."

Chapter Eleven

Max squeezes into the aisle seat of row 22 after hitting his head on the overhead compartment. "Well, you got your wish."

We barely made our connecting flight in Portland, and we're both a little on edge. Everything happened so fast. I texted the girls and called my parents on our way to the airport. Somehow, we were on our flight from Pendleton to Portland within an hour and a half of arriving home from the store opening. Max and I had aisle seats across from each other during the short hour-long flight. He spent the entire flight on his phone or his computer. Now, we're seated next to each other for the next five hours, but his electronic devices are all stored in the overhead compartment, at least for the time being.

"And what wish was that? To be pulled away from my home without being told where I'm going? Or is it missing Thanksgiving with my family?"

"But you're flying commercial. Silver lining?"

"Smart-ass."

I can hear his attempt at humor in his voice, but I'm still

pissed. I'm looking at the screen on the back of the chair in front of me as though it were the most fascinating thing I'd ever seen. My hands are in my lap, and my elbows are pressed to my sides with nowhere else to go. Mr. Window Seat rudely took one of my armrests, and Max, well, Max just doesn't fit in the seat, so my other armrest is all his.

"Sorry," he says when his shoulder pushes me toward Mr. Window Seat while struggling to get his seat belt on. "I know it's close quarters, but these were the best seats I could get at the last minute."

"The seat is fine. I just wish I knew what was going on in my own life."

"Miss Ford..."

"I mean, what could have been so bad that we had to run away like that?"

"Listen, whoever was doing this was in Eastlyn. It wasn't just paparazzi pictures this time. A blocked number sent pictures, only this time they were of you outside your house, at The Verdict, at the bookstore."

"How is it possible that there could have been a stranger hanging around Eastlyn that none of us noticed?"

"Well, what I'm afraid of, is that it isn't a stranger. Thinking it's somebody you know. Somebody who knows where you spend your time. Someone who can get up close and personal without anyone being the wiser. Emmett, they were in your house today while we were at the opening."

"What are you talking about?"

"There was a picture of your bedroom. And there was today's paper on your bed."

"Oh."

A sliver of fear crawls down my spine. My knuckles turn white as I tighten the grip on my interlaced fingers to try and hide the fact that my body is shaking from the inside out. I can't believe there was someone in my house today.

"Right, so we're gonna take a little trip, just the two of us. You can't let anyone know where we're going. Not even Josh. We just need to lay low for a bit."

Hmm...a trip with just the two of us. Twist my arm.

"New York doesn't seem very low profile."

"We're just flying into New York. We're going to Jersey."

"What's in New Jersey?"

"My family."

"I'm sorry, did you say your family?"

Clearing his throat, he tries his best to adjust in his chair. "It's unexpected, and nobody will look for you there. Hell, they wouldn't even look for me there."

"You don't go home often?"

"It's been a while."

"How come?"

"Been busy."

"What's your hometown like?"

"Well, Phillipsburg isn't as small as Eastlyn, but it's a quaint township, just like all the other townships in that part of the state. We sit right on the Pennsylvania border, and it actually looks a lot like Oregon. I think you'll like it. P-burg is the kind of place where the whole town goes to the Phillipsburg vs. Easton high school football game on Thanksgiving Day, but not before they've gone to the bonfire the night before. It's a thing."

"So...we're going to be with your family for Thanksgiving. Does that mean we'll be going to the big game?"

"I haven't thought that far ahead. I haven't even called to say we're coming."

"We're just gonna show up?"

"Yep."

"Well, this should be fun."

"It will be fine."

"So, let me guess, you played football, right?"

"Yep."

"And you were one of the popular kids?"

Modestly, his shoulders lift as if to say, what can I say?

"Do you have any siblings?"

"A brother. Alex."

"Are you close?"

Another shrug.

"Been a while?"

"Yep."

"So, were you homecoming or prom king?"

"How'd you know?"

It's my turn to shrug.

* * *

Two hours into our flight, we're chatting away like it's our first date. We know each other's favorite movies, and I've decided to forgive him for calling Love Actually lame. He's decided to overlook my love of Justin Bieber, but only because he couldn't deny that the Biebs has had some pretty great hip-hop collaborations.

The pilot warned us there was turbulence ahead, but it still startles the hell out of me when the plane begins to shake, and the empty cup on my tray table falls to the floor. Squealing, I grab Max's hand without even thinking about it. "Shoot, sorry," I say, but he only smiles back.

He squeezes my hand, not letting me pull away. And after the stress of the day and the cocktails I consumed during our conversation, I'm too tired to analyze what it means. So instead, I let the day catch up with me resting my head on his shoulder and floating away to dreamland.

* * *

It's late when we pull up to the lovely two-story house in a quiet neighborhood where all the homes have acres of land that I'm sure in daylight is beautiful. Pulling into the driveway, our headlights light up the sedan parked under the car park and a big truck parked uncovered next to it.

We park our rental car next to the truck and sneak around the back of the house. Max messes with the back door and then opens it without a sound.

"I think it's safe to say you've done this a time or two."

"Yep."

"So, prom king and bad boy all rolled into one."

"Shh...remember if you wake my mom up, she'll feel the need to cook, and we'll be up all night."

"Got it. Sorry. Wait, I thought you texted to let your parents know you were coming?"

"I texted my dad, but he promised not to tell Mom until the morning."

We creep through a dark living room and up some creaky stairs that lead to a short hallway with three doors. Max opens the first door on the left and flips the switch illuminating the bathroom, flips it off, and then leads me to the room on the right.

Wood paneling, a short brown dresser, and a full-size bed covered in peach floral are a welcome sight. Hell, the air mattress on the floor for us looks good too. Even after a two-hour nap on Max's shoulder, I'm exhausted. I'm so tired I don't think I have it in me to cover the air mattress with the sheets that were left on top of it.

"I'll take the air mattress, and you take the bed."

"You don't have to do that. I'm fine on the floor."

"Don't start. I'm on the floor, and you're on the bed. Why

don't you do what you need to do in the bathroom before hitting the hay, and I'll get the extra bed made up."

"Yes, sir," I say with not nearly the punch I would usually give my sarcastic reply.

I grab my bag and head to the adorable bathroom full of pink accents against a pink floral wallpaper. I change into a sleep shirt and some leggings, then pile my hair on top of my head and make quick work of washing my face and brushing my teeth. When I get back to the room, Max is sitting on the edge of the bed with his laptop open, but he closes it as soon as I walk into the room.

"My turn?"

"It's all yours."

"Be right back."

"Hey, Max?"

"Yes?"

"Why did you have to pick the lock if your dad knew you were coming?"

"It's his way of saying he knows I used to sneak out and then back in as a kid. He always says he'll leave the back door open for me, and it's always locked. It's just kind of our thing, I guess."

"Like an inside joke. That's cute," I manage to get out through a yawn.

"Just go to bed, and we'll talk more in the morning."

"So bossy," I say, climbing under the covers. The peach comforter may not be my style, but it's downy soft, and this bed may be even more comfortable than mine at home.

What a day.

I woke up to Max barefoot in my kitchen. Opened my own business on Main Street. I was rushed out of my hometown to fly across the country while holding Max's hand and sleeping on his shoulder. Because I apparently have a stalker. Now, here I am, hands dried on pretty pink towels cozy under a peach floral explosion, but the most shocking thing about this entire day is how with all of this running through my mind, I am still too exhausted to stay awake another second.

Chapter Twelve

Stretching myself awake, I adjust my pillow to avoid the bright light blinding me through the small space in the curtains that have opened just enough to do the dirty work of an alarm clock.

I'm slow to fully wake until a few more seconds go by, and I take in my surroundings.

Shit!

I'm in New Jersey at Max's parent's house!

Pulling the comforter up to my neck, I peek over the edge of the bed, but the space on the floor next to me that should be filled with my giant bodyguard is empty. Bed made. No trace of him.

Where is he?

Sitting up in bed, I sigh, and my mouth smiles to find my phone plugged in next to the bed. I know I was way too tired to have had the mindset to do that myself. No, that was all Max. How very thoughtful of him.

My internal clock says it isn't time to get up, but it's already nine o'clock, East Coast time, so I force myself out of bed. I throw on a hoodie, brush my teeth, and make sure I'm presentable before I go in search of Max. I wander down the steps and through the living room we crept through like criminals last night. It's then I notice this part of the house looks like it was added on and was built in a different decade than the rest of the house. However, there are two recurring themes throughout the house, wood paneling, and pictures of Max and his brother, Alex.

Baby pictures, grade school pictures. Photos in the snow and from prom. Max's senior pictures are where you start to see him blossom, but once you get to his military pictures, you begin to see more of the man I know today. A thinner version with fewer scars but definitely, the man I know.

His brother must have kids because there are recent baby pictures and a grade school picture of a little boy clearly taken recently; that is the spitting image of a similar photo of Max down the hall. He must look a lot like his brother to have a nephew who looks so much like him.

Finally peeling myself from the photos, I tiptoe into the kitchen, where Max sits at the u-shaped kitchen table with a man who must be his father. Both of them looking at something on Max's laptop with giant smiles on their faces. His mother is at the stove cooking, but when she swings around to say something, she sees me lurking in the corner.

"Good morning, you must be Emmett. I'm Mrs. Hopper, but please call me Linda. Did you want some coffee or juice? How would you like your eggs? Over easy? I'm guessing you're an over-easy girl. Am I right?"

"Hi, it's nice to meet you, Linda. A cup of coffee would be great, but I can get it myself. Just point me in the right direction."

"Nonsense, go have a seat, and I'll bring it right over. Max says you like mochas, so if you want me to sneak some chocolate in there, I can do that. Now, how about those eggs?"

He told her what kind of coffee I like? Isn't that interesting?

"I'm good with a little sugar and a splash of milk. And over easy would be perfect."

"I knew it!" Linda boasts.

"Morning," Max says with a smile not just on his face but also in his voice. A smile that says I told you it was better to sneak in the back and not wake my mom up last night. "Emmett Ford, this is my father, Donny," he says, closing his laptop.

I see where he gets his barreled chest and broad shoulders. If it weren't for his hazel eyes, he would be the spitting image of his father, but he has his mother's eyes. And from the pictures on the walls, his brother, Alex, got his dad's piercing blues.

Donny offers me his hand. "Pleased to meet you, Miss Ford."

"Thank you so much for having us. I know it was last minute, and I really appreciate you letting us stay."

"Nonsense," Linda chimes, delivering my coffee. "It's been way too long since Max has been home, and the fact that he's home for the holiday is even better."

"Well, still, it's very kind of you. I'm sure it isn't every day your son turns up in the middle of the night with one of his clients."

"Very true, but we'll take a visit from him any way we can get it. Won't we, Donny?"

"I'm afraid these days we will." Max and Donny are sitting side by side in the middle section of the table, so Max is close enough for his dad to put his arm around him and pull him close. "It's been too long, Son. Never again." He kisses him on the top of his head and then releases him. It's incredibly sweet.

"I know, Dad, I promise."

Linda lifts the bottom of her peach apron to her eyes and pats them dry.

I feel like an intruder sitting smack dab in the middle of a private family moment. Max said it had been a while since he'd been home. I wonder what his idea of a while is?

I sit back quietly and blow on my cup of coffee before taking a sip, wishing I could disappear and let them have their moment.

"Well, you're here now, and that's all that matters. I just hope next time you'll bring my grandson with you. Now, Emmett, tell us about yourself."

Grandson?

He has a son?

Max is a dad?

Swallowing the sip of coffee, I nearly spit all over the table when she mentioned her grandson. I hide my shock and tell them what little there is to know about me and eat my eggs, toast, and even some bacon. It's good but not as good as the bacon I had yesterday morning.

How was that just yesterday?

It feels like a lifetime ago.

* * *

After eating, I excused myself to go take a shower. While washing away the gross feeling of a cross-country flight, the idea of Max being a dad continues to sink in. How is it possible to spend so much time with someone but not really know them?

The real question is, why does it matter so much to me? It's really none of my business. Still, it matters.

My shower is done, and I'm fully dressed, but I'm not quite ready to join Max and his family, so I take a seat on the bed in what I guess is my room for the next few days, trying to get my mind off Max. If only I hadn't made the mistake of looking at my phone and, unfortunately, social media to pass the time.

A gentle knock on the door distracts me.

"Emmett, you okay in there? Can I come in?" Max asks from the hallway.

Wiping my face and dabbing my nose with the tissue I stole from the bathroom cupboard, I try to sound like myself. "Sure, come on in."

There's no hiding my tear-stained makeup, red-rimmed eyes, or the worry on his face when the tears start falling again.

"Hey, what happened? I mean, I know it's a lot of pink, but the bathroom isn't that scary, is it?"

I appreciate that he's trying to lighten the mood, but even Max can't get me to laugh right now.

"No, it's this." I hold out my phone in shame. He's going to see it anyway; why prolong the inevitable?

He looks at the picture, and even though his tell-tale sign of anger shows in the ticking of his jaw, he says, "So what?"

"Here I thought I was helping his career. Instead, he's apparently settled for a fat, ordinary woman who isn't worthy of him."

"Stop."

"I mean, I know I'm not a Hollywood beauty, and I know we seem like a strange match, but I didn't think I could make things even worse for him."

"Stop."

"What was I thinking? My fat ass is everywhere. I'm a laughing stock."

"I don't ever want to hear you talk about yourself like that again. Do you hear me?"

I've never heard him sound so angry.

"What?" I say, looking up at him quickly but then averting my eyes from his, embarrassed.

He squats in front of me, not allowing me to hide my face from his.

"Emmett, I don't know how you can look at this picture and not see perfection."

He holds the phone up in front of me, making me look at the picture of me in my yoga pants, but I don't see anything on the page because he just said he sees perfection, and he called me Emmett.

"I love your ass."

"You love my ass?"

"Emmett, your body is a masterpiece. Your curves are a thing of beauty, and that ass of yours...Listen, I know I'm crossing the line, but you'd have me fired if I told you what goes through my mind when I think about your ass."

"No, really, it's okay. Please tell me."

He lightly chuckles. "If one of the other guys on my team behaved this way, they'd be fired."

"I don't mind."

He reaches up, gently brushing his thumb over my cheek. "Emmett, I've said too much, and telling you more or taking this further would be inappropriate. The right thing to do is to remove myself from the job and let Smith take over, but that isn't an option."

"Because he's going home for the holiday?"

He smiles up at me. "No, because there's no way I could give up a single day spent with you."

"So, it's not just me?"

"It's not just you."

Time stops. Our confessions linger in the air. Our eyes search for the answers to questions we don't dare ask aloud.

"Now, let's get going. My brother and his family are on their way." He stands to his full height, and I miss being eye to eye with him. So many questions are running through my mind.

"I'm meeting more family?"

"I don't come home often, so my mom gets a little excited. Thanksgiving is apparently too far away."

"It's the day after tomorrow, isn't it?"

"It sure is. Consider today a practice run for the big day." He winks, offering his hand, pulling me off the bed. "No more crying over bullshit that doesn't matter, okay?"

"I'll do my best. But, unfortunately, I may have to throw my phone away to make it happen."

"Do what you need to do, girl. As long as I don't find you like I just did ever again. It didn't feel good. Now, you, with a smile on your face...nothing beats that."

"Max," I breathe out his name, an emotion in and of itself.

He lets go of my hand, walking backward toward the door. "I'm gonna give you a second to yourself. You're gonna beg for the quiet once the kids get here."

"Max, wait."

He stops at the door.

"Why didn't you tell me you had a son?"

"I didn't not tell you. I tried to tell you at the bookstore, but the minute I mentioned I had a dog, you interrupted me, and then your friends came back, and the conversation ended."

"Sorry I interrupted you." I really am. I would have loved this new bit of information. "Does this mean you're missing Thanksgiving with him?"

"No. Nick is with his mom for the holiday this year. We talk every day, though, and we'll be sure to video chat with the whole family on Thursday."

"Nick. That's his name?"

"It is. He's ten. He loves basketball and video games. He's smart as hell, and nobody makes me laugh harder. His mother hates that I never married her when I got out of the military and makes things harder than they need to be. I only get him on Wednesdays and every other weekend or when she has plans. It sucks, but she's had a new man in her life these past couple of years and, therefore, lots of plans. So, lately, I get him more than my scheduled days. Still, I have an attorney, and I'm working on changing things. I'll give you a few minutes. See you downstairs when you're ready. And remember, no more tears. You're beautiful."

The door clicks closed, leaving me to sit with my thoughts. The past few minutes run circles around my head. Over and over. His love of my ass. The crossing of lines. Not wanting to spend time away from me. His love for his son and his conflict with his ex.

He. Thinks. I'm. Beautiful.

Standing face-to-face with my reflection staring back at me in the full-length mirror attached to the back of the bedroom door, I look at myself. Really look at myself.

Face-to-face with my curves. The curves that trolls online use to call me fat, but those same curves were just called perfection by the person whose opinion means more than most these days.

Turning from side to side, examining the body parts that just had me in tears, I try to see what he sees. I try to see my curves that, before today, I was comfortable living in. Curves that it would appear work for Max. I've seen Josh go through this. I know better than to let them get to me, but it sure is easier to believe the negative.

When I finally make my way up to my face, there's a sparkle in the brown eyes shining back at me, my cheeks are flushed, and it's all because of the man who loves my ass and thinks my body is a masterpiece. Yes, I know he's going a little overboard to make me feel better about myself, but it still feels good. The most important thing, though, the part that feels even better than his sweet compliments, was his confirmation that it wasn't just me.

What I'm feeling isn't one-sided.

The butterflies in my stomach are untying the knots of anxiety that had taken up residence only moments ago and staking their claim.

Gleefully bouncing down the stairs with a smile plastered on my face, I hear Linda singing in the kitchen. Before I've stepped off the last step, a wave of trepidation washes over me. Our moment upstairs was behind closed doors. To the rest of the world, I'm his client. But, an even more significant roadblock than our business relationship is the assumption by the world that I'm engaged to Josh.

The diamond on my left hand suddenly feels like a weight pulling me under, preventing me from breaking the surface. But here I am, walking into the kitchen with a smile on my face while inside, I'm treading water as if my life depended on it.

"Oh, Emmett, perfect timing. Alex and the kids just pulled up!" Linda squeals.

She signals me to follow her to the family room, where I hear our visitors before I see them.

"Uncle Max!"

"Ivy! Look how big you are! You're beautiful, just like your mommy." Max swings around, arms filled with an adorable little girl whose legs and braids fly through the air while her arms squeeze his neck.

"Hey, Max, it's been way too long."

He shifts Ivy onto one hip and hugs a petite strawberry blond woman, but before they get to exchange any pleasantries, they're interrupted.

"Maxipad!" Max places Ivy on her feet, and her mom grabs her by the hand just in time. "Big Bro! It's about damn time you came home!"

The equally tall and dark-haired man who must be Alex throws himself against Max, hugging him so tightly you can see both men's knuckles pale as they grip each other's shoulders. This is a real hug, full of love and emotion.

"Hey, man, how you doin'?" Max replies, barely audible for anyone other than Alex to hear.

I begin to back into the kitchen to give the family some privacy when I'm poked in the belly. "Who are you?"

The room falls silent. All eyes on me.

"Hi, I'm Emmett. Who are you?"

"My name is Brian. It means I'm noble. What does your name mean?"

"Hi, Brian. It's nice to meet you." I shake his tiny hand. "My name means my dad wanted a boy, but he got me instead."

"Huh?"

"Sorry, he's five and full of questions. I'm Malory, Alex's wife. You must be here with Max?" the pretty blond asks, holding a baby in her arms.

I don't know what to say, but luckily for me, Max takes control of the conversation.

"Brian, doesn't your uncle Max get a hug?"

The adorable little guy slowly walks over to his uncle, who squats down to his level.

"When did you get so big? What are you like, fifteen now?"

"No, I'm only five."

"Only five? Wow, you had me fooled."

Brian touches the faint circular scar on Max's cheek.

"You don't remember me do you, buddy?"

He shakes his head back and forth.

"I'm your uncle Max. I haven't seen you since you were two, I think. I'm sorry about that." He rubs his head, and the look he gives his brother expresses his regret.

"I know," Alex replies.

My tears are back for a completely different reason this time. Max hasn't been home in three years. Three years. Of all the places we could have gone to get away from the crazy person stalking me in Eastlyn, why did he choose to come home?

Clearing his throat, Max speaks to the room. "Alex, Malory, Ivy, Brian, and baby Brody, this is Emmett. Emmett, this is my brother, Alex, his patient wife, Malory, and their three beautiful kids."

"It's nice to meet you, Emmett. We're kind of a lot, I know." Malory laughs.

"Not at all. It's nice to meet you too."

"Ivy. Brian. You two let your old gramps know when you're ready to lose at Uno. You know where to find me." Donny walks out of the room, and the kids follow him like he's the Pied Piper.

"Everyone, booth," Linda orders. "I have pies to make, and I need you to eat everything in the fridge so I can make room for Thanksgiving."

I'm just about to ask what she means when Malory and Alex scoot into the u-shaped table in the kitchen, and I see it now. It's actually just like a big booth in a restaurant. Perfect for a big family to gather around.

I slide in next to Max, feeling unsure of myself. He introduced me by name but didn't mention who I was to him. It's also the first time I've been in his space since our last conversation. He's like a magnet my body automatically attracts to. When I realize I'm close enough for our arms to graze, I pull myself away from him—sitting on my hands to ensure no accidental touching.

"So, Emmett, Max tells me you do something with corporate travel?" Linda startles me out of my thoughts about magnets.

He told his mom about me?

"Um, yes. I manage the team who arranges all the travel for my company."

"Who do you work for?" Malory asks.

"HD Communications."

"Oh, wow, so we're talking a lot of international travel," Alex adds.

"Yes, we have business worldwide, and my team plans it all."

"That sounds incredible. So, you must travel a lot for work then?" Linda says, placing a half-eaten casserole dish of lasagna on the table along with a tossed salad before walking back to the fridge to keep making space.

"You'd think so, but sadly no, I've never left the States, except for a couple of trips to Cabo with friends."

She puts a big salad and a stack of plates and silverware in front of us, looking at me bewildered. "Well, that's nonsense. You'd think if you were in charge of planning it all, you'd get to travel to see the places you're sending everyone else off to."

"Nope. I attend a lot of meetings in Denver, Seattle, and Philadelphia, but that's about it. I'm lucky enough to work from home, though, so no complaints there."

"I would say I wish I could work from home, but that would be a lie. I work construction, and it's quieter on the job site than it is at home with three kids and two dogs."

"Alex is being modest; he owns the company." Max brags about his brother.

"Doesn't mean I don't still work hard."

"Never said you didn't," Max says, tossing a cherry tomato from the salad at his baby brother.

"I can't believe there are no fireflies this time of year. Can you believe I've never seen a firefly?" I say on a yawn.

We've had a full day of family, food, and fun, and I can barely keep my eyes open.

Max and I took a walk after his brother and family left for the night. His parents own several acres of land and even built a pool behind the house. It's the wrong time of year for a swim, but that doesn't mean we can't still lay poolside, bundled up, each with our own blanket and lawn chair.

"I guess we'll have to come back in early summer when you'll be guaranteed to fill a jar full of them."

"Yeah? That would be amazing."

It really does sound great, and it warms my heart to hear him talk about me returning to Phillipsburg with him. However, my eyelids grow heavy, closing on their own. The three glasses of wine since dinner may not have been wise. Mixed with the scent of pine trees and the crisp night air, hinting that snow may be on the way, and I'm down for the count.

"Hey, Emmett?"

"Aw, you called me Emmett."

Pulling my blanket tighter, I roll to my side to look at him, but my eyes don't open as I had planned.

"Emmett?"

"Max?"

"If you could go anywhere in the world, where would you go?"

"Hmm...Paris. I've always dreamed of going to Paris. Do you think they have fireflies in Paris?"

I hear him say something, but it sounds like he's whispering with my blanket covering my ears. "Sorry, what was that?"

"Don't worry about it." He's close enough that the warmth of his breath brushes across my cheek. His hands slide under me, picking me up. "Come on, Firefly, let's get you to bed."

Chapter Thirteen

The distant roar of an engine wakes me from my dreams of fireflies, the Eiffel Tower, and Max. Looking over the side of the bed, I'm not surprised to find the bed on the floor is empty and made.

As I burrow under the blankets, my cheeks strain with the size of my smile.

"Come on, Firefly, let's get you to bed."

I keep hearing his words on a loop in my head.

I was in that place between being awake and asleep last night when Max's hands first touched me. The moment they did, I couldn't have been more cognizant. Afraid he would put me down if he realized I wasn't sleeping, I pretended I was. And I'd do it again if given the opportunity to be close enough to snuggle against his neck again. To feel his breath on my face. To smell the fresh, fruity scent of his that has a hint of cinnamon and is all him.

I almost pretended to wake up when he struggled with the back door, but it was too entertaining listening to him curse under his breath. In the end, he managed just fine. But, of course, I don't think there's much he's not capable of.

He sweetly laid me down, removed my shoes, and pulled the blankets over me. He didn't walk away, though. I could feel his stare as he stood watching me while I wondered if he could see the beating of my heart through my chest or, at the very least, hear the pounding of it. How could he not when it filled the room, it was the only thing I could hear?

Thinking back to last night reminds me that I'm still in my clothes from yesterday, and I should probably get out of bed and ready for the day. Although, I'd rather stay wrapped up in my cocoon of covers all day, reliving last night. Unfortunately, I'm a guest, and it wouldn't be polite to stay in my room all day.

Throwing back the covers, I meander across the room to the window, pulling back the dark blue curtain. Through the low-hanging fog, I spot Donny bundled up in a thick flannel, his beanie held on tight with the giant ear protection he's wearing to dull the sound that woke me. His warm breath on the frosty air leaves a trail behind him as he rides his mower over the acreage of his beautiful land.

Yesterday, when I finally saw Phillipsburg in the daylight, I was pleasantly surprised to see how much this part of New Jersey resembles certain parts of Oregon. I've watched too many episodes of Jersey Shore and had forgotten this is the Garden State after all.

The tall trees rising out of the earth doing their best to reach the sky on the edge of the property remind me of The Jumps back home. Listening to Max talk about his childhood here was reminiscent of my time growing up in Eastlyn and the property we spent our days and nights on.

The Jumps is a big, beautiful field of green covered in tiny purple flowers where countless bonfires took place. A peaceful place lined with a forest of pine trees where we rode our bikes. We used tree roots, fallen logs, and raised trails as our bike jumps and obstacles. Mother Nature provided much of our happiness back home, and it appears she did the same for Max and his friends out here on the other side of the country.

My phone rings with the request of someone wanting to FaceTime, and I know it's Josh. This sound used to bring a smile to my face; today, I'm conflicted. Of course, I'm always happy to hear from Josh. Still, there's an underlying resentment matched with the guilt of wishing I had never signed his contract.

I could ignore the call, but I don't.

"Hey."

"Emmy, girl, where the hell are you?"

I open my mouth to tell him exactly where I am when a sense of uncertainty washes over me. What if it is someone inside Josh's inner circle? For the first time in my life, I don't tell Josh every detail of what was going on in my life.

"I'm safe, and that's all that matters."

"That is all that matters. Sorry I didn't call sooner, but Reeves has been updating me and let me know you were okay. I was thinking about you, though. I'm really sorry about all this, Em."

He didn't even push back. He was completely fine with not knowing where I was after waiting two days to even check in on me after some creep broke into my house. I've been so caught up with my one-on-one time with Max that I hadn't even noticed Josh didn't so much as text me.

Keeping a lid on my simmering bitterness, I do what I'm starting to realize I do more and more these days, let him off the hook and make it all about him.

"It's not your fault, Josh. How is it up there in Canada, eh?"

That was all it took, and he's off.

Talking about his life.

His favorite topic.

This isn't new, but I actually have a lot going on for once. I mean, come on, I just opened my own business only to have my home broken into and my life threatened. Now, I'm off in a mysterious location, just my bodyguard and me, and still, all he wants to talk about is himself!

He rambles on.

I drift off.

I don't hear a word he's saying. I have the soundtrack of last night running through my head. I hear the deep timbre of Max calling me Firefly, his heavy breaths as he carried me across the yard, up the stairs, and then put me to bed.

"I mean, it sucks that she broke her leg and needs surgery, but at least it means a break in filming. I can't wait to see you!"

"Wait, what?" No! "You're coming home?"

"Yep, we'll finish up what we can the next few days without her, but then we'll have to break because she's in nearly every scene left to shoot. I thought you'd be glad."

"Of course, I am," I lie. "Too bad you'll still miss Thanksgiving."

"I know, right? But it's not a holiday up here in Canada, so not a hardship to most of the crew. Well, listen. I have to get going, but I wanted to check on you. Stay safe, Emmy, and I'll call you when I head back to LA."

"Bye."

My screen goes black. He's gone, and I'm bummed. Gathering my things, I drag my feet across the hall to the shower. The giddy mood that greeted me upon waking up is gone, as is my racing heartbeat that had accompanied it.

Deflated, I step under the hot water. I've never lied to Josh before. I've certainly never been bummed at the prospect of seeing him. His news should make me happy.

The truth is, Josh being home means less time with Max.

And that sucks.

The shower hasn't helped wash away the funk Josh's call left me in, and when I wipe away the steam from the bathroom mirror, it's clear that feeling sorry for myself is not an attractive look on me.

Enough.

Who knows what today will hold. This is Max we're talking about. One minute he's obsessed with being professional. The next, he's calling me Firefly or professing his love of my ass.

No need to dwell on what I may be missing once we're back in California and Josh is home because today, the Max who calls me Firefly could be gone again.

I think I'll just live in the moment and see what happens.

* * *

"There she is. How did you sleep, Emmett? What can I get you to eat?"

Linda lifts my spirits in an instant.

She reminds me of my mom, always cooking and needing to feed everyone. Showing her love through her need to care for her family.

"I slept great, thank you. The house is so quiet today."

"Except for the sound of Donny's mower. I tell ya. Every three days, no matter the temperature, that man is out there on that mower. He may be retired, but he still has a schedule, and nothing will keep him from it. Except for those grandkids." The smile on her face says she wouldn't change a thing about him.

"Not surprised he's wrapped around their fingers. They're absolutely adorable. They bring such energy to the house."

"They do." Her eyes light up, just thinking about them. "I couldn't be happier for Alex. I sure hope Max finds that same joy one day."

With a flutter in my belly, I tease the hem of my sweater, not sure what to say.

But just like my mom, I don't have to figure out what to say because Linda keeps right on chatting while pouring me a cup of coffee and placing it on the table, which I take as a request to have a seat. "But then again, we don't see much of Max these days, and I don't really know what's going on in his life. So, for him to show up here, with you, at Thanksgiving, was quite a surprise. A good surprise but still a surprise."

"How long has it been since he's been home?"

"Three years. We've been out to California, but he hasn't come home." The spoon in the mixing bowl stops moving as she answers, her gaze out the window as a shallow sigh escapes. "It's really nice to see him with his dad. He's missed him."

I sip my coffee, searching for something to say, but I don't know anything about Max or why he hasn't been home in three years. "I know he's happy to be home."

Her attention turns back to the mixing bowl, a slight smile on her face and an unfocused gaze almost like a wave of nostalgia has hit her.

"Brian reminds me so much of Max. You know how he introduced himself to you yesterday and said his name meant he was noble?"

"Yes, it was precious."

"Well, Max used to do that. His name is Maximus, and it means the greatest. He used to say, 'Hi, my name is Max. I'm the greatest.'" She laughs down at her bowl. "Oh, he was something else."

He still is, Linda. He still is.

"What does Alex mean?"

"Well, Alexander represents physical courage and impulsive energy. It doesn't really lend itself to introductions like Max would give. Brian is attached to Alex just as Max was to Donny. He was his father's shadow, even through his teenage years. Everything changed when he left for the Marine Corps. He's been out for years now, but I'm not sure all of him came back.

He's a little distant. I don't know. I feel like he's been through something that none of us know about. Not to mention everything he's gone through with Nick's mom. It's such a shame he doesn't get more time with his boy. He's such a wonderful father."

The slamming of the front door ends the conversation.

"Morning." I hear the smile in his voice before I see him, just as I have so many times since we've been here, which makes me smile.

"Morning."

He takes the seat across from me, and I see the smile I heard behind me. There's a sexy stubble on his face. Who would have thought he could look even manlier? But he does.

"So, my chores are done, and I was thinking I could take you for a drive and show you my hometown."

"Your chores?"

"Damn straight." Donny's gruff voice says from behind me. "If he's at home, he's gonna help. That's the way it is in the Hopper household."

"Well, I feel bad. I haven't helped with anything."

"Don't you worry. I'm sure Linda will put you to good use in the next day or two. We'll let you off the hook today," Donny says, kissing his wife on the cheek.

* * *

Day has turned to night. The trickling sound of the gentle river water rushing by and the late fall breeze rustling the pine trees are the only sounds aside from the beating of our hearts.

We've spent the day in his dad's truck, exploring his quaint hometown. It's bigger than Eastlyn but still has that small-town feeling. Set on the Delaware River, it's a rural town but also has a quaint downtown waterfront shopping district. He took me to

Walters Park for a walk and to Rocco's for pizza and wings. Somehow, we managed to pass hours and hours driving and talking and skipping rocks.

Now, we've got a pile of comforters under us and a blanket of stars above us. To say I was surprised when Max laid out the blankets and asked me to crawl in the back of the truck with him would be an understatement, but there was no hesitation on my part. He tucked me into his side, and we've been staring at the night sky ever since.

Pensive and quiet, I follow his lead and enjoy the feel of my body against his. The rising and falling of his chest under my hand, resting over his heart, sets a steady rhythm, and the fresh smell of him has me under a blissful spell. I don't dare move a muscle for fear of breaking it.

He sits up, causing me to roll off him and my heart to squeeze at the prospect of leaving this perfect setting. Instead of getting out of the truck bed, he shrugs off his thick blue flannel and folds it up. He takes my hand, pulls me up, placing the shirt below me, and then lays me back down on my new pillow. All my nerve endings fire at once with him so close and the antici-pation of what he might have planned.

The moonlight etches the outline of the treetops across his face, and the starlight in his eyes shines down on me. The cool breeze may surround us, but my body is on fire as he lowers down to his forearms and hovers over me. We've been lying here with so much on our minds and in our hearts, not knowing how to say what we're thinking, but as his lips brush mine for the first time, we tell each other everything.

His kiss, his gentle touch, and his intense stare that hasn't wavered tell me what he's thinking. He's a man of few words, but when he communicates with his lips and his hand brushes the hair off my face, looking at me with adoration, he tells me everything I need to know.

The amplified sound of the zipper of my coat and our heated breaths have drowned out the river. He pulls the scarf tucked into my jacket out at a painstakingly slow pace, and just as the cool night air skims my exposed skin, his lips kiss my neck, leaving warmth in its place. He sets me ablaze with the heat from his kisses down my neck and over my sternum. When his lips land over my heart, he looks up at me, piercing me with his gaze while my heart tries to jump out of my chest just to get closer to him.

We touch, and we kiss until my lips are swollen. We're still fully clothed, but I've never felt so naked.

So open.

So vulnerable.

So in tune with another person.

He rolls to his back, bringing me with him. Now that I'm using him as my pillow again, he takes his flannel and covers me with it.

His arm squeezes me tight to him, and he kisses the top of my head.

"Two years?" His voice is gruff yet still laced with lust and want.

"What?"

"I'm not hiding for two years."

"What?" I ask again, not sure I heard him right. I push up so I can see his face, not believing what I've heard.

"I've tried, Emmett, I really have, but I can't stop this thing between us. My mom's right. When the right person comes along, you just know." His jaw is set, brows furrowed, while his eye contact is intentional and strong. "I knew the first moment I saw you in that dining room. You walked in with Josh laughing like a kid, and then I watched the joy in your eyes turn to fear, followed by worry about being a burden to Josh's staff. Your resolve to deal with the situation. You went through so many emotions in that first short meeting." He cups my cheek, his thumb gently caressing my bottom lip. "When I introduced myself, and you looked up at me, you hit me like a ton of bricks."

"But you..." My confusion prevents me from finding the words.

"You're engaged. I work for you. My job is to keep you safe. Unfortunately, falling in love with your client can be a distraction."

"What did you just say?" I whisper through my heavy breathing.

"You're a distraction."

He rolls us back over, taking control. A new light shines in his eyes as he looks down on me.

"I'm a distraction?"

"Firefly, you are the most dangerous kind of distraction."

Chapter Fourteen

Heaven is waking with his chest pressed against my back, his heavy arm wrapped around my waist, and his leg tangled between mine.

I don't want to open my eyes.

We both have clothes on, but it doesn't take away from the intimacy of sleeping in his arms.

Even with the smell of pine trees lingering in my hair, I'm still afraid I may have dreamed last night. Last night when he said he was falling in love with me. At least, I'm pretty sure that's what he said right before telling me I was the best kind of distraction. This can't really be my life, can it?

He stirs, and I freeze, not wanting the dream to end, but when he kisses the back of my head, my body goes lax with the assurance last night was real. As if the morning salute pressed against my lower back wasn't enough proof.

Clearing his throat, and untangling his leg from mine he speaks first. "Sorry about that." I nearly purr at the sounds of his gravely morning voice. Instead, I press back into him with a little wiggle, I reach my hand around to grab his hip and pull him back against me, but he isn't having it. "Emmett, be good."

"That doesn't sound nearly as fun as what I had in mind."

He places a pillow between us, then his arm is back around my waist, and his leg is wrapped around mine. "There, now we can have a serious conversation."

"The sun's barely up. Do we have to be serious already?"

"There's only serious when it comes to you and me."

Whoa.

It feels like I'm playing catch-up. I mean, I'm glad to know things weren't one-sided, but to go from getting excited to have his hand on the small of my back to the two of us being *serious* is quite an extreme change of pace.

It's a nice change but an extreme one all the same.

"Okay, well, I'm clearly not going anywhere with a lumberjack on top of me, so talk away."

"Lumberjack, huh?"

"Sexy lumberjack."

"As long as I'm your lumberjack?" He nuzzles into my hair, but he pauses when I don't immediately reply. I am unable to answer his question because a part of me isn't sure if maybe I haven't lost all sense of reason.

Did he really just say he was mine?

"You want to be mine?" I whisper.

"I already am, Emmett."

If it wasn't for the weight of his body on top of mine, I might have spontaneously combusted into a million pieces, unable to put myself back together.

Reaching behind me, I move the pillow from between us and roll over to face him. He already knows exactly what I need. He rolls to his back so I can lie on top of him. With my arm around his waist, leg over his, and my head on his broad chest where I can feel his heart beating under me I feel grounded.

"What in the world are we going to do? We're never alone back in LA, and when we are, paparazzi are hiding around every corner. Not to mention the fact that the house has cameras everywhere."

"We need to bottle moments like this one, right here, up. Take sips when we can, and when we can't make new memories like last night, this right here, and every other memory we make, we use these memories to get us through. Take them with us wherever we go. We'll find a way. And if all we have for the next year and seven months are stolen moments, I'll take it. Because just being in the same orbit as you for these past months has changed my life."

I start to sit up so I can look at him, but his arm tightens around me, holding me to his chest. I don't think he often shares this vulnerable side, and he needs a moment, so I give it to him. He's opened up and shared his feelings and never really let me do the same. It's my turn now.

"You're all that's been on my mind since that first meeting. I missed you as soon as you left the room that day. Even though you never talk to me while you sit at your little perch at the kitchen island, I get a little sad every night when you go home. Before last night, I thought just knowing you were in the other room while I was at work or that you might put your hand on my lower back from time to time was enough, but now, I think only having that might kill me."

"I know, baby."

Baby. Max Hopper just called me baby.

"So, what are we going to do?"

"Well, for starters, are you gonna tell Josh?"

"I probably should. I mean, he's with Jace. Why shouldn't I be with someone?"

"What does the contract say?"

Shooting up in the bed, I feel panic course through me. "Oh my gosh, Max! I don't even know! I'm a smart woman. I manage a team of thirty. I know better than to sign something without reading the fine print, but that's exactly what I did. I trust Josh with my life, so I just signed the contract. I know I have an NDA. I know that our situation will stay intact for two years. At that time, Sibby will release a statement that says with all of the distance, we grew apart and remain the best of friends. That's all I know." I press my back against the headboard for support, my legs pulled into my chest. "What have I done?"

He rubs my flannel-clad leg, lying on his side propped up with his head in his hand.

"Hey, we'll be back in California in a few days, and we'll get a hold of the contract and see what it says."

"I cannot believe I didn't read the contract."

"No matter what it says, we'll figure this out. If we wait, we wait. I'm not going anywhere."

Taking his hand in mine, I look at the man who has captured my heart. We're just getting to know each other, and this conversation should seem too serious. Too soon. But it's not. His eyes are the only ones I want to look at for the rest of my life. That should scare the crap out of me, but it doesn't.

I know he's mine, and I'm his.

Not sure how it's possible, but it is.

"You know, if I hadn't signed that stupid contract, I would have never met you."

"Can I tell you a secret?"

"Yes, please."

"Because of the job, I had been looking at pictures of you with Josh for quite some time. Reeves has been assigned to Josh for years, and he's one of our biggest clients. I've studied photos of you for years."

Gasping, realization hits me. "I'm on Josh's list of approved people."

"You are. And besides Jace, Sibby, and the rest of his team, you're with him more than anyone. I've watched you on red carpets with all of your many hair colors, and I have to say this is my favorite." He tucks a renegade piece of hair behind my ear. "You are beyond beautiful, Emmett."

Is it hot here?

I can't imagine how many shades of red I am right now.

"So, I've had a stalker all this time, and I didn't even know it?" I joke.

Jumping to his knees, he pulls on my legs so I'm flat on my back. He's hovering above me, his stare intense and direct. He wants to be sure I hear whatever he's about to say.

"I want to be clear that yes, you are the most beautiful woman I have ever seen, but you were just a job, a job that I had been watching for years, a job that I couldn't deny was captivating from afar, but that all changed the moment you walked into that room. I wasn't there that day in any capacity other than to show Josh and his team we knew the threats were serious and that LPS was doing everything we could to keep you safe."

"What do you mean? That was the day Reeves added you to the team."

"No, I added myself."

"I'm so confused."

He sits up, and I mirror him. We sit with our legs crossed and our knees gently resting against each other. He pushes the same hair behind my ear and looks at me with one side of his mouth slightly upturned, trying to fight a smile.

"Emmett, I am LPS. Lotus Protection Services is my company. I haven't worked in the field in years. Reeves, Smith, Cleveland...they're all my employees. I was in the room that day because I wanted Josh to know he was a priority and that my team and I were on top of things. But as soon as you walked in and sat down at the table, I knew I had to be the one protecting you. As I said, everything changed that day. Molly may never forgive me for leaving her and not taking her to work with me every day, but I'd say you're worth it."

Moments flash through my memory bank of all the small things I didn't see for what they were. The fact that Reeves let Max take over at that first meeting. How every time I saw Max talk with the other guys, he was the one doing all the talking while they all nodded and remained quiet for the most part. And then there are the hours spent at the kitchen island.

"The laptop and files you're always working on! You're running your business!"

His smile is small, but it says I've finally figured it out. "I hate leaving you every night too."

"I'm glad to hear it, I really am, but why didn't you tell me about this?"

"I wasn't hiding it from you. I thought you knew. Josh knows, and I've known him for years."

"That's why he called you *boss man* that first day you were at the house when we were talking about how hot you were. I think I did know, but I was so distracted I didn't piece it together."

"You think I'm hot?"

"Well, originally, I thought you were hot but very intimidating."

"You still thought I was hot. Guess I still got it." He smiles smugly.

"Uh, I think you know you still got it. You can't tell me you didn't see the way the girls were drooling over you back home. You made quite the impression."

"Well, that's nice, but the only person's opinion who matters is yours."

Putting his weight on his hands, he leans forward and gently kisses my lips.

"Does this happen a lot?"

"Does what happen a lot?"

I point back and forth between him and myself in the small space between us.

"You mean, have I ever fallen for a client before?"

I nod reluctantly. Do I really want to know the answer? The furrow of his scarred brow and the thin line his mouth has formed tell me he's not happy with my question.

"Absolutely not. What do you think this is? Just a perk of the job?"

"I hope not."

In a flash, he's off the bed, pacing back and forth, his hands rubbing the two days' growth on his face.

"Emmett, I don't know how to make this clearer to you. When I say you changed everything, I mean you changed everything!" He's not yelling, but he's whispering very loudly and passionately, so the rest of the house doesn't hear. "I haven't been in a relationship in years. Last time, I ruined everything. I came back from my time in the military a different man. I couldn't give her what she needed, and I was too caged up in my own shit to give any of myself to anyone. Hell, I barely come home to see my family because I know they miss the me I used to be. Nick is the only person who has gotten anything real from me in more years than I like to count. My son is my life, no matter how many days a week I see him, but damn if I don't feel like I'm ready to share my life with someone besides just him."

When he stops at the foot of the bed, his chest is heaving, and I'm not sure if it's from explaining all of this to me or if it's his own self-realization. So I stay quiet, letting him work through his emotions.

"You make me laugh. And I haven't laughed in years. Hell, I haven't been excited to go to work for years. I haven't wanted another person in any real way in so long, and Emmett, I want you. I fucking crave you. Do you understand what I'm saying?"

I nod. There's no way I would dare speak and ruin the beautiful flow of his words.

"Baby, you flipped the switch. You turned the lights back on for me. Finally, after years in the dark, things are bright again."

My tears start falling—nothing I can do about it. Getting up, I meet him next to the bed, wrap my arms around him, and bury my face in his chest.

"You're the reason I brought us here. We could have gone anywhere in the world to get away from Eastlyn, but something in me needed my family to meet you, so I brought you home for Thanksgiving. I've selfishly neglected them for far too long, and you reminded me how important the people I care about are to me. I'm glad you're here with me."

"I'm glad I'm here too."

"That reminds me. Happy Thanksgiving, Emmett."

"Happy Thanksgiving."

"I want you to meet my friends."

"I'd love to."

"Word got out that I'm home, and I've gotten messages that the old gang is gonna get together tomorrow night like the old days. They can be a lot. You sure you're game?"

"Will you be there?"

His chuckle vibrates against my ear. "I will."

"Then that's where I'll be."

Chapter Fifteen

"You ready?" He releases a big breath, his grip on my hand tightening almost to the point of painful. But I know we'll have to let go as soon as the door opens, so he can squeeze it as tight as he wants.

"I am. Are you?"

"It's been a long time."

I can't help but wonder if his nerves were a part of the reason he didn't go to the big football game yesterday morning. Instead, we hung back and helped his mom and sister-in-law prepare Thanksgiving dinner. I had thought it was to get some much-needed time with his mom. It was so sweet to watch him with her. Even with the distance, they still seem close. Now I'm wondering if there was more to it than that? I'm glad he got that time with his mom, whatever his reason.

"You got this." I knock on the door. "Might as well rip the Band-Aid off, right?"

The door swings open before he can answer, and he drops my hand. The man on the other side of the door is tall and bald with a magnificent smile and a belly that says he's enjoyed a beer or two in his day.

"Max Hopper, as I live and breathe! Get in here, man!"

"Hey, Nathan."

Nathan pulls open the door, and as soon as Max crosses the threshold, a chorus of his name stops him in his tracks.

It's clear he wasn't expecting such a warm welcome.

He finally continues into the house, and I follow behind him, giving Nathan a nod that he returns as I pass. Max is giving bro hugs to two other men when the one in a baseball cap notices me.

"And who do we have here?"

My stoic lumberjack lets a rare glimpse of emotion brighten his eyes for just a split second at the mention of my presence. So quickly, I'm sure nobody but myself noticed.

"Uh, guys, this is Emmett. Emmett, this is the guys. You met Nathan at the door, and this short, dark, and handsome man is Taylor." He pats the man to his left on the back and signals with his thumb to the man in a New York Jets hat to his right. "And this is Joel."

"Hi, nice to meet you."

"There's no way you came with him. You look way too high class for this chump over here."

"Max!"

An adorable brunette enters the room with two other women chatting behind her. Her mouth falls open, and her big brown eyes are full of delighted surprise at seeing him. So delighted, she runs across the room and throws herself in his arms. He lifts her off her feet, just as happy to see her.

"Surprise!" Nathan yells from across the room.

"I can't believe you're here!" she says, stepping back to get a better glance at him. Then, looking around him, she takes appraisal of my presence, the wrinkle in her brow and tightening of her gaze nowhere near as welcoming as the men I just met. "Who'd you bring with you, Max?"

"Kristina, this is my friend, Emmett."

Well, that was a punch to the gut. I don't want to be his friend. I want the world to know that he's mine.

I still can't believe he's mine. A few days ago, he only called me ma'am and spoke to me in one-word sentences, and now he's mine. It's the best kind of whiplash I could ask for, but still a pretty severe case.

"I know you aren't from P-burg. Are you from Easton? You look so familiar."

"Uh, no. I'm actually from Oregon."

"Really?"

"Last time I checked."

She shakes her head as though it's an Etch A Sketch, and she's trying to clear her screen. "Sorry, you just look so familiar."

"No worries. I think I just have one of those faces."

Please don't recognize me from the tabloids. Please. Please. Please.

"Well, I'm Kristina, and any friend of Max's is a friend of ours." She shakes my hand. Stepping back, she wraps her arms around her friends. "This is Deanna, and this is Jenn. The handsome bald guy over there belongs to me. Welcome to our humble abode."

"Thanks for having me. You have a beautiful home."

"Okay, enough of the niceties," Nathan cuts in. "Let's drink. We've got a DD, so we might as well preflight."

"Who drew the short stick?" Max asks the group as we all congregate around the kitchen island.

Kristina raises her hand. "That would be me." Dropping her raised hand to her stomach.

"No." Max's eyebrows shoot up; his eyes widen with excitement.

"Yes."

"Nathan, you did it again. You're gonna have three kids!

You know this, right?"

"More like oops, I did it again, but I'm glad to see your math skills are still as sharp as ever."

"Congratulations, you two! That's great news. Crazy, but great." He hugs them both, not letting go of Nathan. Instead, he leaves his big arm around his neck.

He's happy.

It's nice to see.

"Crazy is right. I'm gonna be forty this spring."

Kristina doesn't look a day over thirty. She's glowing and has one of those faces that you just know looks even more beautiful without makeup.

"Uh, pretty sure you guys know what causes this whole pregnancy thing, right?"

"We sure do, but your idiot friend over there never went in for his vasectomy like we planned, and here we are."

Taylor fills seven shot glasses with tequila and one with water. "Everyone, take a glass, and let's toast to the lucky little baby who will get to call these two mom and dad."

Glasses in hand, "Cheers!" is shouted by all, followed by the slamming of shot glasses back down on the kitchen counter.

"Shit, I haven't had Jose in years. Tonight should be interesting."

"What? They don't have tequila in LA?" Joel asks.

"I'm sure they do, but I'm always working or with Nick on the weekends. So, I don't really get a chance to partake too often."

"Well, it's nice you were able to get away for the holiday. I'm sure your parents were thrilled. Maybe Nick can come with you next time," the shorter blonde with long hair named Jenn says. "At least these days you can just assign your jobs to your employees. You must be relieved you don't have to give every second of your life to your clients anymore. I really don't know how you used to do it. Spending all that time with the rich and famous."

I'm feeling a little queasy, and it's not the tequila. Everyone in the room will hate me if they find out who I really am, that's obvious. The sick feeling is also one of the guilt I have hearing them reinforce what I already knew. Max has given up much of his personal life by assigning himself to me. But, I remind myself I've turned the lights back on for him. I sure hope I really am worth it.

I may have turned the lights on for him, but he doesn't realize that he has blinded me with the bright beams of his own spotlight. I can't see anything but him.

"It's no wonder you were single for so long." Deanna's eyes open wide, and she gasps. "Oh, my goodness! I just figured out why Kristina thought you looked familiar! You aren't just Max's friend; you're his client!"

"Wait, what did I miss?"

Deanna ignores Kristina, still staring at me like I have three heads. "You're Emmett Ford, aren't you?"

"Emmett Ford? As in Josh West's fiancée?" Jenn asks before covering her mouth with her hand.

"No way?" Kristina says, disbelieving. "So you aren't Max's date. You're his client."

Oh, Kristina, I sure do wish it was the other way around.

"Guys, let's all just calm down." Max finally steps in and places himself in front of me like they're paparazzi or something. "Emmett is a client, but she's also a friend. So how about we treat her like we would anyone else? Sound like a plan?"

I move away from Max to the other side of the kitchen under the pretense of putting my shot glass next to the sink. It's impossible to be that close to him and not touch him. Especially when I'm feeling insecure, and my natural instinct is to grab his hand for stability.

"Well, I guess those rumors about him weren't true, after all." Taylor's comment slices through my heart but serves as another example of why I'm doing this. "I mean, who really gives a shit if they're true or not. But I sure hope they aren't because you guys are gonna make some pretty babies one day."

Okay, I like Taylor. If only everyone felt the way he does about all the rumors.

Except there won't be any babies.

Nope.

That's never gonna happen.

Blech, just the thought of what it would take to make a baby with Josh makes my tequila want to come back up.

"I knew there was no way she was your date," Nathan kids with a wink in my direction.

Max's friends remind me of The Crew back home. It's a shame he's kept himself away from them. Hopefully, he'll make more of an effort to stay in touch after tonight.

Kristina wraps her arm around Max's waist. "Don't listen to him. One day, you're gonna meet the right girl, and when you do, she'll be damn lucky you did."

Ain't that the truth, Kristina, I think to myself as Max watches me from across the room. His intense stare reminds me to think back to the past three days together. His confession under the stars. Sleeping in his arms every night.

I could be that lucky woman if the world didn't think I was engaged to Josh.

Afraid someone will notice our stare, I look away, and I'm met with Deanna's knowing gaze when I do. Shit. This was a bad idea.

She must see the fear in my eyes because she gives me a smile that says I got this. "So, are we gonna sit around here all night, or are we going to take Emmett out and show her a good time?"

"Yep. Let me just go grab my purse. Be right back." Jenn runs back down the hall.

"You ready, babe?" Nathan asks Kristina, rubbing her barely-there baby belly.

"I am. Are you?"

"Let's see...clean T-shirt?" He looks down at himself. "Check. Shot of cologne?" He lifts his shirt to his nose. "Check. Folding money? Check," he says, patting his wallet in his back pocket. "Smokin' hot date? Check." He kisses Kristina on the side of her head while she rolls her eyes.

They're so sweet. On the way here, Max told me that they've been together since their senior year of high school. It's really cool to see they still have it. She may have rolled her eyes at his antics, but the sparkle in those same eyes said she loved his silly compliment.

"To the minivan!"

"Minivan? Nathan, tell me it's not true?" Max says with his hand on his chest over his heart.

"Oh, it is true, but it's mine," Kristina says, putting her purse over her shoulder. "You wait until you have two kids in sports and tell me you don't see why a minivan isn't a necessity. Besides, it seats eight, so we only need to take one car. You're gonna love it, Max!"

We all turn to head to the front door when Joel stops us, standing between the group and the door so nobody can leave. "So are we all going to pretend we don't want to know why Max brought a celebrity client home for Thanksgiving?"

My heart begins to race, but I guess I've gotten good at lying on the spot because there's no hesitation when I answer. "Josh was stuck working in Canada, and Max was nice enough to invite me to spend the holiday with his family."

"No offense, Emmett, I know we just met, but I call bullshit." Joel's back is pressed against the door, and his legs are crossed at the ankles. It's clear we aren't going anywhere until he gets the truth. "You don't have a family to go home to or any friends in Los Angeles? I seriously doubt that. Max hasn't been here for Thanksgiving in years, so why would he suddenly turn up?"

"Joel, stop it," Jenn whispers.

Standing behind me, I can feel his breath on my hair when Max speaks up. "You're right, T. There is more to it than that."

My racing heart stops beating altogether.

He wouldn't, would he?

He's signed an NDA too.

Is he about to out Josh?

"We had to leave Oregon before the holiday. I can't give you any details, but there's some asshole out there threatening Emmett, and we had to get away from the West Coast. I figured nobody would look for her here, so I brought her home." In a protective move, he steps around me. "Nobody knows where she is, not even Josh. It has to stay that way."

Somebody in the group says, "Shit," and then the room goes silent.

Joel pushes away from the door, moving until he's standing in front of Max. "Was that so hard?"

"Joel, come on." Jenn tries to quiet her husband.

"I'm sure, for her safety, you weren't supposed to tell us any of that. Thanks for trusting us, man. You know we always have your back. Everything you just said stays right here in this house. Right, everyone?"

What I wouldn't give to be holding Max's hand right now so I could give him a squeeze as the rest of his friends agree with Joel. Hearing them each give him words of support warms my heart. I know I just met them minutes ago, but something tells me we can trust them.

"Listen, you guys. I know I haven't been good at staying in

touch, and I'm sorry about that. I'm gonna to do better, okay?" His hand clasps Joel's shoulder. "Thanks for still being here."

"Don't sweat it. Just don't let it happen again. Besides, we ain't going anywhere except to the bar to get college girl drunk." Nathan focuses on me from in front of the door next to Joel. "And Emmett, it's really shitty you've got some asshole out there messing with you. Even shittier, you had to miss turkey day with your family. We're happy to meet you, though. And here's to hoping that, after tonight, you'll be glad you had to hide away here in our little town. We're kind of awesome." He winks. "I sure hope you like to drink."

"Thanks, Nathan. Phillipsburg has been pretty good to me so far, and yes, I do like to drink. Now, do I get to check out this minivan or what?"

* * *

"I really can't believe we're sitting here with Emmett Ford. You're marrying the biggest star in the world. What's he like?"

"Deanna, really?" Taylor asks, embarrassed.

"It's okay. I'm used to it. The thing is, I've known him my whole life, so he's really just Joshy Washy to me."

"Oh, my goodness. Is that what you call him?"

"That's what we all call him."

"Who's we?" It's obvious Taylor isn't going to get his sweet wife to stop asking questions, and I don't mind. I've been dealing with it for years now, but the ticking of Max's jaw would indicate he's a bit annoyed with all the talk about Josh.

"Oh, well, Josh and I have a group of friends back home who are like family. Back in middle school, we started calling ourselves 'The Crew', and it stuck. In fact, you guys remind me a lot of our little group of friends. We've all called him Joshy

Washy since grade school. It gets under his skin, which makes us do it even more."

"I can't imagine anyone calling Josh West, Joshy Washy. That's so weird," Jenn says to Kristina.

"Jesus, he's just a dude who happens to make movies for a living. He's not the second coming!" Max punctuates his statement with the clank of his beer bottle on the table. I've never seen this side of him, and I feel awful. However, there's no denying a part of me loves that he's affected by the conversation.

"He's right. Josh and I grew up in a town half the size of Phillipsburg. We're just a couple of small-town kids living a pretty extraordinary life."

"So when's the big day, or is it top secret?"

"There's nothing to keep top secret at the moment. We've been too busy to even think about planning." I hate lying to my new friends.

Even more, I hate what it's doing to Max.

"Okay, ladies, let's give Emmett a break. She's got to be tired of talking about Josh, and she's gonna be doing it for the rest of her life, so we should give her a night off. Besides, I have two pitchers of Eastlyn, a round of shots, and a lemonade for the prettiest girl in the place."

Kristina blows Nathan a kiss. "He's right. Sorry, Emmett."

"Don't worry about it." I know just the thing to change the topic of conversation. "You know what's even cooler than Josh West?" Max lifts an eyebrow, curious about what I might be referring to.

"Not sure there is anything cooler than that, but you can try," Jenn says from across the table.

"The guys may disagree." Max looks even more confused now. "That beer in your glasses...that beer comes from my hometown of Eastlyn, Oregon, and our friend Miles, who's a part of The Crew I just told you about, his family not only grows the hops, but they also own the company."

"No, shit? So you could have married a beer God or a movie star. I'd say you might have chosen poorly."

"Of course, you'd think that. I think Emmett made the right choice." Jenn sticks her tongue out at her husband, and he rolls his eyes just like she knew he would.

Turning to the girls, I wonder if I can blow their minds just a little bit more. "Have any of you read The Manhattan Diaries or watched the TV series based on the books?"

"Uh, you're looking at Nina Patrick's biggest fans. We've read all the books multiple times, and we used to have viewing parties every week when the show was on. Why? Are you marrying Nina too?"

"No, but my friend Miles, who owns EBC, is engaged to her, and she and I just opened a bookstore together earlier this week back home. So she's kind of a part of our crew now."

"Shut up!" Deanna yells.

"Nope." I laugh. "I will not."

"So..." Jenn scoots to the edge of her seat, leaning closer to me. "What you're saying is that as of tonight, we all have one degree of separation from the sexiest man alive and our all-time favorite author?"

"I guess I am."

My face hurts from smiling. Their reactions are so natural, and so big. I've grown so accustomed to Josh's celebrity that I've become somewhat immune to the rich and famous. I hadn't read Mason's series until after I met her, so her celebrity didn't impact me at all. I'm enjoying living this excitement through them.

"Damn, Max. It's too bad she's already taken because she's kinda great," Kristina says with a defeated sigh. "She could have been one of us."

"Yep, Mr. West is a lucky man. Shots?" Max stands abruptly, sending his chair squealing behind him.

"Hey guys, I'll be right back." I get up to walk away, and Max follows me. "I can go to the bathroom by myself, you know."

"Just doing my job," he says, trailing a couple of feet behind me.

Thank goodness the green letters above the doorknob say VACANT. I push my way in; only when I try to close the door, it's met with a force that pushes it open wider. Before I know it, his hands are on my hips, and the click of the door closing behind me sends adrenaline shooting through my veins.

"What are you doing?"

He lets go of me to lock the door, and when he turns around, he looks like he might eat me alive. "Max, somebody is going to notice you're in here."

"After all that talk about you and Josh, I need to taste you." His big hands cup my face, and he bends down, taking my lips in a slow, seductive kiss. "Emmett and tequila. Fuck."

With barely a fight, I succumb to his lips on mine and press myself against him until his back thuds against the door. His hands leave my face, trailing over my breasts and down my sides until he reaches my hips and finally my ass. After grabbing his final destination, he pushes me even closer to his growing erection. I can't help but pull back enough to get my hand between us, rubbing my hand over his length.

We've had our moment in the back of the truck, and yes, I've spent the past two nights in his arms, sleeping between kisses, but this is the first time I've felt this kind of desperate need for me from him.

"Fuck, Emmett. Do you have any clue what you do to me?" he says against my lips.

Giving him a squeeze, so he knows I've noticed just what I

do to him; the result is not what I had expected when he pulls away from my mouth. My heart drops when he pulls my hand away. Rejection seeps in, but understanding replaces the momentary rejection when he drags my hand from his jeans, up to his firm stomach, over his magnificent pec, and finally holds it in place over his heart.

"Seriously, Em. It's killing me not to tell everyone you're mine. Keeping my hands off you is harder than anything I ever faced during the war."

"Max." His name on a sigh is all I can get out.

He's exaggerating, and I love every bit of it.

"Emmett, you're all I think about. Touching you is all I dream about. Twenty-four-seven, my whole world is about you."

"You're all I think about, Max." His shoulders sag in relief. He needed to hear that I'm just as obsessed with him as he is with me. "I'm so sorry we're in this mess, but I would have never met you if we weren't. I want nothing more than for you to announce to all of Phillipsburg that I'm yours." It's my turn to hold his face. "Remember what you said. We need to bottle these moments up. Every touch, every word..." I press one hand against his chest. "...every beat of your heart I'm keeping bottled up so when we have to spend nights like tonight, not touching each other, trying not to stare at each other from across the room, I can take a sip when I need to, and it will remind me that we'll get these moments again."

"We shouldn't have to." His hands circle my wrists, assuring I keep my hold on his face.

"I know, but it's the fate I sealed for us when I signed that contract." He kisses me gently, his tongue tracing my upper lip when he pulls away. "Don't you think it's going to look suspicious if you don't go back before me?"

"I'm gonna need a second."

Stepping away from him, I lean against the sink and watch him.

He watches me right back.

I've never felt as wanted as I do at this moment.

The heat in his stare searches my eyes. It's as if he's searching the depths of my soul for the meaning of life.

As if *I* am the meaning of life.

He pushes off the door and stalks toward me. The pace of my heartbeat accelerates once again, and on their own accord, my thighs press together in want. He kisses me softly but quickly turns me around, so I'm between his arms, and we're facing the mirror above the sink.

"I like seeing you in my arms. Even in this dingy warped mirror, seeing us together gives me life." He lifts his phone in front of us, and the reflection of the two of us wrapped up in each other is now on the small screen as he takes our picture. He slips the phone back into his pocket. "For those moments when I need to take a sip."

With that, he's gone.

Turning to face the mirror, I see a light in my eyes and a smile on my face I've never seen before. I'm not just happy. I'm in love. But I have to dim my light and erase the smile so his friends don't catch on. If they haven't already.

* * *

"Woo! C'mon, Max. Try it. It feels so good," I yell with my head hanging out of the back seat window of the car Max called to take us home.

His huge hands pull on my hips, ending my fun when he pulls me back into the car, and I land on his lap. "We're almost home. We need to keep it down. You're gonna wake the entire neighborhood, and it's freezing out there, Emmett."

"Oh, sorry," I whisper yell.

His laughter vibrates through my inebriated body. "I like your hair like this. It's cute."

"Cute?" I pull on my hair that ended up in a high ponytail at about the same time my heels were kicked off. "I didn't know Max Hopper used words like cute. I'd rather you think I was sexy." I pull the hairband out of my hair and whip my hair around, trying to be sexy but instead making myself dizzy. "Whoa," I say, realizing just how drunk I am.

"What am I gonna do with you, Firefly?"

In a moment of clarity, I find his eyes in the darkness of the car. "I can think of a few things."

He kisses my nose. "We're home." He lifts me off his lap, climbing out of the car only to lean back in, and in one swift move, he grabs me, throwing me over his shoulder as if I weigh nothing.

Sneaking around the side of the house to go in the back door like we've done most nights in P-burg, he carries me like a sack of potatoes. My limp body is flopping around and my giggle disappears into the still night air.

My feet touch the carpet, and the loss of his body heat hits me, and I realize just how cold I am. My shivers sneak up on me, and I wrap my arms around myself, trying to warm up.

"Cold?"

"Y-y-y-e-e-s-s."

"Emmett, there's snow on the ground, and you're walking around barefoot."

"My feet hurt."

"I bet they do. You girls danced for three hours straight. That is, when you weren't throwing back shots."

"Those were warm."

Another chuckle. I love the sound of his happiness.

"I bet they were."

Sneaking through the moonlit family room, I stop in front of the picture of who I now realize is his son, not Alex's.

"He looks just like you."

"That's what people say."

Next is a picture of Max and his friends at his graduation. "I really like your friends," I say. Then, tapping on the photo, I cause it to swing from side to side like it's going to fall off its nail, but Max stops it, keeping it from falling.

"I'm glad, baby. But how about we don't touch anything and just keep moving." He's standing against me with his hands on my shoulders, guiding me to the stairs that lead to our own little part of the house that seems like it must be abandoned when we aren't here. "There you go. Up the stairs, little lady."

"I'm not little. I've got a fat ass, remember?"

His hand smacks my butt playfully. "What did I tell you about that? I don't want to hear it, Emmett. Your ass is perfect. Just keep it moving all the way to the bathroom. You aren't getting in bed with those dirty feet."

"I don't want to take a shower unless you're getting in with me."

"Don't tempt me, woman." His growl is feral, heating me up from the inside out. "Neither one of us is taking a shower. I'm just gonna wash your feet and then put you to bed."

And he did just that. Washed my feet, and gave me the T-shirt he had worn under his flannel all night so I could sleep in it. When he took his shirt off, I couldn't help myself and licked his bare nipples offering myself to him, and even then he was a gentleman, refusing my advances.

The last thing I remember him saying was something about our first time not being like this. Instead, he wanted me to remember every second. And with his promise of our first time, I closed my eyes and drifted away to dream about Max and his smile.

Chapter Sixteen

The roar of the plane's engine is trying to lull me to sleep. Still, every time I close my eyes, I have flashes of pine trees across his face in the back of his truck, the sound of his voice calling me Firefly as he carried me to bed, looking at ourselves in that dirty bathroom mirror, the feel of his hands washing my feet, and the weight of his heavy body holding me tight to him, as if he may lose me in his sleep.

We're once again in the public eye, but back here in row 23 with my P-Burg Stateliner baseball cap on, I'm tucked away from prying eyes in the window seat. Poor Max is stuck in the middle seat, but I happily let him spill into my space with the arm lifted between us, knowing this may be our last chance to touch for quite some time. As cramped as we are, I hope the plane never lands. With blankets over our laps, our thighs pressed together, and our hands interlock, holding on for dear life. As soon as the plane lands, we know all we'll have are stolen moments and memories.

As much as I love the feel of him, it's too hard to look at him. The moment we left his parents' house, the old Hopper mask was put in place, and his smile that I had grown so familiar with while we were hidden away from the real world was nowhere to be found. Instead, he's quiet and in his head. I'm afraid if I ask him what he's thinking, he'll tell me it's not his job to share that kind of information with his client. Because that's what I am, after all—his client.

Worse than that, I'm afraid he's having second thoughts. That he's starting to think all of this isn't worth it, and maybe he's changed his mind.

I have to believe in what he said these past few days. That we would figure this out. We'd make it work. I just wish he hadn't gone quiet on me. His silence is filling me with doubt.

Squeezing his hand, I cuddle up against him, resting my head against his broad shoulder. His returned squeeze and kiss to the top of my hat relaxes me, and even though I don't want to miss a moment of his hand in mine, I feel myself drifting off to sleep.

* * *

My head bobs from the bump of the plane's wheels touching down on the tarmac. I'm instantly disappointed with myself for sleeping so long and missing my time with him, but I'm happy to feel his hand still holding mine. When I finally brave a look at him, I expect to see Hopper, but instead, I'm met with a sweet smile and his deep whisper.

"Hey, Firefly. How'd you sleep?"

My Max.

"I don't want to get off the plane." I feel the moisture gathering in my eyes, and he shakes his head, telling me not to let the tears fall.

"We're gonna be okay. We will figure this out."

The other passengers have released their seat belts and are gathering impatiently around the aisles to grab their bags and flee the plane while the two of us don't move an inch. Locking our gazes on each other, we soak in the last moments we'll be able to do this.

"Emmett, this is LAX. The moment you step off this plane, there is a good chance you'll be recognized, and you know there will be paparazzi waiting outside. You ready?"

"As long as I have you by my side, I'm good."

The man in the seat next to Max is up and grabbing his bag from the overhead bin. Max takes this as his cue to release my hand and scoot away from me. I go to follow him but haven't taken my seat belt off. I fumble with it while Max grabs the bags, finally releasing myself from my seat and scooting toward the aisle. He moves to let me out into the aisle, whispering, "I've got you," into my ear as I pass by.

And he does.

All the way through the airport to the waiting cameras, who aren't sure I'm somebody, but they assume I must be, because of Max's presence. Even with my sunglasses on, the flashing lights from the cameras that wait for us at the terminal exit is enough to throw me off my balance. I do my best to hide behind Max as he pushes our way through the swarm of paparazzi and finally to our waiting car.

When he opens the back door to the black sedan, I'm breathing heavily, not from exertion but from adrenaline and fear. I don't know how Josh ever got used to being hounded by the press. It sends a heart-pumping fear through me every time.

Not to mention pictures of me mean whoever is messing with me will see I'm home. Know where I am. Hearing the trunk of the car slam shut sends a wave of relief through me because it should mean he'll be climbing in next to me.

But I'm left disappointed when Max takes the front passenger seat, leaving me alone in the back seat. He's checking in with our driver and asking about details not only about Josh and myself but his other clients too.

What Jenn said back in Jersey about Max not having to spend time with clients and assigning jobs to his employees runs through my brain. I'm afraid his being in the field with me again will impact how he runs his business. We really need to have a conversation about all the logistics of what this is doing to his company when we get home.

Home.

I don't even know where that is anymore.

It should be Eastlyn, but instead, it's LA, where I couldn't feel more alone and further from where I should be. Only now, after spending the past few nights in Max's arms, I'm not really sure even Eastlyn is home. At least, not if Max isn't there with me.

If I'm this miserable with Max within reach, how will I handle being unable to touch him once we get out of this car?

I have to talk to Josh.

He should know more than anyone how hard this is. He has to hide his relationship with Jace from the world. If there's anyone I can talk to about this, it's Josh.

* * *

I was put off by the white wreath covered in gold bows and bulbs hanging on the front door when we walked up to the house, but it was all I could do not to rip each and every pretentious decoration off the interior walls.

"How is it gaudy and boring at the same time?"

Max chuckles behind me.

We haven't spoken since getting in the car at the airport, but friendly banter shouldn't give us away. And walking into what is sort of my home already decorated for Christmas without my input—and so poorly decorated at that—requires conversation. My list of conversations that needs to be had seems to be getting longer.

Unfortunately for Greta, she enters the foyer to welcome us home. "Greta, who did this?"

"Did what, Miss Ford?"

"Who decorated the house? And why didn't anyone wait for me? I love Christmas, and I had a lot of ideas!"

Am I yelling?

I think I'm yelling.

What is wrong with me?

Her mouth hangs open. She's either shocked, offended or both. But she regains her composure. "Mr. West always has the house decorated the day after Thanksgiving. He uses the same service every year."

"He uses a service?"

"Yes, ma'am."

"So, he doesn't even own this stuff? This is all just brought in by a decorator?"

"Yes, ma'am."

"I don't even want to know how much he paid the person who thought fake white trees covered in nothing but gold would make the house feel like Christmas. It's so pretentious."

"I'm sorry, Miss Ford. Would you like me to call and have them come back and add some color?"

Max steps in front of me. "Greta, it's lovely to see you. I'm sure the décor will grow on Miss Ford if it's what Mr. West wants." Then, turning to me, he cautiously asks, "Shall I take your bags to your room?"

He's looking at me as though I'm a wild animal he's trying to wrangle into a crate or something.

Is he trying to handle me?

"Fine." I storm off toward the staircase that leads to my

luxurious room. I'm pissed at him for trying to end my tantrum but not so mad that I don't see a moment to have five seconds alone with him. "I mean, come on. All white garland on his already all-white walls. And I'm sure he paid thousands for it." I scoff at the décor lining the hallway leading to my room.

"The gold looks nice. It may not be how you decorate, but the house looks pretty."

He's talking under his breath as we enter the room, playing it safe, but I've lost all sense. "Really, Max? Oh wait, we're back in LA. We're back to Hopper and Miss Ford again, aren't we?" I swing around, hissing at him. "You think the house looks good?" My back is stiff, and I'm up on my toes trying to get face-to-face with him, begging him to disagree with me.

Ready to fight.

"I think you're upset because you don't feel like you have control over your life at the moment. The last straw was not getting to have a say in how the house you live in is decorated for your favorite time of year."

Deflating back on my heels, I feel a painful lump forming in my throat, preventing me from saying he's right, but he is. Looking down at my feet to avoid his knowing eyes, I'm embarrassed by my behavior.

"I was a jerk to Greta. I need to tell her I'm sorry," I say to the hardwood floor.

"Hey. Look at me." Doing as he asks, I lift my face and meet his golden eyes. "I'm here. I got you. Yes, you need to apologize to Greta, but you also need to remember I'm not going anywhere, and you and I can control what we can control when it comes to us."

With the bedroom door open, I can't do what feels natural: raise up on my toes and kiss him. So, instead, I nod my head in understanding as Jace's voice travels up the stairs, reminding me that I should probably go say hey to Josh.

"Listen, I'm gonna go catch up with Reeves, and you need to go check in with Josh. I'll be sure to say goodbye before I leave."

"It's just a couple of days, right?"

"It's gonna be a bitch, but I promise I'll stay in touch."

With that, he leaves me alone in the middle of my luxurious room. It's cold compared to the wood-paneled house in snowy New Jersey. What I wouldn't give to be back there already.

Heading downstairs in search of Josh, I know I'll feel better once I talk to my best friend.

We will figure this out.

Entering the kitchen, Greta is going over a list of some sort at the island when her eyes lift in anticipation.

"Greta, I'm so sorry. The house looks beautiful. I'm just tired, and I took it out on you."

"I don't even know what you're talking about, Miss Ford." She winks.

"Well, thank you for being so sweet and putting up with me. Is Mr. West in his office?"

"He is, but I believe he's on a call. I can check for you."

"No, that's okay. I'll go pop in and see if he's available."

She's right, he is busy, but he waves at me through the doors as he paces back and forth like he usually does on business calls. He must be talking to his agent.

Jace starts to rudely close the big French doors in my face without so much as a hello. I put my foot in his way and stop the doors from shutting completely.

"Jace, I need to talk to Josh when he's off his call."

"You'll have to wait."

Thump.

The doors close in my face, the wood grazing my nose.

Wow, what's gotten into him? I sure hope things are okay with the movie.

Oh my God, do they already know? Did Jace shut me out because somehow Max and I were already noticed by someone? If so, does that mean the paparazzi know?

The squeak of the new leather couch outside Josh's office echoes off the walls when I plop down in a pout. It's new, like everything else in the house, just like me.

Even as his oldest friend, I feel like a kid waiting outside the principal's office, wondering what her punishment will be.

Fortunately, only a couple of minutes pass before the door swings open.

"Emmy! I'm so glad you're home!" He holds his arms out wide, and the couch squeaks again when I jump up and hop into the arms of my best friend.

Seeing his warm smile waiting for me when he walked out of his office reminded me how much I've missed him. He's my person, and it's felt strange keeping what's going on with Max from him. He doesn't even know where I've been for the past five days.

"Oh, I've missed you so much, Josh. We have so much to catch up on. Do you have a few minutes?"

"Always for you."

Jace walks into the room. "Hey, Emmett. Good to see you, girl," he says with a much different attitude than when he closed the door in my face, pulling me into a hug.

"Hey, you. Good to see you too."

"Are you doing okay? I'm really sorry to hear about the nonsense that happened when you were in Eastlyn. Even more sorry you missed Thanksgiving with the fam." He releases me, and Josh puts his arm around me.

"I'm fine. Did you have a good holiday with your family?"

"It was great. I hated to leave Josh on his own, but it was really good to see my mom. It had been way too long. But listen,

I'm gonna let you guys catch up. Maybe we can all do dinner later this week?"

"Dinner sounds great, Jace."

"Oh, and don't forget you two have dinner with the Smiths tonight."

Shit, we really are back from our bubble in New Jersey. Dinner with other celebrity couples is already happening on my first night back. Great.

"I'll be there," I say, deflating inside at the thought of having to be with anyone other than Max.

As much as I like Jace, I'm happy to see him leave the room. It's always nice to get time alone with Josh. Unfortunately, it's rare these days.

"Hey, come talk to me while I finish up a couple of things." I follow him and close the French doors of his office, looking for some privacy. I'm relieved when he sits down on the white microfiber couch instead of behind his desk and pats the seat next to him. "Talk to me, Emmy."

"I thought you had some stuff to finish up?"

I take the seat next to him, doing my best to delay the conversation about to take place.

"It can wait. I can tell you have something on your mind." Yes, he can be selfish, but he can also be that sweet boy who knows me so well. "Let me just say, I am so sorry all of this is happening. If I had known there would be psychos out there just waiting to make your life miserable, I would have never agreed to this."

"I know. We didn't know this would happen."

"How can I make it up to you?"

"Well, actually. You've already given me something; you just don't know it yet."

His furrowed brow says he's confused, and his silence says he's waiting for me to spill it.

"I know this is going to sound crazy, but somehow, during this mess, I've actually met someone."

"I'm sorry, did you say you met someone?"

"Yes, you heard me right. I, Emmett Ford, met someone. Crazy, I know."

As if in slow motion, he rises from the couch and walks the length of the room. When he turns around, the face aimed at me isn't one I've ever seen before. He's a mixture of angry and disgusted. Why do I get this sick feeling that this conversation isn't going to go quite as I had anticipated?

"What do you mean you met someone?" he growls from across the room.

"Hey. Don't freak out. I haven't been in public with this person, and it's all very new."

"Don't freak out? You're my fucking fiancée, Emmett! What the hell are you thinking?"

Standing to meet his rage with my own, I walk toward him, but he backs up until his desk is between us. "I thought you, of all people, would understand."

"What exactly should I understand? That you signed a contract and only a few months in, you've already broken it. I never would have thought you could be this selfish!" he all but spits his words at me.

"Selfish? Are you serious right now?"

"That's exactly what you are, Emmett! I mean, come on! How could you do this to me?"

"It's not like I planned it. I didn't sign my life over to you for two years, lie to everyone in my life about our engagement, and move to Los Angeles so I could throw a wrench in it all. Life happens sometimes, you know?"

"You may not have planned it, but here we are."

"Josh, I'm sorry, but you need to give me a chance to explain."

His arms are crossed over his heaving chest, his nostrils are flaring, and his seething glare cuts right through my heart.

I have no idea who this man in front of me is.

Where did my best friend go?

"Go ahead, explain."

"Listen, I...I...we have no plans to go public."

"I thought it was 'new.' Now you're a 'we?'"

"Josh, what is going on? I know I have well over a year and a half left on the contract, and I can keep it private until that time is over. It sucks, but if you and Jace can make it work..."

"Do not compare me and Jace with whatever this is." He waves his hand at me, dismissing Max and me before he knows a thing about our relationship. He finally sits down. Hopefully, this is a good sign, and he's calming down.

"Josh. Why are you reacting this way? You know I wouldn't do anything to jeopardize your career. I know how important our engagement is."

"Who is it?"

Thank God I didn't blurt Max's name out when this conversation started. There is no way I'm telling him now.

"Nobody."

He jumps out of his seat, sending it crashing into the floor-to-ceiling bookcase behind him, pounding his fist into the desk before bellowing. "Tell me!"

"Why do you get to be with someone, and I don't?"

Still screaming, he ignores my question. "Emmett, tell me who the fuck it is!"

"You're irrational. Do you really think I would tell you anything right now when you're behaving like this? I don't even know who you are."

My phone rings, scaring me half to death, and I drop it on the floor. I'm shocked when Josh jolts in front of me to grab it, but he doesn't get what he was hoping for. I'm so glad I changed

Max's name to The Greatest in my phone after his mom told me the meaning behind her boys' names.

"Is that him?" he says with a sneer in place, making fun of the nickname.

I grab my phone from his hand, silencing it as I head to the door to end this conversation that isn't going anywhere. "Josh, you know I would never hurt you."

My phone lights up.

THE GREATEST

You okay? Need me?

ME

I'm fine. We're just about done here.

"You're seriously going to walk away right now?"

"I came in here to talk to my best friend, but he isn't anywhere to be found. I think this conversation is over."

"I really can't believe you're doing this to me, Emmett!" he yells at my back.

"Right back at ya, Josh," I whisper to myself. Then, take the back staircase to my room, to avoid Max and everyone who may have heard the humiliating scene.

Chapter Seventeen

Once locked inside my room, I slowly unpacked and took a long hot shower. Much to my dismay, the twenty minutes under the water didn't wash away the hurt. My chest still feels tight from the pain.

Sitting cross-legged on my bed, I've just started towel-drying my hair when I hear a knock on the door.

"Emmy, it's me. Can we talk?"

I don't care how pathetic he sounds on the other side of the door; he's the last person I want to talk to.

"Please, just leave me alone."

"Come on, Emmett. I've had some time to calm down, and I'm ready to talk."

Huh, so he's ready to talk. As long as he's ready, then by all means. Jerk.

"Well, I'm not. Go away."

"What about dinner with the Smiths?"

Is he kidding me right now?

"You're on your own tonight."

I walk into the en suite bathroom and shut the door behind me. If he has anything else to say, I don't want to hear it. I turn on the blow dryer for good measure, blocking out the possibility of him hurting me further.

I don't bother putting on any makeup or doing anything with myself but still stall long enough that Josh has probably given up trying to talk to me. Finally, I crack the door to my bedroom to take a listen, and when I find things are quiet, I leave the bathroom and crawl into my bed.

Not two minutes later, there's another knock on the door. This time, it's Jace on the other side.

"Sweetie, can I come in?"

I really don't want to talk to anyone, but Jace didn't do anything wrong, so I tell him he can come in.

The door opens slowly, and he sheepishly walks in. "Hey, girl."

"Hey."

He closes the door behind him and walks over to the bed. "Can I sit?"

"Sure."

The bed dips when he sits down, causing me to readjust my pillows and find my balance. We're both quiet for a second, but eventually, he speaks.

"Emmett, he told me what's going on."

I don't dare speak. First, I need to feel this out and see where the conversation is headed. Jace is a nice guy, but he's not only Josh's manager; he's the love of his life. Jace is Team Josh, and no matter how nice he is, he isn't on my side right now.

"You surprised him."

"We know how he hates surprises."

He chuckles. "He knows his reaction was a bit much. He feels awful, Emmett."

"He should."

"You know he loves you, and he wants you to be happy more than anyone in his life."

"He has a bizarre way of showing it."

"Em, you know he does. Do you see him showering anyone else with a clothing allowance and trips on private jets?"

My body tenses, breaking out into a cold sweat at his insinuation.

"Jace, I don't care about any of that. I would hope after all these years you would know that." Teeth grinding, I force myself to take a deep inhale through my nose in hopes that I can calm myself and not start screaming at Jace like Josh did to me. "I also don't consider throwing around disposable wealth as a real way of showing how much you care about someone. If this is your take on the situation, I think you should leave."

Hanging his perfectly coiffed head, he doesn't look at me when he starts speaking again. "Emmett, I'm sorry. I'm not good at this. That came out all kinds of wrong. All I know is he loves you, and because he loves you, I love you, and I'm really sorry." He takes my hand in his with sincere regret in his eyes.

Maybe I reacted a bit too harshly. Unfortunately, there seems to be a lot of that going around today.

"He hates that he reacted the way he did, and he knows what you were willing to sacrifice when you signed that contract. If he could take it all back, he would. He got scared. He assumed you wanted out when you said you had met some-one, and his career flashed before his eyes. He freaked the fuck out, Emmett. He's had a chance to breathe, and I think he's seeing things clearer now."

"Well, I'm gonna need a bit of space before I'm ready to talk to him."

"I get it. I do."

"Thanks, Jace."

He pulls his hand back and stands to leave, but instead of heading toward the door, he turns and faces me. He doesn't speak, almost like he wants to say something but doesn't know how to get it out.

"What is it, Jace?"

"You sure you won't change your mind about dinner?"

"Oh, Jace. Here I thought you came in here concerned about Josh and me."

"Ugh, I'm sorry." His shoulders lift. "It's the manager in me. Tonight was a bitch to plan. I was just hoping to salvage it."

"Well, sorry to be a bitch as well, but there's no way I can fake it tonight. He's gonna have to entertain Hollywood royalty on his own this time. He's a great actor, Jace. He's got the shelves of awards to prove it."

"You're right. It's too soon. No problem. It'll be fine." He leans in and kisses me on the top of my head.

I stop him just before he reaches the door. "Jace, I don't know how you do it. Balancing loving him and managing him. You're in a tough position, and you do a great job. I'm not sure what he would do without you. Thank you for taking care of him, even if that means you have to try to manage me too."

His cheeks redden, and he nods as he walks out the door.

EMMETT

You still here?

THE GREATEST

I am. I'll be there in a few minutes. Josh is getting ready to leave.

EMMETT

I miss you already.

THE GREATEST

Me too, baby.

* * *

I'm watching Sense and Sensibility like I always do when I'm depressed. There's nothing like crying alongside Emma Thompson to cleanse one's soul. However, I've been staring blindly at the TV, not really hearing the words, too wrapped up in the day's events to focus.

When I hear Max's gentle knock on my door, my insides warm, knowing he's here.

"Come in."

His six-foot-four frame fills the doorway, and his handsome face melts my heart, but a piece of my heart breaks as I watch him sneak in and quietly shut the door behind him. This isn't fair to him, and I hate that he's in this position because of me.

Josh may be right about me being selfish.

Because I'm too selfish to let him go.

He crosses the room and slips his shoes off, joining me on the bed. He tucks me into his side like he always does and doesn't say a word.

He simply holds me.

His way of being there for me without forcing me to talk.

I breathe in the clean scent of him and do my best to wrap my arms and legs around his massive body. There's no way I could ever get close enough to him.

"I missed you so much."

"Missed you too, baby. Want to talk about it?"

"He didn't take it well."

"So I heard."

"I've never experienced him like that, Max. I have no idea who that person was today. Honestly, I've known him my whole life, and I've never seen him like that."

"I'm sorry." He kisses the top of my head.

"He didn't even let me explain."

"It sounded like there was furniture flying. It took everything I had in me not to break through the door to make sure you were okay."

"Thank God you didn't."

He sighs heavily, not liking that I didn't want him to step in.

"He has no idea it's you. That's what really enraged him. He wanted to know who I had met, and I refused to tell him."

"Why is that?" There's hurt in his quiet question.

Sitting up, I make sure he sees my eyes when I answer him. "Max, he's my best friend, and I was so excited to tell him all about us, but the moment I said I had met someone, he morphed into a person I could no longer trust with us." Reaching down, I tickle the salt and pepper at his temples and let my fingers trace his rugged jawline. "Max, he was so reactive at that moment, he would have fired you and your entire team, and if we think this is gonna be hard with you in the same house every day, imagine if you weren't here. I couldn't take that risk."

His hand reaches behind my head, tangling in my hair gently and encouraging me toward him. When our lips meet, they tell me he understands. Then, after what could never be long enough, he pulls away, adjusting so he's lying on his side, and I follow suit facing him.

"Listen, you know I have the next couple of days off."

"Why now?" I whine. The reminder deflates me, and I roll over onto my back, stomping my feet into the mattress. "I know you deserve your time off. I really do. I'm being a big baby. Hopefully, you get to see Nick, and I am sure Molly will be excited to see you?"

"I know, the timing sucks, but I'm gonna be working on trying to figure out exactly who it is that's fucking with you. All we know is that the threats only seem to happen after a public outing when your picture has been out there, but the twist of someone breaking into your place in Eastlyn changes things. Eastlyn is nowhere near LA, but it's clear it was orchestrated by the same person. I need the time to focus and figure this out, and you have lots of meetings this week that you need to prep for over the rest of your weekend." His fingers trail up and down my arm in an easy rhythm, relaxing me. "So we'll both focus on work, and the time will fly by. I'll also be a part of the security detail for the party you two are going to tomorrow night, so I'll be close by."

"What about Nick?"

With a tight smile, he says, "It's not my weekend."

It's not his weekend, but he wishes it were. He misses his little boy.

"I don't want to go anywhere with Josh right now, but if it means I'll get to see you, even if from a distance, then it'll be worth it." I sound like such a brat, but it's how I feel.

I am selfish, after all.

He grabs my hip and turns me, so I'm facing him again. "Kiss me."

I do as instructed, and my tantrum fades away; in place of it is the taste of the man who already owns my heart. He eases me like no one ever has.

My phone pings from my bedside table, and it's Josh.

JOSH

On my way home. Can we talk?

I hold the phone up for Max to see.

"Talk to him. You don't have to tell him anything you don't want to, but hear him out. He's your best friend."

EMMETT

Okay.

"Well, that's my cue. I'm gonna get out of here, but I'll check in later, okay?"

"I don't want you to leave."

"I don't either, but you and Josh need to talk, and I don't think him finding me here would start that conversation off any better than the one you had earlier today."

"I'll text you after we talk."

"Okay, baby."

He slinks out of the room, and I'm left to wait for Josh.

Chapter Eighteen

I'm waiting in the kitchen, drinking a glass of wine and snacking on pita chips when Josh gets home. I'm surprised to see Jace isn't with him.

"Hi," he says with his hands in his front pants pocket.

"Hey. How was dinner?"

"It was good. They can't wait to meet you at the party tomorrow night."

"That's nice." I grab a stemless wine glass out of the cupboard and pull the cork out of the bottle of red I've been sipping on, and pour him a drink.

Rounding the massive kitchen island, he grabs his glass in one hand and my hand in the other. He leads us to the living room, where we sit on the plush white couch facing each other. Everything in this damn house is white.

"Red wine on a white couch means you have to keep calm, or you'll ruin more than just my mood."

"Emmy, I am so sorry about today. My reaction was uncalled for and frankly unacceptable. I'm not sure what got into me, but I freaked out, and there are no excuses. Forgive me?"

"Always. But Josh, what in the world was that?"

"I thought for sure you were going to back out, and my job, my career, my fans, Jace, it all flashed before my eyes, and I snapped. The thing is, I was only thinking about myself. And I know everything is always about me, Em, I do, but today was next level selfish of me. I am so, so sorry."

"I get it, but a violent reaction like that can't happen again, Josh. I know you would never hurt me; it's not that. I just don't deserve to be treated in such a way. Especially by you."

"Of course, you don't. You don't have to tell me that. I don't know what I would do without you."

"Hopefully, you never have to find out."

He sets his glass down on the coffee table and then takes mine, setting it beside his. "Come here." He pulls me into a hug. "Love you, Emmy."

"Love you, Joshy Washy."

Releasing me, he gets our glasses and settles back into the couch. "Now, tell me everything."

"I'm not ready to tell you who it is just yet, but I can tell you he's a good man. He makes me feel things, Josh. Things I've never felt before."

"And the sex?"

"You and your one-track mind."

"Sorry, I can't help it."

"Well, we haven't gotten there yet. I think we both want to do this right. Well, he does, anyway. I've tried, but he shoots me down every time. We've slept together, but we haven't 'slept' together."

"Well, I like him already."

"Josh, we didn't plan for this."

"I know."

"I'm willing to keep it under wraps. I have no intention of breaking the contract."

"Well, it's not like there's a clause that says you're not allowed to fall in love. But, I do think it would help if you told me who he was. And not to make it about me, but he's going to have to sign an NDA at some point. I know it's a shitty thing to ask, Em, but in this crazy world I live in, I don't really have a choice."

The man looking back at me is the man I've known my whole life. He hates bringing this up, and it shows in his eyes. He's right about keeping it real. If only he knew that he didn't have to worry about his request. The man who has complicated our lives has already signed an NDA. Of course, knowing Josh, he's already figured it out. He knows everywhere I go, and the only time I would have been alone to meet someone would be my time away with Max.

Is he just being nice and letting me tell him when I'm ready?

"I'm gonna keep him to myself a little longer, but I promise to keep it on the D.L."

Josh and I spend the next hour talking while we slowly drink our wine. Just like the old days. When we finally go to bed, I feel like things will be okay.

I text Max, telling him things went well with Josh and that I'm going to turn in for the night. When I've finished my night-time routine and climb into bed, I can see that he's read my message, but he hasn't replied. Turning out the light, I do my best to get comfortable, but these down pillows are no match for Max's shoulder.

Tossing and turning, I do my best not to analyze why he might not have returned my text. Did he already figure out I'm not worth it? I get it. He's a grown man sneaking around like a kid. I don't blame him if he's having a change of heart.

Lying on my side, every muscle in my body tightens as I watch my bedroom door slowly open. I hold my breath, knowing it would be nearly impossible for my stalker to have gotten in the house, but what if? Not a heartbeat later, I see the backlit outline of a body I already know by heart.

Silently, he removes his shoes and pants, then climbs under the covers with me. He holds himself over me and then slowly lowers himself and slides down my body burying his face in the silk covering my stomach. His teeth graze my abdomen as he bites his way back up, following the path of teasing he left on his way down. Stopping when he reaches my breast, he brings my nipples to attention nipping at them through the silk I wish he would rip off my body so I could feel his lips against my flushed skin.

My wish is granted when his mouth finds my sternum, his lips blazing a red hot trail over my neck and shoulders thanks to the two-day scruff adorning his handsome face. A kiss here. A nibble there. And finally, a luscious lick up the side of my neck to my earlobe, where he finally speaks.

"How did I ever breathe before you?"

I gasp, arching my back, spreading my legs for him, and digging my fingernails into his back as my body acts on its own accord. Longing to be closer to him. To feel all of him.

All the while, my heart swells with love.

He swallows the gasp that follows when his hand begins to travel up the inside of my thigh. His kiss is slow, his fingers just as relaxed as they stroke and squeeze each of my curves. My greedy hands find their way under his shirt, desperate to touch him, but he stops me and holds them above my head, regaining his control as his fingers intertwine with mine.

He deepens the kiss with a growl. Tasting, pushing, stroking as our tongues dance to the beat of our overflowing hearts and lust-filled libidos.

"Fuck," he breathes into my mouth. Then, slowing our kiss,

he lets go of his hold on my hands, and I instinctually begin to gently stroke his back.

He rolls off me and situates us until we're lying with his front to my back, his chest lifting and falling against me as he regains his composure. "Why do you always throw me off my game? I came here to say good night and to lay with you until you fell asleep."

"You sure that's all you wanted?" I wiggle my butt against his erection.

"I didn't say that was all I wanted, but it's the reason I'm here. Now, be good and go to sleep."

"Thanks for coming back."

"Don't get used to it. I won't be able to sneak in here on my days off. Thought I would get one last sip to try to hold me over."

"I don't even want to think about it."

He doesn't reply. Instead, he holds me as he had intended to do all along. Several minutes go by before he whispers into my hair.

"Hey, Emmett?"

"Yeah?"

"I'm really glad you met my family. My friends. My hometown. Besides Nick, they're the only part of my heart that isn't yours, and I'm glad I got to share them with you."

"Max..."

"Shh...go to sleep."

I'm not sure how he expects me to go to sleep with his words floating around my head and caressing my heart. Still, he seems to have the magic elixir needed to do just that because I drift off to sleep in his arms.

Chapter Nineteen

I'm not asleep, and I'm certainly not ready to be awake yet. Because, I know when I open my eyes, he'll be gone, and I'll be back to pretending, so I keep my eyes shut a few moments longer.

I can hear him asking how he ever breathed before me. Feel his breath in my hair as he holds me from behind, and the weight of his arm pulls me tight against him. Only in this space between sleep and wakefulness he doesn't simply hold me until I fall asleep.

In my dream state, after Max wonders how he ever breathed before me, he punctuates the emotion by slipping his fingers under the lace of my panties. Brushing over the spot that sets my core on fire for the quickest of moments before plunging two fingers deep inside me, causing my back to arch and a moan to slip from my mouth that he quickly covers with his hand, so we aren't heard.

While his fingers wind me up into a frenzy, his mouth replaces his hand, swallowing my moans. Once he's quieted me, he removes his fingers, and I whimper in protest. He pulls the top of my nightgown down to expose my right breast, the warmth of his tongue smothering the cold air on my nipple. While he devours me, his hand pulls down the other side of my nightgown to gain access to my other breast.

He lifts up, so his weight is on his forearms, hovering above me. His eyes convey love and respect and ask permission at the same time. I give him a small nod, letting him know I want this as much as he does, and he wastes no time getting his boxers off.

He kisses me deeply, passionately, and I breathe his name into his mouth. I've been waiting for what feels like a lifetime for this moment. The firmness of his length pressing against me, the anticipation of feeling him inside me, has me writhing beneath him...

Ping.

The sound of a text message coming through on my phone effectively shuts down what was about to be one of the best dreams of my life. Instead, I'm met with the stark reality that it's time to get up, and when I do, he won't be here.

He deserves his time off, but I'm wondering how *I'm* going to breathe with *him* gone for three days. Just the thought of the next three days without him somewhere in the house sours my mood and pushes away the memories of last night.

Stretching awake, I'm met with the darkness thanks to the black-out window coverings in my room. I fumble for the remote, and the hum of the motor that opens the curtains lets me know I found the right button. Gradually, the bright SoCal sun fills the room. When Josh first moved to LA, I loved waking up to the bright sun, but I've grown immune to the bountiful vitamin D, and it no longer invigorates me like it once did. Now, it leaves me feeling exposed.

Rolling over to face the empty pillow next to me, I'm surprised to find a piece of paper filling the space where his scruffy face had been last night. My stomach flutters with anticipation as I snatch the folded piece of paper and sit up against the headboard to read it.

Firefly,

I hope you have a good day. I'll be doing my best to breathe while I'm away. If you need me, just call.

XOXO,
M

Twenty-five words and the letter M.

This was all I needed.

With this, I'll be able to get through my day with a smile on my face.

Bounding out of bed, I throw on an oversized sweater and float on air to the kitchen, where I find Josh sipping his coffee in Max's usual perch, which annoys me. We may have to make that spot reserved seating only.

He notices me and stands up straight, crossing his arms and lifting a perfectly manicured eyebrow. He's up to no good.

"What?"

"Oh, my sweet Emmy. You are always full of surprises, aren't you?"

No, no, no. Please tell me he didn't figure it out.

"Josh, what in the world are you talking about? I just got up. Haven't really had a chance to do anything surprising yet."

"Speaking of sleeping, did you sleep well?"

"I did. How about you?"

"I bet you did."

"And what exactly is that supposed to mean?"

"Well, you see, I *didn't* sleep well. Had a lot on my mind. You know, like how I could have been so awful to my best friend. I guess you could say the guilt was getting to me." I try to speak, but he wags his finger at me and continues. "Around 4:30, I finally gave up and got out of bed."

Crap, I know where this is going.

"Imagine my surprise when I see a large man creeping away from your bedroom door. I thought we had an intruder for the briefest moment, but when I got a better look at him, it turned out it was a certain brooding member of our security team."

The flaming hot blush burning my cheeks says it all.

"Maximus Hopper. I get it now."

"Josh..."

"Emmy, I mean it. He's hot as hell, smart, and from what I know of him, a pretty decent guy."

"Josh, he's everything." My insides tumble around when I hear myself say it out loud because it's true, and I can't believe I've found him.

The smile on Josh's face is the one I know and love. Not the fake one seen on red carpets and magazine covers. No, this is a smile that says he couldn't be happier for me. He rounds the island and pulls me into a hug.

"Tell me everything."

* * *

"My feet are killing me, but man, was it worth it. The McKinleys know how to throw a charity gala." I pull my three-inch heels off my feet and prop them on Josh's lap, moaning when he begins to rub them. My eyes fall shut, but I can still see the bright flashes of the paparazzi who ascended on us in just the twenty feet we had to walk from the exit doors to the car. I really don't know how Josh does it.

"Tonight was fun." He squeezes my foot, and I open my

eyes to look at him. "I've missed you, Emmy. I'm glad we were able to spend the day together."

The passing headlights of the cars going in the opposite direction on Santa Monica Boulevard highlight his features as they go by. He looks content. Happy.

"It was a perfect day." I sigh, as he continues to rub my feet.

It's true. It was a perfect day. Josh and I were simply two best friends from Oregon hanging out like we always have. We sat in the kitchen and drank our coffee while I shared all the details about how Max and I became an us. The idea of the two of us being a couple is still new and still so secret. It was the first time I had said any of it out loud, and it felt really good.

After coffee, we went for a swim.

Outside.

During the first week of December!

Southern California temperatures and the heated pool and heat lamps next to the poolside tables made for a perfect morning topped off with lunch prepared by Greta. We ate, we talked, and we tried to dunk each other in the pool. We even scored each other's dives off the diving board just like we used to with The Crew back home on the lake. We may get a lot more height with a diving board, but it's not the same without the rest of the gang here with us. But it was still fun.

It was nice not to have Jace around today. I know it's selfish of me, and I really like him, I do, but it was still nice.

Jace has always welcomed me with open arms, and if Josh loves him, then I do too. It's just so rare that I'm in a room with Josh, and he isn't there. It's understandable; he's not just his manager, he's his person. If I could be with Max every minute of the day, that would be just fine with me. So, there aren't any hard feelings, but it's been great to have a day to ourselves.

We may be in a blacked-out SUV, being driven by a member of Josh's security team. And he may be decked out in an Armani suit while I lounge in the back seat in my black strapless Chanel gown, but we're still just a couple of small-town kids living an extraordinary life. At least for the moment.

"I hate that production is delayed, but I'm really glad I got to come home for a little while."

"I wish we got to hang out like this more often, especially if it means I get foot rubs." He pinches my foot. "I'm just kidding. I'm glad you're home too. Do you think you'll get to come home for Christmas now that your schedule is pushed back?"

"It's up in the air right now, but I know Jace is trying to work his magic. At least now I won't feel so guilty about you being alone here in La La Land while I'm gone. You have your boy toy now."

"Josh!" I hiss, nodding my head toward Reeves in the driver's seat, who I can only assume doesn't know about Max and me.

"Shit, that's right. I'm so sorry, Emmy. This whole thing really sucks," he says in a quiet voice I can barely hear.

"It's fine. It's only a year, eight months, and three weeks."

"But who's counting, right?"

Distracted by a phone call, Reeves isn't paying attention to us. Dropping my feet to the floor of the car, I take his hand in mine and hope that even in the darkness of the back seat, Josh can see the sincerity in my eyes.

"When this all started, I didn't know something might be waiting for me on the other side. Now that I do have something waiting for me, I can't help the anticipation. But Josh, I will always be here for you. As much as I hate that the world is such that we have to be in the situation we're in, I couldn't be happier to be here with you. Please don't doubt that."

Kissing the back of my hand, he whispers, "Love you."

"Love you right back."

Pulling up the long driveway to Josh's house, it's strange that

Reeves doesn't pull up to the front door like usual. Instead, he pushes the button to open the garage door and pulls the car inside.

"Everything okay?" Josh asks, loosening his tie and undoing the top button on his pristine black shirt while I slip my shoes back on.

"Mr. Hopper is waiting inside, sir, and he'll explain."

A sinking sensation in the pit of my stomach hits me without warning. Why is Max here, and why did we have to park inside the garage? Max hadn't been able to attend the gala since he got Nick at the last minute and sent Smith in his place, so he shouldn't be here.

Reeves opens the door for me, and I wait for Josh to come around to my side of the car before following him into the house. He takes my hand, guiding me through the garage and into the house. All the while, the tapping of my red-bottomed shoes and the swooshing of the yards upon yards of fabric of my beautiful gown echo in my ears like a surreal soundtrack.

I hear him before I see him. His voice is low. Angry. My free hand gathers my heavy dress, lifting it, so I don't trip on it. I'm ready to run into his arms, but the gentle squeeze from Josh reminds me that he's the only hand I get to hold tonight.

Entering command central, also known as the dining room, all conversation halts with our presence. I feel my heart plummet when his beautiful head lifts and his gaze finds mine as if there is nowhere and nobody else to look at.

His eyes say everything I'm feeling.

That his instinct is also to rush to me and pull me into his arms, but that's not possible, and that hurts my heart.

"Just tell us what's going on. Don't sugarcoat it. Just spit it out," I blurt out before anyone else has a moment to speak.

Smith begins to fill us in, but Max cuts him off.

"Miss Ford, we aren't exactly sure what's going on. There

was a threat left on the front steps of the house, but we have no idea who left it there. Smith was walking the perimeter in anticipation of your arrival home. The package was there when he finished his loop."

"But you checked the cameras, right? You must have gotten a good look at the asshole?" No longer holding my hand, Josh stands with his feet shoulder-width apart and his arms folded across his chest.

This is his stubborn, I'm not moving until you tell me what I want to hear, stance. I haven't seen it in years. The last time was when one of the guys back home was trying to drive home after too much beer, and he stood just like this in front of their truck, refusing to move until they got out and handed over his keys.

"Mr. West, somehow, they hacked into the security system because about ten seconds are missing from the video we pulled. Sir, I am sorry for the breach, but I assure you my team is on top of it."

"How can someone hack into our security system? How is that even possible?" I ask. Not accusingly but in real wonder.

Max's eyes plead with me to forgive him. He feels responsible. He's in charge of our safety, and he feels like he let not just me but also Josh and everyone else down.

"The truth is it's either a computer expert who can breach a system like the one Mr. West has on-site, or it's somebody on the inside with access."

The air whips out of my lungs, and my dress billows under me as I drop down into the closest chair. Thank God for that chair because my legs weren't going to hold me up a second longer.

Looking around the room, I find it impossible to think it could be anyone present. Reeves was with us. Smith was here and outside at the time. He does have access to the system, but he's been with Josh for so long. I can't imagine Max would have anyone working for him who he couldn't vouch for, and I know I haven't known him long, but I trust him with my life.

Then there's Jace, who always has his face in his phone and his thumbs moving a mile a minute. No, it couldn't be Jace. He's the love of Josh's life, and his entire life is centered around taking care of him. I drop my head and give it a shake, trying to ward off the dark thoughts going through my mind about everyone in the room. I know it's not Josh, and it certainly isn't me.

Greta went home early since we were eating out, and the housekeeping staff wasn't in today. But they do have access to the security room—we all do. I don't know how to do anything with the cameras, but I have access to it just like everyone else does.

No!

Stop it, Emmett!

It's not anybody on the inside. That is just crazy.

"Bullshit!" Josh yells at Max.

"I'm sure you're right, Mr. West, but we have to explore every possible theory."

"You hearing this shit, Jace?"

"Kinda hard not to when I'm standing right here with the rest of you." Never lifting his eyes from his phone, he almost seems annoyed with Josh for interrupting him.

Josh moves closer to him until he's standing directly in front of him. If looks could kill, Jace would be dead on the floor. "What the fuck are you working on that is more important than this?" Josh taps Jace's phone, and it falls to the ground.

Whoa.

I've never seen the two of them share a cross word, but I, too, would like to know what in the world he could be working on at a time like this.

"Josh, calm down. I'm trying to figure out which slimeball

paparazzi took the pictures. Whoever this is has to have a contact with one of the paps. I'm trying to see which websites have posted these exact pictures. If I can figure that out, then I can reach out to my contacts and see if I can get them to spill who they bought the shots from." He holds up his phone, and even I can see from my seat that he's got the pics of Josh and me tonight walking the red carpet at the gala. He's on Online Buzz because the site's name is plastered across the top of the screen. "I don't need the debrief, I've been here all night. I was here when it happened."

Josh wipes his hands over his face in frustration. "Fuck, Jace. I'm sorry. Ba...dude, you know I'm just freaked out, and it looked like you weren't listening."

My soul sags at the sound of Josh wanting to call Jace "babe" but stopping himself. God, I hate that he has to hide who he really is. Everyone in this room knows the truth, but he still can't let himself go there.

"I get it, but you know I'm always looking out for you. Your best interest is always my top priority. Now, if you don't mind, I'd like to get back to it?"

The sound of pinging phones bounces around the room, and my clutch vibrates. I open my bag to grab my phone, but Max rounds the table and puts his hand on top of mine just as Josh curses under his breath.

"Don't."

He's so close.

His touch sends a wave of heat over my body, and his scent is like aromatherapy to my libido. Leaning in front of me, he's so close that I can see each beautiful detail of his face, the salt and pepper at his temples, and each one of his tiny yet beautiful scars.

When I don't reply, he pleads with me again in a whisper that I'm not sure the rest of the room can hear. "Please don't."

"Is it that bad?"

"Sweetie, just don't. Let one of us delete it," Josh, white as a ghost, says, siding with Max.

Even though it goes against every fiber of my being, I let Max take the phone out of my purse, and with his big palm over the screen, he holds it out to me so I can unlock it with my thumb. The look on his face is serious and apologetic. I'm not sure how these new images could be worse than what we've already seen, but they must be bad if they're all protecting me like this.

He nods his appreciation, but his eyes don't linger when he walks away.

"Mr. West, we need to discuss how this will change the red carpet tomorrow night," Max says, standing at the other end of the table.

"Should we just skip it altogether?"

"No, I don't think we need to go to that extreme, but we do know this only seems to happen when Miss Ford is in the press. Maybe we should see what happens if she doesn't walk the carpet with you."

"Works for me. I would certainly rather go alone if it means keeping Em safe."

"But I promised Nikki. It's her first film," I whine in protest.

"No offense, Emmy, but I think she'll survive if you aren't there." He tugs on the tie that's been hanging loose around his neck. The joy of our day has been washed away and replaced with fear and exhaustion.

Countering, I stand to get my point across. "Bullshit! Why should this scumbag get to control my life? We'll bring extra security instead of just Reeves."

Jace excuses himself when his phone rings.

"Miss Ford is right. If she insists on attending, we will make sure Reeves is assigned to you. I'll be with Miss Ford, and then we'll have Smith and Cleveland at the front and back entrances. If we need more men, I'll call them in." He shifts his feet, his hands in the front pockets of his jeans as he speaks to Josh, but his attention focuses on me. "But it would be ideal if you arrived in different vehicles, and you did the carpet on your own, sir. Then, we could have Miss Ford meet you inside."

"So you're gonna sneak me in the back door or something?"

"Something like that." His stance reflects calm, but his tone and the intensity in his eyes are deadly serious.

"Works for me. I hate the red carpet anyway, and I still get to be there for Nikki. Josh, does that work for you?"

"Only if you're sure, Emmy. You don't have to go at all."

"I want to go."

"Okay, thanks, man. I appreciate it," Jace interrupts as he enters the room, concluding his call.

"You got something?" Max asks him before he's hung up.

"Maybe. The pictures were sold to a celebrity photo agency that sells them to the highest bidder. So I have to work backward. My contact at Online Buzz told me the agency they bought the pictures from, and luckily, I know a couple of the paps over there. So I'm gonna head into your office to start making calls if that's cool with you, Josh."

"Of course. Thanks, Jace. I really appreciate it."

"I know you do." He smiles at Josh. His eyes project just as much love as Josh's do. I'm such an ass for thinking that Jace could be the person behind all of this for even a split second.

"What about Eastlyn?"

Huh?

Why is Josh asking Max about Eastlyn?

"I have connections in Portland that are a few hours away, but I'll reach out to them as well as the local authorities. We'll be sure things are secured there too."

"Why, what's going on in Eastlyn?"

"We're just taking precautions, Emmy."

"What was on the text?" I ask the room, only to be met with silence.

When nobody answers me, I stand, holding my hand out to Max. "Give me my phone."

He hands it over to me, but the text is already deleted from my phone.

"What was it?"

"Miss Ford. We're still verifying if it is a recent picture or not. We think it's old and just being used as a scare tactic. Let us clarify things before we share the details with you. We don't want to upset you if it's just smoke and mirrors."

Yes, I see the pleading in his eyes, but I don't care. I'm not a fragile woman who can't handle the truth.

"Don't leave me in the dark on this."

Josh pulls me into his side. "Let's get changed out of all of this bullshit, and I'll fill you in, okay? We won't leave you in the dark. Let's just give Hopper and his team some time to do a little research. I promise I'll fill you in."

"Fine, but tonight. No exception."

He looks at Max before he relents. "I promise. Let's just give them some time. But it will be me who tells you. Is that clear to everyone?"

Everyone in the room nods their agreement.

Max and his team spend the next few minutes going over how we're going to clear the hair and makeup team, not to mention Josh's stylist for tomorrow's prep for the movie premier with Sibby on speakerphone. Of course, Sibby has her role just as the rest of us do. Josh will fill Jace in later, and in no time flat, a plan is in motion.

Max asks his team to convene in the security room, which is just a bedroom with an en suite that was originally built to be live-in quarters for a housekeeper or nanny. Since Josh doesn't require any of his staff to live on-site, Reeves turned it into their home base. It also houses all the security monitors.

I now know that Max sits at the island because he can see all the cameras on his laptop, not requiring him to be in the security room to monitor things. He may be running his business, but he's also keeping an eye out. Of course, I also know now, that he sits at the kitchen island to be closer to me.

Smith and Cleveland leave the room, but Reeves hangs back to let Josh know he will stay on-site tonight.

Max is almost out of the room when Josh stops him. "Hey, Hopper. A word?"

I break into a sweat, my heartbeat picking up speed as I wonder what he has to say to him.

"Sir?"

"Listen, I just want to say how sorry I am for behaving the way I did yesterday when Emmett told me she had met someone. I was an asshole, and even though she's already forgiven me, I hope you will as well?"

He extends his hand out to Max, and I swear it feels the same as watching my dad and my high school boyfriend meet for the first time.

"No need to apologize, and there's nothing to forgive, Mr. West."

Not releasing his hand, the Josh I've given two years of my life up for says, "You make her happier than I've seen her in a very long time. Take care of our girl." Then, letting go of Max's hand, he turns to me. "I'll give you two a minute. Come find me when you're done."

"Thank you," I whisper.

Josh wipes a tear from my cheek with his thumb. "No tears. Come find me once you've changed, and we'll watch Friends until we fall asleep. Deal?"

"Deal."

Josh leaves the room, and the right corner of Max's mouth lifts, easing the insecure anxiousness beginning to creep in. "You told him about me?"

"Well, he saw you sneaking out this morning and kind of busted us. But yes, he knows everything, sorry."

"Don't be sorry. If I had my way, the whole world would know."

"Are there cameras in here?"

"Yes, ma'am."

"So the guys can see us on the monitor right now?"

"Yes, ma'am."

"Can they hear us?"

"No, ma'am."

"I really want to touch you right now."

"Miss Ford, I know exactly what you mean."

"I suppose since Reeves is staying over tonight, you won't be sneaking into my room?"

"No, ma'am."

"Text me?"

"Yes, ma'am."

He lowers his head, bowing to me as if I'm some kind of royalty, and starts to leave the room. But then I remember he hadn't been there tonight because he got his son at the last minute.

"Hey, Max?" He turns back to me. "I thought you had Nick tonight. Where is he if you're here?"

"He's in the security room."

I gasp, a thrill rushing through me at the thought of meeting his son.

"He's here?"

His brows furrow ever so slightly. "Is that a problem, Miss Ford?"

"Not at all. In fact, I'd love to meet him."

"Ma'am, I think it might be a bit odd if you were to follow me to the security room to meet my son."

"Well, I don't need to follow you. I know the way. Besides, he doesn't need to be in there while you guys discuss what was so horrible you couldn't even let me see it. I'll take him to the kitchen and get him a snack. Then, we can go to the theater room and watch a movie until you're done."

He smiles. "We won't be meeting long enough for you to watch a movie, but I'm sure he would love a snack."

"Great!"

I may portray confidence leaving Max to trail behind me as I march through the halls of the house, but I should be the one with the Oscar. Anxious doesn't even begin to cover how I feel about meeting the most important person in Max's life.

Rounding the corner to the short hallway, I enter the open door at the end of it, and there he is. Spinning around in an office chair, he's adorable. The spitting image of his father, he has long, gangly ten-year-old legs and feet he hasn't quite grown into yet, but that indicate he'll be tall like his daddy. His hair is dark brown, just like his dad's, but he's got a faux hawk that says he's cool and maybe a little rebellious but not such a rebel that he'd actually go full mohawk.

Seeing him in person made the fact that Max is a dad all too real.

I don't waste any time getting to the room before Max, so I don't chicken out. "You must be Nick? It's nice to meet you. I'm Emmett."

I offer him my hand, and the sweet boy stands politely, shaking my hand. "Nice to meet you, ma'am."

"I'm here to rescue you from the boring work about to be discussed. How does ice cream sound?"

His eyes grow large, but he looks at his dad for permission before accepting my offer.

"Fine, but only one scoop."

He turns his steely gaze on me, trying to appear firm, but all it does is turn me on to see him in his role as dad.

"Yes, sir."

"Miss Ford, it's late. One scoop, no more," he warns.

"Yes, sir."

The corner of his mouth fights the smile he wants to release when I call him sir. But, with an audience of his employees standing a couple of feet away, he manages to win the battle.

"Come on, Nick. Let's leave your dad and the guys to their work while we go have our *one*"—I give him a conspiratorial wink—"scoop of ice cream."

As I usher the sweet brown-haired boy out of the small dark room full of monitors, the fear creeps in. I've never been so nervous about making a good first impression. He takes a couple of small steps ahead of me, then turns and waits for me to reach him. For a few short moments, the only sound is the swishing of my dress as it swings back and forth while I try to think of what to say first, but Nick breaks the silence before I get a chance.

"So is Mr. West here too? My dad said this was his house. Is that true?"

Damn, it's always about Josh.

"Yes, this is his house, and yes, he's here. Should we see if he wants to have some ice cream too?"

He shrugs, playing off the excitement I can see brewing under the surface. I've seen it a million times before. The feeling is almost palpable.

"This house is huge," he says with quiet awe.

"Don't tell anyone, but I've gotten lost more than once. It's way too big, if you ask me."

"Whoa."

Yep, kiddo. That was my reaction the first time I saw this place.

When we reach the kitchen, I pat the counter where Max's laptop usually takes up residence. "Here, have a seat while I get our ice cream."

I wish I hadn't left my phone in the dining room so I could text Josh and have him come back down to meet Nick. If there were ever a time I would be willing to use Josh for his fame; this would be it. But, even without the celebrity, his charm and ease with people might make things a little easier.

"Sorry, we ruined your night with your dad."

"You didn't ruin it!" He spins in his chair and looks at me like I've lost my mind. "I'm hanging out in Josh West's house. I mean, how cool is that?"

"Pretty cool?"

"Uh, you could say that. It's sure better than going to Dad's office. That's usually the only place he takes me. Not that he's been working in the office much. This is a lot more fun, that's for sure. Besides, I was already in bed, so you won't hear me complaining."

"Does your dad usually take you to the office a lot?" I ask while reaching for bowls to add to the ice cream and spoons I already have out.

"Dad and I do everything together. It's been strange with him working here at Josh's house, but he says this is a really important job."

"He said that?"

He's up on his knees trying to look around the house, I'm sure to catch a glimpse of Josh, when he answers me, but he's not really paying attention. "Yep."

Along with his bowl and one giant scoop of vanilla ice cream, I slide chocolate sauce and a can of whipped cream in front of him.

"Your dad said one scoop, but he didn't say anything about toppings. I forgot to ask. Do you like vanilla?"

He chuckles and lifts his hand for a high five. "That is the biggest scoop I've ever seen! Thank you!"

"You're welcome," I say, slapping his hand.

Taking a seat across from him, I try not to stare, but it's like watching Max as a little boy. I can't take my eyes off him. Now that I'm up close, I see that he has his dad's hazel eyes and the longest lashes. He's a beautiful little boy.

His long lashes lift, and he looks right at me when he asks the question I had been dreading.

"So, is Mr. West your boyfriend?"

Shit!

I want to yell, "No! Your daddy is my boyfriend!" but, of course, I can't.

I'm struggling to come up with an answer that isn't a lie but also isn't the truth when Josh enters the room and saves the day.

"Well, who do we have here?"

Nick's eyes grow big, and his full mouth of ice cream hangs open, unable to answer.

"Josh, this is Hopper's son, Nick."

Now it's Josh's eyes that bulge. "No shit?"

"Josh, language!"

Looking sheepish, he mouths his apology to me.

"Hey, Nick, how the heck are you, man? It's nice to meet you."

Suddenly quiet, Nick takes Josh's outstretched hand and says, "Hi, Mr. West. It's nice to meet you."

"Well, with manners like that, I'd say your dad is doing a pretty good job." He lifts an impressed eyebrow in my direction. "But please, call me Josh."

A smile stretches across his face, and I'd say this is much better than going into his dad's office.

"So, how old are you, Nick?"

"Ten."

"So what grade would that be? Fifth?"

"Yep."

"What's your favorite subject?"

"Social Studies."

"Nice. You get good grades?"

"Yes, Dad will take away my X-Box if not."

"Your dad sounds like a smart guy."

"He is. He has his own company and everything."

"He sure does." Josh shoots me a small smile, recognizing how cute it is that Nick is bragging about his dad. "And lucky for me, he's helping me out. Sorry, we interrupted your night, though."

"That's okay. Miss Ford gave me the biggest scoop of ice cream ever, and your house is pretty epic."

"Hey, why didn't you get me any ice cream, Miss Ford?" he teases me with a smile.

"Here, have mine. I'm not hungry, after all. Besides, I'm wearing Chanel. I shouldn't tempt fate." I push the bowl over to where he stands at the end of the island between Nick and me.

I'd give him anything he wants right now as long as he keeps this easy conversation going with Nick.

"Dude, hit me with that chocolate sauce." Nick slides the plastic bottle to Josh, and he proceeds to douse my ice cream in chocolate. "Don't tell my trainer." He winks in the ten-year-old's direction.

"So, got a girlfriend?"

Nick blushes, his full mouth fighting the giant smile trying to break free when he shakes his head vigorously.

"How about your dad? Does he have a girlfriend?"

I gasp in shock, and I can feel my eyes bugging out even more than Nick's did when Josh walked into the room.

I smack him on his arm. "Josh!" But Nick has no problem answering the question.

"I don't think so, but he seems really happy lately. Kinda like my mom did when she first met her boyfriend. So maybe?" He shrugs.

"Do you like your mom's boyfriend?"

I don't hit him this time, but I shoot him a warning glare. He looks at me, confused, as though he doesn't know what I'm freaking out about.

"He's okay. He has season tickets to the Lakers, and sometimes when he can't go, he'll give mom and me the tickets."

"So he's nice to you?"

"Yep. Randall's nice, and the more he's around, the more I get to see my dad, so that's cool."

Josh casually eats but keeps asking all the questions I would have been too afraid to ask.

"Why do you get to see your dad more?"

"Mom and Dad don't really like babysitters, so if mom is out with Randall, I get to stay at Dad's, even if it's not his night. As long as he's not out of town. Then they have the sitter come over."

"You like your sitter?"

"She's cool. She likes video games. I'd rather be with Dad and Molly, but she's not bad." Another shrug.

Aw, he loves his daddy.

"What else do you like besides video games? You look pretty tall. You like sports?"

"Basketball is my fave. I'm on a travel league."

"Whoa. Travel league is no joke. So you must be good?"

Nick blushes. "I'm pretty good, but don't tell Dad I said that. He says it's not nice to brag."

"Your secret's safe with me. How about you, Emmett? You won't tell his dad, will you?"

Josh is trying to involve me in the conversation because, at the moment, I'm just sitting here observing them much like a tennis match. My head goes to Josh in fear of what he might ask and then over to Nick, waiting with bated breath for every answer.

"Promise."

"Hey, Nick? You know who was a stud basketball player?"

"Who, you?"

"Nah, I was a baseball guy, but Emmett here was all-state in high school."

"Really?" He furrows his little brow, skeptical.

"Don't let her fancy dress fool you. She's a badass."

"Language!" I scold him again.

Nick laughs. "It's okay; I hear my mom and dad cuss."

It's then I realize I'm still in my dress and heels from the gala, whereas Josh is in sweat shorts and a T-shirt.

So not fair.

"Chocolate sauce and whipped cream? Really? I thought I was pretty clear."

Hopping off my chair, I stand at attention, addressing Nick's daddy. "You said one scoop. You didn't say a thing about toppings."

"Semantics, Miss Ford."

He's trying to be firm, but there's a smile in his voice and a softness in his eyes.

"Next time, you'll have to be more clear."

He shakes his head, but I can tell he's happy to see us all getting along.

"Well, things are in order, so we should get out of your hair. Take your bowl to the sink and rinse it out, buddy."

"Aw, do we have to go?"

"Nicholas..."

"Okay, okay." Nick slides off his chair and heads to the sink.

"You've got a pretty cool kid there, Hopper."

"Thanks, Mr. West. I would have to agree with you."

Josh gives him a nod, and Max replies with a barely-there one of his own.

The moment gives me goosebumps.

The sounds of Nick rinsing out his bowl come to an end, and he joins his dad near the kitchen entrance.

"Thanks for that one scoop of ice cream, Miss Ford." He beams, and so do I.

We already have our own little inside joke or secret, or whatever it is. The point is we have it!

"You're very welcome. It was nice to meet you."

Josh chimes in next. "Yes, come by again and bring Molly. I haven't met her yet."

Nick beams a smile from ear to ear at the invite. "That would be awesome!"

"Well, we'll have to make sure it happens then."

"Thank you, sir." Max nods to Josh. "Miss Ford." He nods to me as well, and then he and Nick leave the room, taking my heart with them.

Josh and I stare at each other, silently acknowledging the weight of what just happened. I just met the son of the man I'm falling in love with. It's a pretty big deal.

I open my mouth to say something, not sure what, but Josh stops me.

"Go change and meet me in my room. Friends will have to wait. We've got some serious shit to talk about." He takes a bite of ice cream. "Like, how it's possible he's even hotter when he's being a dad. I mean, talk about a DILF?"

Chapter Twenty

"You still sure you want to do this?"

I'm helping him with his tie. The most beautiful man in the world can't go to a premiere looking disheveled, now can he? It's my job to make sure he doesn't. Even if it's not in the contract.

If you had asked me last night, I would have said that there was no way I was going. In fact, for a good hour or two, I was moving back to Eastlyn and ripping the contract into pieces.

When Josh finally showed me the text Max had deleted from my phone, I went through all the emotions that would go along with a picture of my grammy sitting in her favorite chair looking out the window in her room at the retirement home along with a cryptic message.

GO BACK HOME OR WE'LL PAY GRAMMY A VISIT.

LOUISE FORD

RIVERWALK RETIREMENT

PENDLETON OR

ROOM 52

When he handed me his phone, my entire body trembled with fear, and my first reaction was not one of fight but of flight. That was it. I was going home.

It wasn't until I realized I had posted that picture over two years ago on my social media account with a message that just said Grammy next to a little red heart that my fear turned into seething rage. Of course, it helped to know it wasn't a recent picture, and that they knew I called her Grammy because it was in the post. All it took was a quick Google search of her full name and sure enough her address was right there on Josh's phone. So it wasn't that serious of a threat, but still, knowing someone would stoop that low was not okay.

With security in place in Eastlyn, I decided to give this sicko a big F you and stay the course. There were moments all night when I thought I was making the wrong decision. That I should just go home to Eastlyn and pretend to be Josh's fiancée from afar, but in the end, I decided the assholes didn't get to win.

We called Max and filled him in about where the picture had come from, but he had already figured it out. He was way ahead of us and already had additional support headed to Oregon.

So, here I am, helping Josh get ready to go to a movie premiere.

"Josh, it will be fine. Besides, I'll have Max with me."

He smiles. "That's why you're in such a great mood! You get to spend time with Hopper." He proudly busts me. "No hanky-panky in the car, Emmy."

I tsk him, playfully smacking him on the shoulder. "Do you

really think after all the time I just spent getting my hair and makeup done that I would do anything to ruin it?"

One of his eyebrows lifts. "Uh, I have a feeling a few minutes in the back seat with a man like Hopper would be completely worth it."

He's right. Five minutes with Max would be worth it.

"Okay, you're right. Maybe on the way home."

"That's my girl."

We leave Josh's primary suite both decked out in Tom Ford because, you know, that's how we roll. He looks sexy in his black suit, and I'm a perfect match in my little black dress. It's classy yet sexy, and I love it. I'd love it even more if Max got to take it off me tonight when I get home. I haven't even walked out the door yet, and I'm already fantasizing about what will happen when the night is over.

Too bad Reeves will be coming back with Josh, and Smith is here for the night shift. It looks like I'll be the one slipping my little black dress off tonight.

Jace, Max, and Reeves wait for us in the foyer when we come down the stairs. Max is closest to the door, placing himself behind the other two men. When he catches my eye, his chest lifts on a big breath, and his head ever so slightly moves from side to side. His fist lifts to his chest to rest over his heart for a beat before dropping it and returning to his usual stoic posture.

It's a small gesture, but it's plenty to melt my heart.

Josh squeezes my hand, letting me know he saw Max's small show of affection. "Wow, Emmy. The man has got it bad," he whispers out of the corner of his mouth. Then, just before we reach the last step, he lets go of my hand as the team guides us silently out the door.

Tonight, two black SUVs are waiting out front. Josh and Jace follow Reeves to the car in front, and I follow Max to the one behind theirs. Sibby is already there with another client.

Smith and Cleveland also left early to make sure things were secure before we got there. Smith will head back to the house once we all arrive. This means Max and I will get some much-needed time together, even if I am in the back seat while he's in the front.

"Ma'am," he says, holding my door open for me.

I don't dare look at him when I pass him to get it. I'm not the actor in this dysfunctional family, and I'm afraid I'll give us away if someone is watching.

Once he's in the driver's seat and the door is closed, he wastes no time telling me what he tried to convey inside the house.

"Emmett, you look absolutely stunning," he says, pulling away from the house behind Reeves. "I swear, I thank God every time you walk in a room."

"Max," I say, not knowing how to reply to such a beautiful compliment.

"As beautiful as you look in that dress, I'd give anything to climb back there and take it off you. Because, God, I missed you last night."

"I missed you too."

His eyes meet mine in the rearview. "You staying for the after-party tonight?"

"I thought I might be a little too tired to stay. I may need to sneak out the back door just as soon as the movie is over."

"Is that so?"

Thinking back to Josh's comment in the house, I giggle to myself. "I'd rather have five minutes with you in the back seat of this car than to go to a stuffy Hollywood party."

"Well, you are the boss. So whatever you want, Miss Ford. I aim to please."

* * *

The crowd is on its feet, applauding the film that has left me in a puddle in my red velvet theater seat. Nikki, the star of the show, is sitting in the row in front of me with her face in her hands, doing her best to conceal her tears. But, not even she could have expected the performance we all witnessed here tonight. It was stunning. Gut-wrenching. She absolutely transformed herself into her character, and I forgot I was watching my friend up on the screen. I couldn't be happier for her.

After a few minutes, the crowd finally begins to disperse on their way to the after-party. Standing, I step in front of Josh and tap the star of the hour on the shoulder.

When she turns and sees it's me, she gasps. "I'm so glad you came. Thank you."

"Oh, Nikki. You were brilliant!"

She stomps her heeled feet in glee, opening her arms to me. We both lean for the other over her chair and hug.

"I don't think I embarrassed myself, so that's good."

"What are you talking about?" I pull back from her so I can see her face. "It was absolutely wonderful. I'm so proud of you."

"Nicolette, she's right," Josh says from behind me, pulling my back to his front with his arms around my chest, holding me like any loving fiancé would. "You're on your way, my friend."

Nikki's manager interrupts, letting her know people are waiting for her.

"Hey, I have to go. I'll see you at the after-party, right?"

"I'll see you there, but Emmy's gonna head home."

"What? You aren't coming?"

"I'll explain later, but I swear there's a good reason."

"There better be. Call me tomorrow and fill me in. Promise?" she says over her shoulder as she's ushered away by her people.

"Promise," I say, waving goodbye.

"Um, Em. I believe there's a brooding bodyguard waiting at

the end of the aisle for you." Then, taking me by the shoulders, he turns me in the direction of Max, who is just where Josh said he would be, hands clasped in front of him as per usual. "You should head out and get those five minutes."

"Executive protection associate."

He chuckles. "Well, I think he'll let you call him whatever the hell you want." He continues guiding me through the aisle to Max, who's now waiting with Reeves.

"Miss Ford, are you ready, or did you need to socialize before leaving?"

"Nope. She's ready, Hopper. Get her home safe."

"Thanks for speaking for me, Dad."

"Ma'am, did you want to stay?"

"No, I'm ready. I just prefer to speak for myself." I stick my tongue out at Josh.

"I'm just looking out for my girl. Reeves, you ready to party?"

"Sir." Reeves nods his readiness to party.

Josh steps around me, stopping to give me a kiss on the cheek, not to put on a show but with complete sincerity. "Love you, Emmy."

"Love you."

And I do.

I love Josh, but nothing like how I think I might love Max.

Josh and Reeves head down the theater stairs, leaving me with my executive protection associate.

"Ma'am."

He extends his arm, inviting me to walk ahead of him, and I do. Wanting to touch him yet resisting.

With his hand on the small of my back, he leads me to the side door where we entered when we got here. The car is waiting close by, and without a word, he opens the door for me to climb inside.

Once he takes his place in the front seat, the nerves take hold. Do I have the guts to ask him to pull over somewhere and climb in the back with me?

"Emmett, tonight might be our only time alone without the cameras in the house watching us. Would you mind a pit stop?"

He eases my mind before I have to find the words to ask for what I want.

"I would love a pit stop."

The rest of the drive is quiet. Neither of us speaking.

Eventually, we pull into the driveway of a beautiful home in a beautiful neighborhood. It's one of those houses in the hills that look like a simple brown one-story from the front, but you just know it drops down in the back. It's sleek and contemporary, yet something about it is rugged. If a house can look manly, this one does. It looks like Max.

Still, without a word, he parks in the garage and pushes the button on his rearview mirror to close the garage door, jumping out to make his way around the car to get my door.

"Ma'am."

"Max, do you live here?"

"This is home sweet home and the only place I know we can have complete privacy." he says. Then taking me by the hand, he pulls me in a rush through the garage. "We don't have long before the team is expecting me to check in to confirm you're home, so we'll make this quick, but there's someone who wants to meet you."

As soon as he says the words, I hear the tapping of excited paws on the other side of the door leading to the inside of the house. As the door opens, I can hear the sweet snorting of his beloved Frenchie, Molly. The minute I see her adorable squishy face, I make a note to demand she come to work with him every day.

"I know, sweet girl. I missed you too." He leans down and picks Molly up. "Calm down, girl. I want you to meet someone."

He holds the door open with his foot, and I scoot past him while petting his sweet pup on the head.

"Oh, Max, she's adorable!" I hold my hands out so she can give me a sniff and decide if we're gonna be friends. She's tan but has a silvery charcoal color that covers parts of her face and all the way down the top of her back. "I've never seen her coloring before; she's beautiful."

"She's a blue fawn, and yes, she is beautiful, and she knows it. I've done my best not to let it go to her head, but this is Holly-wood. You know how starlets can be." He puts her down and brushes the dog hair off the front of his suit. "I'm gonna let her out real quick. Be right back." He starts to walk away, then stops midstep. "I know I said it earlier, but you look fucking beautiful tonight, Emmett."

He turns on his heel and is back out the door to the garage with Molly before I can thank him, but not before my cheeks redden from his compliment.

Shaking off what his words do to me, I take advantage of being alone in the house and look around his space. Stepping into the ample open space of his living room, I can't believe how much this home feels like its owner.

The room is large with dark gray granite floors. The far wall is nothing but floor-to-ceiling windows overlooking the city. In contrast, the rest of the walls are a kind of textured gray wood paneling that doesn't look like old 70s type of wood paneling but instead is chic. Very expensive looking. It's such a nice contrast to Josh's all-white home.

A floor-to-ceiling stone fireplace takes up a corner of the room. There's a giant TV hanging on the wall directly across from an oversized leather couch—large enough for a man the size of Max—with large cream throw pillows in each corner and a matching blanket thrown over the back. On either side of the TV are blown-up black and white photographs. One of Phillipsburg and one of Hollywood. Below the TV is what looks like a TV stand, but since the TV is on the wall, Max has it filled with pictures of Nick, Molly, and the rest of his family.

It warms my heart to see them here. But it hurts my heart to think he's stayed away from his family for so long. Especially, when they clearly mean so much to him.

I hear the tapping of paws and the snorting of the other woman in Max's life headed toward me before I hear the door close.

"Sorry about that. Can I get you something to drink? Wine? Water? Whatever you want?" he says from across the room, from too far away.

All I want is him.

"A glass of wine would be nice if we have time for that?"

"We have time. I told Smith we were stopping for you to spend some time with a friend."

"Is that so?"

"It is. I know it's only been a couple of days, but I missed you. Hope you don't mind."

"I couldn't be happier."

"Good. Stay there. I'll be right back."

I know I've spent many nights sleeping in his arms, and his lips have left their imprint on mine. Still, as I stand here in his home watching his beloved pup follow him over to the kitchen on the other side of the open space of what seems to be the main floor of the house, it feels like I'm in a dream.

Max Hopper missed me.

He wants to be alone with me.

He's surrounded by beautiful, wealthy women all the time, yet he wants to be with mea A small-town girl from Oregon whose fake fiancé happens to be a Hollywood A-lister. I have a crazy stalker and a job planning people's trips around the world, but I've never been abroad. Max has been everywhere and lived more in his lifetime than I could dream of, and he still chooses me.

He not only chooses me, but he sees me.

He really sees me, and he still wants me.

"That picture was taken when he was four. Taking my little boy to Disneyland for the first time was one of the best days of my life."

I didn't realize I was staring at a picture of Max and Nick both adorning Mickey Mouse ears and smiling sweet smiles in front of the castle at Disneyland. It's a selfie, but it's perfect.

"You're a great dad, aren't you?" I bring the glass of red wine he hands me to my lips and take a sip. It's good and tastes like my new favorite bottle I've been hoarding from World Market every chance I get. I may be engaged to Josh, but I still buy my wine on sale or with discount coupons at World Market.

You can take the girl out of Eastlyn...

"I don't know about that, but I do my best, and I love him more than I thought it was possible to love another person. He's a great kid, and no matter what happens, I'll always know I did something good in this world as long as he's in it."

"He loves you too, you know. We had a pretty deep conversation over ice cream the other night."

"You mean over the two scoops of ice cream you gave him instead of the one I told you he could have?"

He pushes a button on a small wall console, and blinds cover the windows on their own.

"It was one scoop. I swear."

"It was two scoops rolled into one giant scoop."

"It was still one scoop."

Taking my hand in his, he pulls me across the room to the couch. He picks up one of the cream pillows and tosses it on the loveseat a few feet away. Sitting in the corner spot, he pulls me down with him. Naturally, I snuggle into place, kicking off my heels and pulling my legs under me. He reaches around me and pulls the blanket from the back of the couch over us. Molly hops into her dog bed in front of the fireplace and spins in circles for a few seconds before settling.

"Nick really liked you."

Oh, how my heart swells to hear his little boy liked me.

"Really?"

"He said he felt like he was eating ice cream with a princess."

"What?" I ask, confused.

"It was your dress. I mean, that dress you wore to the gala was something else. You looked more like a queen to me, but princess works too."

"It's amazing what some fancy clothes and a hair and makeup team can do."

"I like you better without all that, but I'll take you any way I can get you."

"Max—"

"I'm glad he liked you," he interrupts me but doesn't elaborate.

"I really like him too."

He squeezes me a little tighter into his side. I take a sip of my wine and then lean forward to put it on the table in front of us, but he takes it from me and sets it on the side table next to him.

He places a kiss on my head. "I could get used to this," he says, sounding uncharacteristically defeated

I should be overcome with joy to hear him say this, yet I can not only hear the underlying frustration that this can't be our new normal, but I also feel the same.

And it hurts.

My chin begins to tremble, but before I let my emotions get the best of me, I take control and change the mood.

Twisting out from under his arm, I sit up and maneuver myself onto his lap. I take his glass from him, and when I rise up to set it next to mine, I purposely make sure my chest is mere centimeters from his face. This is all it takes. And much to my pleasure, his big hands glide up my thighs under my dress to my ass.

"Whatcha doin', Emmett?"

Wine glass in place, I sit back down on his lap and take his handsome face in my hands. His eyes close in contentment for the briefest of moments, and when they open, the golds and greens of his hazel eyes shine back at me with want. Or maybe it's need?

"I'm taking advantage of the moment."

His hands move over my backside and land on my hips with a firm grip.

"And what is it you'd like to do?"

"Well, if I had my way, we'd make out here on the couch like a couple of school kids, and then you'd carry me to your bedroom and make love to me all night long. Then I'd fall asleep in your arms, and you'd wake me in the morning when you crawled on top of me to do it all again. But since I can't stay the night, the make out on the couch, and then the trip to your bedroom will have to do."

Before I've gotten my last word out, one of his hands is back on my ass, and the other is out from under my dress and tangled in my hair as he sits up. His mouth colliding with mine. Within seconds, I'm moaning, he's growling, and our hands are all over each other. I've desperately untucked his pressed shirt and am trying to undo the buttons while he rips my lace panties from my body in one hard tug.

He rolls me onto my back, and my legs wrap around his

waist, but before he continues, he surprises me by pulling back just before our lips are about to come back together. His eyes search mine for something, but what, I'm not sure?

"I didn't bring you here tonight for this." I try to speak, but as he usually does, he keeps speaking without giving me the opportunity. "I just wanted you here with me. I needed time alone where I could hold you in my arms and call you mine."

His words hold so much love and respect and make me want him all that much more.

"I am yours."

"You sure the hell are." His voice is gruff. "I just wish the rest of the world knew that."

I hate that our situation is hurting him. He's the last person on earth I want to make feel anything more than joy. I, too, want the world to know that he's mine, but it's out of my hands. All it took was one signature, and our fate was sealed.

"Max, please kiss me." My hands wrap around his neck, urging him forward so I can feel his beautiful lips on mine. "Claim me."

"Emmett, I'm not sure I can hold back tonight. Are you sure?"

"I've been sure for weeks, Max. Please, don't make me wait any longer."

Much to my surprise, he stands up with me still wrapped around him. "Sorry, but we're gonna have to cut the make-out session on the couch short. I need you in my bed."

As we start walking out of the room, I vaguely hear the sound of Molly following behind us, but all I see is Max. All I feel is the scorching of my skin every time it connects with his.

Since he decimated my panties, his hands under my dress are now on my bare backside, and I'm trailing kisses up his neck. When I reach his ear, there's no feigning my heated breath when I beg him to take me.

In a flash, my back is pressed against the wall. The weight of his body holds me in place as his hands stroke up and down my thighs and find their way back to my ass. Finally, he pulls back just enough for one hand to caress my hot, wet center, and my body trembles from his touch.

After a few short strokes, he removes his fingers and sucks them clean. I nearly orgasm from the visual.

"Emmett, do you know how it makes me feel to know I did this to you? That the woman I dream about every night could be even remotely as hot for me as I am for her?"

My answer is to attack his mouth with mine while I circle my hips against him, letting him know I'm more than hot for him. I'm ready.

"Bedroom," he says against my lips and continues our journey down the hall.

He's only taken a few steps when I feel his pants vibrating. "Is that a phone in your pocket, or are you just happy to see me?"

"Shit." He walks us into a dark room and sets me on a bed.

He pulls the phone from his pocket, his face aglow from the bright screen, and his brow furrows.

"Sorry," he says with a look that says I wouldn't take this if I didn't have to.

"Of course," I say, as though I'm not bothered, but inside, hating to lose the heat of his body against mine.

"Hey, buddy. What's up?"

He sits down next to me, and I hear Nick on the other end.

"Dad, it's happening. I knew it would, but it's really happening now."

"Slow down, Son. What's happening?"

"Randall is gonna ask Mom to marry him. He just asked my permission."

"I thought you liked Randall?"

"Well, I do, but I don't want to live with him."

"Buddy, he's a good guy. He treats you and Mom well, right?"

"Yes, but..."

"What is it?"

"I have a dad. I don't want another dad," Nick confesses with a whimper.

Max reaches for my hand, and we sit in the dark, listening to his whole heart on the other end of the phone. He's confused and scared and doesn't want his dad to think he would ever betray him.

My heart breaks for both of them.

"Nick, Randall won't be your dad, but he can still be an important person in your life. And, buddy, I'm not going anywhere."

"Is court still next week?"

"It is, but I don't want you to worry about that. That's something your mom and I will take care of. So you don't need to lose any sleep over it."

He's such a good dad.

"Dad, if it's okay with Mom, can you come get me? I kinda just wanna sleep at your place tonight."

"Bud, I'm working tonight, and it's already nine o'clock."

"Does that mean you're with Emmett at Josh West's house?"

Holding my breath, I wonder how Max will answer.

"It does."

"Cool, she's awesome! I don't mind hanging out with her again."

The smile on my face is almost painful, and I bounce in my spot on the bed with the knowledge that Nick finds me awesome!

"Hang on, Bud."

He puts the phone down and looks at me, but I whisper my order before he can say a word.

"You're taking me home right now, and you're going to go get your boy. He needs you."

"Thank you for understanding."

"There's nothing to understand. Now, I'm going to go find what's left of my panties, and I'll be ready to go," I whisper before kissing him on the cheek.

Leaving him to talk in private, I make my way down the stark hall that needs a woman's touch. The front room is manly yet, homey and full of things he loves. It's perfect. I have no idea what the bedroom looks like, but he needs some life on the walls in the hallway. Of course, the blank space gave him the room to seduce me mere moments ago, so maybe the bare walls should stay.

When he joins me in the living room, my shoes are on, but I'm digging through the couch cushions in search of my underwear.

"Looking for these?"

Max is headed in my direction with my destroyed lace dangling from his finger. He's lost his hot and bothered look, but his eyes still smolder.

"As a matter of fact, I was."

"Well, I'll buy you a new pair because these are mine." He shoves them in his pants pocket. "I'm really sorry the night is ending this way."

"Don't be sorry. Nick needs you, and it's kind of hot seeing you as a dad." I meet him in the middle of the room taking his hand in mine. As we walk to the door leading to the garage with Molly hot on our heels. "Did Lauryn say it was okay for him to come stay with you?"

"She did. I think she's so wrapped up with Randall that she will take all the time alone with him that she can. Nick's been at my place more and more lately. And I love it, but I need it to be permanent and not just because Lauryn needs a babysitter. I want it in writing. Signed by a judge."

Once we're in the garage, he opens my door for me but takes me tightly in his arms, kissing me long and hard.

"When I finally do make love to you, it's gonna be a beautiful thing. But, until then, I'll have to hold on to tonight's taste of you to get me through."

Chapter Twenty-One

"Earth to Emmy." Amelia waves her hand in front of my face.

"Sorry. What was that?"

We're at Tell Me About It getting our holiday manicures before our hands are on display at the annual Eastlyn Holiday Festival Dance tomorrow night. My parents talked Amelia and me into working at the raffle table. Seeing how much people will spend on raffle tickets to win prize packages from local businesses and amateur bakers always amazes me. It's one of the biggest fundraisers for the Eastlyn 4H Club every year. So we decided if we were stuck at the table most of the night, then we, at the very least, deserved to treat ourselves to manicures.

"Where were you?"

"Right here, I heard you."

"Oh, really? Then who did Cara just say got engaged last night?"

Shit.

When I don't reply, Cara giggles and Amelia gives me a look that says I know who you were daydreaming about. She can't disguise the pity in her eyes, and I hate it.

"Okay, I lied. I was off in my head somewhere. So who's getting married?"

"Well, it feels like everyone these days with Miles and Mason and you and Josh. Now we can add Scheanna and Adam to that list. He proposed last night, and of course, she said yes," Cara chirps.

The pity in Amelia's eyes intensifies with the mention of my engagement to Josh.

"Aw, that's great news. I'm happy for them," I say sincerely.

I'm actually jealous, truth be told.

I see Max every weekday and some weekends, but I can't even touch him. Every night when he and Molly leave, I fall into such a deep well of self-pity. Wishing I could have kissed him goodbye or, even better, that I could have left with him. What I wouldn't give to go home with them every night. Josh's place is great, fabulous even, but I'd rather live in a tent with Max than have to stay away from him in Josh's mansion. It's shocking how attached I became so quickly. I guess when you meet the right person, this is how it's supposed to feel.

Yes, we have our moments in the security room during the day when we're alone, but it's not nearly enough. Smith is a nice guy, but every night when he arrives and signals it's time for Max and Molly to leave, I have an unwarranted desire to throat punch him. With Josh gone these past couple of weeks, I spend most of my time sulking in my bedroom once they leave.

"Speaking of weddings, do you and Josh have a date picked out yet?" Cara asks.

"Nope, he's been way too busy to even think about it."

"So, what had you off in a faraway land then, if not planning the wedding of the decade?"

"Oh, um...I was thinking about getting a puppy. My security guy brings his French Bulldog to the house on the days I don't have anything planned, and it's so nice having a dog around. With Josh gone so much, I think I might get a dog."

Amelia saves me and changes the subject from my wedding, that will never happen, to the litter of puppies her neighbor just had. She's the best kind of friend.

It's not a lie. I was thinking about Max and how sweet he is with Molly when I wasn't thinking about being pressed against his wall while he sucked his fingers dry. There are constant flashes of sweet and sexy flickering through my head day and night.

His adorable pup spends her days going back and forth between the two of us. I have a bed in my office for her now, and I got one for Max to have near his perch in the kitchen. She spends time with him, then she'll visit me in my office, and then she goes back to her daddy. She does this all day long, and I love it. However, I do have to kick her out when I have meetings. Her snoring is so loud that one of my employees commented on it one day during a conference call. Since then, I have taken her out to her daddy when I have calls. Every time I drop her off, he picks her up, sets her on his lap like a toddler, and gives her a belly rub.

She's spoiled rotten, and it's adorable.

My moments of watching him with Molly are just one of the many I keep bottled up and take sips of when I'm missing him. Like I am today.

* * *

When Miles and his dad built Eastlyn Brewing Company, they not only built the brewery but also created a place where everyone in town could celebrate all the events of their lives in one place. There is a restaurant, a bar, meeting and event rooms, and the banquet hall we're using tonight for the final event of the season. The Eastlyn Holiday Festival Dance.

As it's more commonly referred to, *The Dance* takes place every year on Christmas Eve. When you're from a small community, the people of your town are like family, and you share family events, like Christmas Eve. Sure, some are that drunk uncle you hope you don't get seated next to at dinner, but he's still family, and you love him. Some are the sweet grandmothers constantly squeezing your cheeks and telling you to eat more. And there are always the little cousins running around screaming. All of those family members— blood members or not—come to *The Dance* every year. It doesn't go too late, so kids are home in time to get tucked in, and parents can put together those big gifts from Santa without staying up all night.

Nights like tonight couldn't be more small town, and I love every second of it.

I've always loved knowing I had Eastlyn to come home to, but now I wonder how that will work out with Max and Nick back in Los Angeles. Not sure why I'm even thinking about that when there is still so much time on my contract. Who knows if Max will really wait that long? So tonight, I need to push that aside and remind myself how excited I am to be home for Christmas and the big dance.

Growing up, the Dance took place at the rotary club, and I couldn't wait to get dressed up for it every year. Now that it takes place at EBC, it may be a little more modern, have a bit more space and a staff of people assisting, but it still has that hometown feel. There's still a big table full of home-baked desserts, and all the raffle prizes are from business people in the community and put together in fancy baskets. Miles insists that it is still decorated like it always had been with homemade, simple decorations.

Nobody loves this town as much as Miles Montgomery, and

it's never more evident than on nights like tonight. He takes such pride in being able to provide for his community while keeping things as close to how they've always been as he can. You could almost call him the unofficial mayor of Eastlyn, but don't say that around Mayor Sheeran. She takes her job very seriously, and you can see her bristle when Eastlyners go to Miles for help instead of her. She loves Miles and what his family has brought to the community, everyone does, but I think she's waiting for the day that the townsfolk ask her to step down so he can take her job.

It's a shame Josh isn't here for the dance, but he does change the atmosphere when he is in the room. No matter how everyone here at home likes to pretend having a famous world-renown star from Eastlyn isn't a big deal, they still can't help but get excited when he comes home. It's sweet but also a little sad. Eastlyn is the one place he should be able to be himself, but you can always see the star-struck emotion lying just under the surface when people outside of The Crew and his parents talk to him.

Josh left to resume shooting a couple of weeks ago, and he was supposed to be home today. I told him to meet me here, but he hasn't shown up yet. I'm just about to text him when Margie Brown, the widow of our beloved barber, Mel Brown, approaches the table. I haven't seen her since she lost the love of her life just two short months ago, and I rise to meet her in front of the table.

"Oh, Margie. I'm so sorry for your loss. We all loved Mel so much."

She squeezes me tight. "Thanks, darlin'."

It's her first Christmas without him, and I can't imagine how hard it must be on her. just as I release her from our hug, her kids walk through the door, and I'm glad to see her support system is here. She may have the entire town behind her, but it's nice her immediate family is here tonight, too, since they haven't stayed in Eastlyn. I would hate to think of her alone this time of year.

Pulling back from our hug, I stand with my arm around her shoulders while Amelia lightens the mood. "The shop's raffle prize is pretty great this year. You guys went all out."

"It was fun to put together. Not sure Mel would have approved of throwing in the six free cuts, but I thought it was a nice addition."

"You're right. He wouldn't have approved of the free cuts"—Amelia laughs—"but I know the lucky winner will."

"How's the shop doing, Margie? Everything okay? Do you need anything?" I ask, trying not to change the conversation back to Mel but wanting to make sure she's doing well.

"You're sweet, but things are going fine. Miles made sure of it. That friend of yours sure does have a big heart."

"That he does," I agree.

"It's nice to see he's found someone he can share it with. You too, honey. I'm real happy for the both of you."

My stomach instantly sours, a cold sweat coating my skin with her kind words. The anguish I feel at moments like this is more than I could have ever imagined when I suggested the ridiculous fake engagement idea to Josh. I've turned myself into a fraud. A liar. I'm disgusted with myself as I perpetuate the sham that is my fake engagement.

"Thanks, Margie. Josh and I couldn't be happier for Miles and Mason too. They're great together."

"Hey, Mom, how many tickets do we want this year?" Margie's son, Mark, asks with his wallet open, waiting to pay Amelia for his raffle tickets. "Hey, Emmett, good to see you."

Mark and I hug, and then I round the table, getting back to my duties.

"Emmy, dear, I'll have twenty dollars in tickets, please." She turns her attention to her oldest. "But, Mark, I'm not sharing. You'll have to get your own."

"That's fine, Mom. But you just remember you said that when I come up with a winning ticket, and you want to share my prize with me," he says paying Amelia for his tickets.

Margie hands me a twenty, and I tear off her red raffle tickets placing their matches in the spinning metal basket usually used for the rotary club's BINGO balls. "Good luck, and have fun tonight!"

"Thanks, honey, and send that fiancé of yours my way to say hi before he jet sets out of town again."

"I sure will."

As if on cue, my phone pings with a text from Josh.

JOSH

> Hey. I made it home, but I think I'm just gonna lay low at your place. I don't really feel like being at The Dance tonight.

EMMETT

> Everything okay?

JOSH

> I'm fine. Just not in the mood.

EMMETT

> Okay, well, I'll do my best to get out of here at a decent hour. Love you.

JOSH

> Love you too. Give my best to everyone and have fun. No need to rush home. See you when you get here.

I guess I'm not the only one who notices the change in people when Josh arrives. But, I can't help but think there's more to it than just not wanting a night full of attention. I hope he's okay.

"Emmett, do you mind if I steal my sister for a second?"

"Of course not. Things have been pretty slow since most everyone is here already. I have it covered, Melly, so go enjoy the rest of the night."

"Thanks, but I'll bring her back. We just need to take our annual picture with Santa Montgomery before we forget."

"Thanks for the reminder; we need to get one with The Crew too. Melly, we can't forget."

"I'll rally the troops, and we'll come grab you shortly."

Miles' dad, Mitch, has been playing Santa for the past twenty or so years, and we always get a group picture with him. Parker and Audrey are home for the holiday, but Reece and Rachel are still in Africa for another month. And with Josh staying in tonight, we'll be short three Crew members this year.

I finish my time at the ticket table, take a few spins around the dance floor, then pose with Santa. And as I'm sipping my punch and hanging with the girls I can't help but feel like something or someone is missing.

What I wouldn't give to show all of this to Max and Nick. I haven't spent much time with Nick, but I know they're a package deal, and I love that.

When Max won his custody battle a couple of weeks ago, I had never seen him so happy. He had already been getting Nick more than usual, but now it was official. He'll have Nick full-time for one week, and then he'll be with his mom for a week. It seems crazy to me, but Nick is apparently thrilled. He's the one who said he wanted to do the weekly schedule so everyone is happy. Oh, how I wanted to celebrate with him, but alas, it wasn't a possibility.

They still have to work out the holiday schedule, but this year, Max has Christmas Eve, and Lauryn has Christmas Day. Which is why I'm here with Cleveland hovering in the corner instead of Max. But he's exactly where he should be, with his boy.

"Well, that's just about a wrap on this year's dance. What's going on for the rest of the night?" Parker addresses the group.

"No plans, man. What did you have in mind?" Miles replies with his arms around Mason's waist and her back pressed to his front.

"I have an idea," I chime in.

"Do tell," Miles says with a lifted brow.

"Well, Josh flew home but didn't feel up to a crowd and is just sitting alone at my place waiting for me. What do you say we surprise him and go hang out? I have all the fixins for hot toddies."

"Perfect!" Amelia and Audrey answer in unison.

"Don't text him, Emmy," Parker says excitedly. "Let's surprise him. Everyone get your shit together and meet in the parking lot in five."

"Sounds good, Parker. Meet you out front," Miles proclaims.

We all scatter to gather our coats and say our goodbyes to the few people still here. Miles already let his staff go, and with all the food put away, the rest of the cleanup can wait.

It may not be everyone's typical Christmas Eve, but The Crew together is ours. We don't care where we are or what we do as long as we're together.

Chapter Twenty-Two

"Emmy. Wake up."

I'm in that place between being awake and asleep, and I'm not sure if Josh's voice is a dream or if he's really in my bedroom. But it's way too early to find out. So I roll over and shove a pillow over my head to drown out the sound in case he really is trying to wake me up at such an ungodly hour after the late night we had last night.

"Emmy, come on. Wake up. Santa came." This time, I feel the bed dip and the pillow ripped off the top of my head

Guess it's not a dream.

Bummer.

"Why are you up so early? And why did I ever give you a key to my house?"

"Em, it's almost nine."

"You've got to be kidding me? It feels more like five. Remind me never to drink hot toddies again."

"Well, I'll promise not to let you drink three of them when Parker is bartending. How does that sound?"

"Deal. But I don't have to be at my mom's until later this

afternoon. Why are you making me get up? You can wait for your present."

"I can, but you can't. You need to get up, Em. Santa brought you a present."

"Josh, I'm thirty-one, Santa doesn't bring me presents anymore."

"Well, he did this year. Get up, brush your teeth, and meet me in the living room. And an Altoid doesn't count. Brush your fangs, lady." He smacks me on my butt and disappears, closing the door behind him.

I'd be lying if the thought of something fun waiting for me under the tree didn't light a little fire in me and have me popping out of bed. However, popping out of bed was a bad idea. The room tilts ever so slightly, and my head begins to throb before taking my first steps, but I push through. I throw a long sweater over my red tank and gray pajama bottoms covered in little Santa hats.

When I pull open my bedroom door, Josh is standing in the hallway with his hands on his hips, blocking my view into the living room.

"Go brush that nasty dragon breath."

"Merry Christmas to you too, Josh."

Following his instructions, I shuffle my slippered feet into the bathroom and freshen up, but when I open the door, he's no longer in the hallway, so this must mean I have the all-clear to venture to the living room.

"Okay, Santa West. What have you done that couldn't wait..."

My heart skips a beat, and my headache all but disappears when I see the most beautiful man and the prettiest girl in the world standing next to my tree.

"What are you doing here? What about Nick?" I'm frozen to the spot for a few beats, and just when I take my first step in their direction, Molly comes running my way, her butt wiggling with excitement.

I reach down and pet her real quick. "Molly, girl, it's great to see you, but I need to kiss your daddy!"

Walking around the grunting Frenchie, I rush to Max and jump in his arms, my legs going around his waist. His massive arms wrap around my back, and I kiss him like a woman starved.

"Merry Christmas, Firefly," he whispers against my lips.

"Merry Christmas, my handsome lumberjack," I whisper back.

"Okay, okay. You two aren't alone. Let's take it easy with the face sucking."

Max pulls back. "He did let me borrow the plane to get here, so..."

I unwrap myself from Max and make my way over to my best friend, hugging him tightly. Stepping back, I look into the eyes of someone who has always been there for me. Who loves me as much as I love him. I can see him warring with himself, between setting me free and saving his career. It's a decision I don't want him to make. I got myself into this, and I have to deal with the consequences.

Josh is worth it.

So is Max.

I have to find a way to make things work with both of them.

"You knew he was coming?"

"I did."

"You planned this with him and let him borrow the jet to get here?"

"Ho, ho, ho."

"You made one of the pilots work on Christmas morning?"

"Captain Lerman is Jewish. He was more than happy to. Besides, he has another flight in a few hours. It's all good.

"I love you, Joshy."

"Love you right back, Emmy." His gaze glances over my shoulder, and he gives a tiny nod to Max. "You've gotten my gift, and now I have to go spend the day with my parents before I fly out tomorrow to meet Jace back in Los Angeles." He embraces me in another big hug and then takes me by the shoulders and turns me around to face the man who has lit up my world with his mere presence. "Besides, I think Max has something for you."

"There's more?"

"There is," my best friend whispers in my ear. "I love you, Emmy. Have the best New Year ever."

What in the world is he talking about? I hate New Year's Eve, and he knows it. Still, he kisses my cheek and pushes me toward Max, who gives Josh a nod. A couple of seconds later, I hear the door shut behind him when he leaves.

"Are we really alone?"

"Well, there's Molly, but yes, we're alone."

He meets me in the middle of the room, and standing face-to-face, we interlace our fingers and smile at one another.

"You know, that first night I met you, I would never have imagined you even knew how to smile, let alone have a smile that would light me up from the inside out. And now, here you are, standing in my living room, on Christmas morning, and I feel like the luckiest woman alive. *You* are the best Christmas present I've ever gotten."

"Baby, you have no idea how happy you make me. I never thought there was anything outside of Nick that could make me feel this full. This happy."

I can't get past the lump in my throat to respond to his lovely words.

With the lights from the tree twinkling in his eyes, he leans down and kisses me ever so softly, then speaks against my lips. "You know I'm head over heels mad about you, right?"

"Right back at ya," I breathe into his mouth. "Now kiss me. I've missed you so much."

He pulls me against him with one hand on my lower back while he caresses my face with the other. Kissing me slow and lazy while keeping his gaze locked on mine. Each movement is deliberate.

Meaningful.

Life-changing.

Every bite of my lip and flick from his tongue fills me with lust and passion, but what I have found in him is so much more than this. He is my missing piece. I feel it in my bones. I haven't told him so, but I am in love with this man.

He releases my bun from the top of my head, and his hands tangle in my hair. I'm practically climbing him when Molly lays down on our feet, making her presence known. We come up for air, both of us smiling, but I'm still pressed tight against him with my cheek on his chest and his heart beating the same cadence as mine.

"What's this I hear about you and a hangover?"

"I think I found the magic cure."

He gives me a squeeze.

"Wild night last night?" he asks into my hair.

"It didn't start that way. I worked the raffle table all night at the Dance, but then everyone came over here, and hot toddies happened."

"Oh, I love a hot toddy when it's cold out."

"I used to. I think I've had enough to get me through the winter. But like I said, I feel better now."

"Well, let's see if I can make you feel even better."

"I like the sound of that. I've been waiting forever to have you in my bed."

"Well, that's not exactly what I was talking about."

"Oh. Well, don't I feel silly."

More like dejected but no need for dramatics.

"Don't you worry, you're going to get that too. Soon."

"How soon?"

"Shush, woman, and go sit down on the couch."

"What in the world are you up to?"

I grab Molly, and she and I wait for Max on the couch while he grabs a beautifully wrapped box from under the tree. The paper is white, adorned with large red snowflakes and a matching red bow. He doesn't say anything when he hands the box to me, and when all I do is stare up at him, he gives a slight lift of his chin, telling me to go ahead and open it.

Under the beautifully tied ribbon on top of the box is an envelope. My fingers are shaking as I pull out a note that says...

Firefly,

It's time someone planned a trip for you.

I hope to see the world with you, and I think this will be the perfect way to get started.

Yours,

Max

My heart is beating out of my chest in anticipation as I pull on the ribbon and let it fall from my lap, only to have Molly grab hold and try to take off with it. Her daddy takes it from her and then sits next to us with his body turned to face me while I tear open the perfectly wrapped gift.

His arm is stretched out on the back of the couch, and he's playing with my hair as I remove the lid.

"What in the world?"

It's a black beret.

"Here, let's see how it looks," he says. Then, taking the hat out of the box, he adjusts it on my head so it fits to his liking.

"Thank you. I've never owned a beret before. I feel so Fr...."

Stopping mid-sentence, my mouth falls open because it can't be true.

Can it?

"You feel so what?"

"No way, Max."

"No, you don't want to spend New Year's Eve in Paris with me? Here I thought maybe you could take some of your own pictures to use as your new screensaver."

My gasp is so loud Molly stops chewing on the corner of the box and gives me side-eye that asks what in the world is wrong with you, woman?

The tears filling my eyes blur my vision. "Max, is this real?"

"If you agree to go with me, it will be. I sure hope those are happy tears?"

"The happiest!"

I leap up from the couch and jump up and down like an idiot. Molly barks at me, sharing my excitement, even if she has no idea why.

"So, that's a yes?"

"Yes! A million times, yes!" Then my gift to him, that is nowhere near a trip to France, flashes through my head, and it hits me how big this gift is. Too big.

"What? What's wrong? Why do you look like you're about to change your mind?"

"Max, this is too much. I can't accept this."

"I would give you the moon if I could. You will accept it."

"Max, last-minute plane tickets to Paris this time of year have to cost a fortune!"

The corner of his mouth lifts. "We've got our own plane."

"Josh?"

"When I told him my plan, he insisted."

"But..."

"I know, I know. We'll fly commercial and make sure we work on our carbon footprint from here on out."

And just like that, I tumble a little further in love with this amazing man who already knows me so well.

"What about Nick?"

"Well, he's off on vacation in Hawaii with his mom and Randall for the next week and a half, so the timing is perfect."

"What about Molly?"

"Josh is gonna take her back with him tomorrow morning when he flies out. And then Greta will take her."

"Wow, you really thought of everything."

"Oh, I have." He lifts an eyebrow.

"When are we going?"

"Twelve hours. Give or take."

"I'm sorry, did you say twelve hours?"

"That I did."

"It's Christmas."

"It is."

"But..."

"No buts. Josh already told me that your family eats early, so I figure if you get ready now and start packing, we should still have time to get you to see Grammy before heading to your parents. Then we'll drop Molly off with Josh and head out."

"Whoa..."

"Impressed?"

"Turned on."

He laughs. "Go get in the shower, baby."

"Wanna join me?"

"You better believe I do, but we're twenty-four hours away from me having you alone in a plush five-star room with a view of the Eiffel Tower from our bed."

"Sounds incredibly romantic for a lumberjack."

He stands from the couch. "You have no idea what you're in for. This lumberjack is about to woo the hell out of you, but he's also not going to make love to you for the first time in the shower when Paris is waiting for us."

He's right. I know he's right. But we're alone, and I can't help but want him. I mean, I'm only human. But my libido goes cold when I think about being in Paris and not being able to hold his hand and kiss him and act like a couple.

"What if we're seen?"

"Well, not having Josh there will certainly help. Besides, it's Paris; nobody is looking around for celebrities nor do they care that much. They also have much stricter laws since the death of Princess Diana. It's winter, so we'll cover you up in big coats and scarfs, and we'll make sure you have lots of hats. We'll be discreet, but if you think I'm taking you to Paris and I'm not going to hold your hand as we walk along the Seine, then you are seriously mistaken."

Chapter Twenty-Three

"Bonjour? Vérifiez-vous, monsieur?"

"Yes, we have reservations under Slim Shady."

I chuckle to myself as I hear Max checking us in behind me, but I'm so mesmerized by the beauty of the Shangri-La Hotel the hilarity of the pseudonym he's used for our reservations barely registers.

Corporate travel and booking trips for the bigwigs at my company is what I do for a living, yet here I am, all wide-eyed and mouth agape as I take in the opulence surrounding us. I know how much a hotel of this caliber costs, and I cannot believe this is where we're staying.

I've stayed in beautiful hotels with Josh in the States and a couple of times in Mexico, but this isn't a beach vacation. On the contrary, this is the vacation I've always dreamed of. But this is even more than I could have imagined. The Shangri-La is grand, luxe, and home for the next week. And the fact that a place this beautiful is smack dab in the heart of Paris intensifies my excitement.

I'm in Paris.

The City of Love.

With Max.

I'm so lost in my head that I jump when he whispers in my ear. "C'mon, Firefly."

He takes my hand in his, claiming me publicly, and there is no longer anything more beautiful than the feeling of being his. Because I am, heart and soul. I know this already, and our relationship has only just begun.

We're on the elevator with the bellhop who has all of our luggage on a rack. The ride to our room is so quiet that when Max brings our interlaced hands up to his mouth and kisses the back of my hand, all I can hear is my thunderous heart beating to the new rhythm it seems to beat to when Max's lips touch me. No matter how sweet the act, it still sets me on fire.

The bellhop opens the door to our room and steps aside so we can enter. Once we're all inside, he steps around us and opens the French doors that lead to a terrace. I'd say I was tired from the overnight flight we were just on, and this is why my eyes well up when I see our view, but that's a lie. I slept soundly in Max's arms for at least seven hours of the flight.

No, it's the perfection of it all that has me tearing up. There are floor-to-ceiling windows on one entire side of the room with a view of the city, in particular the Eiffel Tower. I'm standing next to the bed, and it's right there.

I hear Max thank the gentleman for helping us to our room, followed by the door clicking shut. Within moments, his body is pressed against mine from behind as his arms wrap around my waist.

"You've been quiet since we got here. What's going on in that beautiful head of yours?"

"Max, it's just...I don't even know what to say. It's beautiful."

"So, you like it?"

I turn in his arms so I can see a view even more stunning

than the one from our terrace. Golden eyes, scruff littered with flecks of silver, and every rugged scar on his face takes my breath away. My fingers instinctually reach to touch the scar above his eyebrow and then trace his jawline until I reach his mouth. My thumb gently pulls on his bottom lip.

"It's perfect, Max. You're perfect."

When I lift up on my toes to kiss him, he bends to meet me. Kissing me softly, he searches my soul with his gaze, telling me so much more than words ever could.

His large hands hold my face as though I'm a fragile piece of china. His thumbs are caressing my cheeks when he pulls his lips away, pressing his forehead to mine.

"Emmett Ford, I am so fucking in love with you it hurts."

"Max..."

"Shh...just let me love you, Emmett. I don't want to wait another minute."

"Yes," I say.

He steps away and pulls the covers back on the bed, then kicks his shoes off, stepping to where I'm frozen to the spot, unable to comprehend that he's finally going to take me. I've been dreaming about it for three months now, and the moment is not only here, but the Eiffel Tower will have a full view.

He pulls on the end of the cream scarf Josh gave me for Christmas, and the feel of it sliding across my neck ever so slowly sets the tone for what's to come. He drops it to the floor before slipping my wool coat off my shoulders, letting it join the scarf at our feet.

He removes his coat, throws it to the floor, and quickly adds his charcoal cashmere sweater and undershirt to the growing pile of discarded items. I've slept on his bare chest in the past, but seeing him give himself to me is a sight to behold. He's broad and solid and all muscle. Only his muscles aren't for looks; they serve a purpose.

To protect.

He has a six-pack, but not like a starved model has a six-pack. He's thick at the same time. Standing in front of him while his barreled chest rises and falls with each of his lust-filled breaths leaves me unable to find air myself. The need I feel is one close to desperation.

Leaving me completely covered, he removes the rest of his clothes until he's left in only his black boxer briefs. Reaching out my fingers, I trace over one of his pecs. I can feel the sexual tension coursing under his skin. I step closer until I'm near enough to press my lips to where his heart beats within his chest.

As I pepper his chest with my kisses, he keeps his hands down at his sides, letting me push us forward. My hands flatten as they drag over his chest and down his abdomen until they reach the waistband of his briefs where one of my fingers teases along the edge.

Stepping back, I kick off my shoes and pull off my leggings. Now farther back from him, I can see what my caresses have done to him as he strains against the one article of clothing still covering him.

Pulling my sweater over my head and adding to the ever-growing pile of winter clothes on the floor, I stand before him in just my bra and panties.

Reaching behind me for the clasp on my bra, I look up, and his eyes are on mine. Not on my body but on my face. Telling me this is more to him than just sex. With the clasp undone, I stop before fully exposing myself to him. I need to make sure his feelings are matched.

Closing the gap between us, I rest my hands on his chest, and my head tips back to look up at him. "I love you, Max." His eyes close, and his face softens in relief. "So much," I say, kissing his chest once again.

His hands finally touch me, caressing my back.

"Make love to me, Max."

His rough fingers trail up to my shoulders to my bra straps, where he slips them off my shoulders, and I drop my arms to my sides, letting my bra fall to the ground.

Stepping over the clutter below us, he turns me so the back of my legs touches the mattress, encouraging me to lie back on the bed. I scoot back and lay my head on the mountain of soft downy pillows offering myself to him as he stands above me, drinking me in.

For the briefest of moments, my insecurities about my body sneak into my conscience, but I remember the first time he told me he loved my ass and that he thought my body was a master-piece. The memory of his words gives me the confidence I need as I lift my hips just enough to slip off my panties, hiding nothing from him.

"You are perfect, Emmett. There is simply no other way to describe you."

Lifting up on my elbows, I quirk an eyebrow that says, are you going to leave me here on my own, or are you going to join me? No words are needed. He knows what I'm asking.

He finally slips off his briefs, and his erection springs free when he does. He climbs into the bed but leaves the covers pulled back, not hiding either of us. Instead, baring ourselves to one another body and soul.

Except to call out each other's names, no other words are spoken as we give ourselves to each other. He explores every inch of my body, and by the time the sun sets on the Parisian streets below, I know his by heart.

* * *

Famished, from spending all day making love, we ordered half the room service menu and ate in our hotel robes. Now we're lounging in the large luxurious bathtub. The signature Shangri-La scent surrounds us as the hotel candles flicker their ambient light in the dark room. Vanilla, sandal, musk, and highlights of ginger tea intoxicate us as if our self-induced bliss wasn't enough.

We've talked about our childhoods, first kisses, proms, hangovers, and broken hearts. I've listened to him gush about Nicholas and how proud he is of the young man he's turning into. We've even talked about his ex and how much better they've gotten along since she found love again. As open as we've been, I'm hesitant to ask my next question, but I want to know everything there is to know about him.

"Max, why did you stay away from home for so long? You seem so close to your parents and your brother. I just can't imagine anything keeping you apart."

My question is met with silence. With my back lying against his chest, I can't see the expression on his face to know what kind of emotion my question has evoked. So I keep my head resting on his shoulder and give him the privacy not being able to see his face can give him. But when he still doesn't answer minutes later, I start to change the subject but stop when his arms come out of the water to wrap around my shoulders. He places a soft kiss against my temple before speaking quietly.

"You're right. I am close to my family, and I was away from them for far too long. At first I did go home when I would get leave after deployments, but I was no longer the eighteen-year-old boy I had been when I left. I had seen things. Done things. Things that changed who I was inside. Don't get me wrong, I wasn't ashamed of my time in the military. My time serving my country made me the man I am today."

"I quite like the man you are today, if you don't mind me saying?" I interject as he pauses in thought.

"And I'm glad you do, but I was no longer my mom's son, at least not the one who left Phillipsburg for the Marine Corps. When I would come home to visit, she wanted to wait on me hand and foot and treat me like I was still her little boy, but I had grown into a man. A man who had fought and killed to keep not only myself but also my brothers-in-arms alive. For some reason, it got under my skin to be treated like I always had been. In fact, when I would go home, I tended to get into fights at the local bars and even got kicked out of a few. One night, I overheard my parents talking about how worried they were for me. How they couldn't believe I was behaving this way in my hometown, in the community I grew up in. Emmett, hearing their disappointment sent me into a spiral of shame. I told myself I wouldn't go back to Phillipsburg until I was the kind of man they could be proud of."

"Oh, honey. They were just worried about you. I'm sure they've always been proud of you."

"Well, after that, I stopped going home on leave, and I stayed in California instead. I used Lauryn as an excuse not to go home. When Mom and Dad found out she was pregnant, they did come visit to meet the mother of their grandchild, and then they've come back a couple of times a year since Nick was born."

"But you said it had only been three years since you had been home. That seems like a lot more than three years ago that you stopped going home."

"Well, first I went home when Alex and Malory got married. Come to think of it, most of the times I went home seemed to be for a wedding since I was a groomsman in all of the guys weddings. I was there for Dad's retirement party and then again when my grandmother passed away. I've gone back when there has been a reason to, but I never stayed long, and I never missed the look of concern my mom would have every time I would go out in the evenings. She was so afraid I would tarnish the family name, and it hurt. Mostly, it hurt knowing I caused that kind of concern."

"What about Nick? Did you ever take him back to Phillipsburg?"

"No, and I'm ashamed of that. Alex and his family have been out to LA and stayed with us. They did the whole Disneyland thing, and I played tour guide. So they've met Nick, but I haven't taken him home. I'm not sure why either. After taking you there and spending real time with everyone, I can't wait to take him. I want him to see where I grew up, meet my friends, and spend more time with my parents and Alex's kids. It couldn't be more different than LA, and I think it would be good for him."

"He'll love it so much. And with your new custody schedule, I would imagine it will make things that much easier."

"It will, and I already plan on taking him out for spring break. I don't want to put it off any longer."

"I think that's a great idea."

Feeling the hard part is over, I break from his embrace and turn to face him. Sloshing a bit of the water over the side of the tub.

"Thanks for sharing that with me."

"There isn't really much to share. I was stubborn and stupid and let my pride get in the way. It was selfish and immature." He shrugs. "Thanks to you, I went back, and I'm putting an end to all of that bullshit." He lifts my fingers out of the water and kisses the tip of my forefinger. "Now, let's get out of this tub before we shrivel up. We can plan the rest of the week and get some sleep. We need to get an early start in the morning."

He's not looking at me when he talks, staring at my fingers instead. Embarrassed by his behavior.

"I love you," I say, hoping to get his attention.

"I don't deserve you, but I love you too, baby."

He stands, water trickling off his body. I stare in a trance watching the masterpiece before me. He grabs a towel but doesn't dry himself off. Instead, he unfolds it, holding it open to me. Standing, I step out of the tub, and he wraps the towel around me.

He dries me off, then himself, before covering my body in lotion. The rest of the evening is spent in bed planning our week before making love again.

We fall asleep in each other's arms.

Curtains open with the City of Love surrounding us.

Chapter Twenty-Four

Stopping on the stone steps outside the grand Paris Opera House, I pull one of my gloves off with my teeth and shove it in my pocket before calling Josh. I've learned how to do things with one hand this past week because one of them is always in Max's hand, and I'm not letting go for anything.

Opening the FaceTime app, I call Josh, watching a cloud of my warm breath float on the cold Parisian air while I wait for him to pick up.

"Well, there she is! How's my girl liking France?" Josh's tired face beams up at me from the screen.

"Bonjour!"

"You've already taken up the language. I like it." He yawns.

"I'm so sorry. Did I wake you up?"

"Nah, I have to get up soon anyway, and I haven't talked to you in days. Tell me all about it, Emmy."

"Oh, Josh, this place is amazing. I can't believe it's taken me so long to get here. To leave North America, for that matter. I've been missing out on so much. Thank you for letting us borrow the plane. It's been a dream trip, and it was an incredibly extravagant yet sweet gift."

A toddler runs up the stairs behind us, scaring a group of pigeons, causing them to fly away over my head and me to duck for imaginary cover.

"Ha! Even in Paris, you can't escape your nemesis, le pigeon!"

He's right. I hate them, and they hate me. Max can also attest to this because they seem to be everywhere we go this week.

"Ugh, they are so evil!"

"Only to you. Now, tell me what your favorite part of the trip has been so far?"

"Well, if I'm being honest...I probably shouldn't share with small children around." Max lifts my gloved hand and brings it to his lips. We have seen all the city sights, but we've also spent plenty of time to ourselves in our hotel room, falling deeper and deeper into one another.

Josh's eyes grow large, but his smile says it all. "Now, that's what I like to hear. Speaking of the man of the hour, where is he? You aren't out on the streets alone, are you?"

Tugging on Max's hand, I pull him down next to me, and he rests his chin on my shoulder. "Hey, Josh. How's it going?" he asks, waving into the camera phone.

"I know I don't need to ask, but are things as quiet on your end as they are here?"

"Yep, I've been checking in with the guys daily. There hasn't been a picture in the press or any threats since Emmett left LA for Eastlyn the week of Christmas."

"Good, that's what I like to hear. Take care of my girl, Hopper. She means the world to me."

"I know exactly what you mean. I've got her, I promise."

Max steps out of frame but continues holding my hand

while I go on about our week. Sharing everything with him just as I have since we were kids.

"It's such a romantic city, Josh. I wish I never had to leave. Right now, we're standing out in front of the opera house. Here, take a look, isn't it gorgeous?"

I hold my phone up so he can see the beautiful green-domed building with its grandiose pillars and gold statues. Napoleon commissioned it in 1861. It's magnificent.

"So, where else have you been?"

"We've been everywhere. We were kinda stuck in the Louvre for about five hours, but we made it out eventually."

"What do you mean *kinda* stuck?"

"Well, the first four and a half hours were great, but then we spent thirty minutes trying to find the exit."

"Why didn't you ask for help?"

"We did! But no matter what we did, we just kept passing the same Greek statues over and over. I thought we would never get out of there."

"Max, did you let her navigate?" He yells so Max can hear him. "I should've warned you, never let her navigate!"

Max pops his head back into frame. "I wish I could blame her, but the two of us were a disaster. It was just as much me as it was her." He lands a peck on my cheek before stepping out of frame again.

"See. Be nice. Besides, I'm not that bad." I stick my tongue out at him. "We've also been to the Eiffel Tower during the day and at night. Oh, and Josh, we can see it from our terrace in our room. She watches over us every night when we go to sleep. It's the most magnificent thing I've ever seen. Did I mention how romantic this week has been?"

"You did." He chuckles, and Jace cuddles up next to him and gives me a wave.

I wave back and carry on, unable to contain my excitement.

"Let's see...we've had croissants and macaroons, and they really are better here. We went to a cheesy dinner show at the Moulin Rouge, and we shopped on the Champs-Elysees after going to the Arc de Triomphe earlier today, and now we're gonna go take a break somewhere and have a bite to eat."

I feel something cold land on my bare hand holding up the phone and notice tiny snowflakes beginning to fall around us, and can't help but look to Max, who is smiling back at me because he feels it too. The trip just keeps getting better and better.

"Hello...where'd you go?"

When I hear Josh looking for my attention, I realize I've lowered my hand to gaze at Max. I lift on my tiptoes and press a kiss to the round scar on his cheek before returning my attention to Josh.

"Sorry, it started snowing, and I got a little distracted."

"Emmy, I couldn't be happier that you're distracted and in love. It's all I've ever wanted for you, babe. I'm so sorry we're in this situation, and the three of us will have to sit down and talk about things when you get home. We'll figure this out, Emmy."

"Thank you, Josh. I know what I signed up for, though, and I don't want to let you down."

"I don't want you to give any of that another thought until we're both back in LA, okay? So just enjoy yourself and have an amazing New Year."

I'm glad I have these oversized sunglasses on, and he can't see that his words and the possibility of more with Max has me misty-eyed.

"Talk to you later."

"Have fun, Emmy."

With that, he ends the call, and I put my phone in my pocket.

When I sniffle, Max pulls me into his side because he knows

me well enough by now to know I'm tearing up. My arms wrap around his waist and his arm is around my shoulders when he speaks into my hair. "Listen to Josh. Don't think about it now. We'll figure it all out when we get home. Right now, it's just you and me. Can you just think about here and now, for me?"

He's right. When will we be somewhere so romantic, just the two of us, again in the near future? I would be a fool to waste another second thinking about anything else.

"I can do that. Now, how about a drink."

He turns, so we're facing each other, still holding me in his arms, and kisses me sweetly. "I love you."

"I love you too."

"Good, now that that's settled, let's get you a glass of red wine and me a Kronenbourg 1664."

Chapter Twenty-Five

"Baby, wake up."

As I stretch myself awake, it feels much too early to be getting up. "What time is it?"

"It's early, but babe, we need to get ready to head out."

"What do you mean? It's New Year's Eve. Head out where?"

"I'm sorry, we're gonna have to miss New Year's Eve. I have a car picking us up in fifteen minutes."

It's then I hear the anxiety in his voice, and I spring up to a sitting position. Then pulling the covers up to my chest thinking the worst, I wait for him to tell me who's died, but instead, he hands me his phone.

My body begins to shake even though I'm covered in a fevered sweat as my world begins to crumble, and the bliss I've been living in the past five days vanishes without a trace.

GOLD DIGGER, EMMETT FORD, CHEATS ON JOSH
WEST WITH BODYGUARD!

JOSH WEST CHEATED ON WHILE ON PHONE WITH FIANCÉE!

FIANCÉE CHEATS ON HOLLYWOOD HEARTTHROB

Along with all of the bold proclamations, there are pictures of me Facetiming with Josh on the steps of the Opera House while Max stands to the side holding my hand. There are pictures from every angle, but of course, no pictures of Max also talking to Josh, or Max kissing me on the cheek in front of him. From every angle, it looks like I'm cheating while on the phone with him.

Not behind his back but right in front of him!

I look like an evil, conniving whore, and Max looks like he's cheating with his employer's fiancée. This could ruin him.

"Oh, Max. This is terrible. I'm so sorry."

He stops throwing his clothes in his suitcase, frozen mid-motion. "You're sorry? Why in the world are you sorry?"

"Because this affects your business. Your clients trust you with their lives, and this could destroy that trust."

He sits on the bed next to me. "Baby, it's my job to keep you safe. I'm the one who should be sorry. I was too wrapped in you and what we've had this week, and I let my guard down. This is all on me."

Leaning forward onto my hands and knees, I crawl to him. "This has been the best week of my life. Can't we just stay in here and not venture out anymore? We can order room service and stay a little longer."

"Emmett, as much as I'd love to do exactly that, it's not possible. Besides, I don't think management would be too happy with that decision. The street in front of the hotel is crawling with paps and blocking the entrance.

Throwing my robe on, I sail out of bed. "Are they kicking us out because of the press?"

"No, but paparazzi from all over Europe are waiting for us . So, I've arranged for a car to pick us up around back."

"Shit."

"Yep. That about sums it up."

My phone vibrates, and I jump at it thinking it must be Josh, but it's not. Instead, it's my mother, and I drop the phone as if it's on fire and let it fall to the bed, staring at it until she hangs up. Once the phone stops ringing, the screen is left filled with text messages. Forty-eight messages, to be exact. I think the entire population of Eastlyn has texted me. The only person who hasn't is Josh.

"What have I done?"

"Hey, hey. Don't do that. This isn't your fault."

"The whole world thinks I'm a lying whore. And poor Josh. He looks like a fool who got screwed over by his gold-digging friend. I can't even believe what my family must think of me." I gasp when another person crosses my mind. "Oh, my God, Max! What about Nicholas? He's going to think I'm a monster."

Strong arms engulf me from behind, and I turn, burying my face in his chest, and begin to sob. Sobs of regret for ever agreeing to lie to my family, but if I had never done so, I wouldn't be in Max's arms right now, even if it's under these circumstances.

"Nick is not going to think you're a monster, and we will figure this out. Sibby will work her magic, and we'll make this right. I love you, baby. I got you. No matter what happens."

His words help enough for me to take a deep, cleansing breath. I knew this was the risk, and I took it. Now, I need to suffer the consequences.

Hating to step out of his arms, I do, then take two seconds to gather myself before rushing to the already open closet to grab my clothes.

"Have you already talked to Josh?"

"No, just Sibby. She's already working on things and reaching out to Josh. Luckily, he's out of town and working so he should be out of the spotlight for now."

I empty my drawers and set out a few things to change into before grabbing my phone off the bed and dialing Josh's number.

He doesn't answer, so I text him.

EMMETT

I am so sorry.

JOSH

...

Oh, thank goodness he's replying. Max sets my bag on the bed, and I put the phone in my robe pocket and begin haphazardly shoving everything inside.

I check my phone, and there's no reply from Josh. Then the dancing dots start again, and the knots tightening in my stomach ease up a bit, but then they disappear again without a reply.

I try calling him again, but it rings once, and he sends me to his voicemail.

"Josh won't answer, and he keeps starting to reply to my texts and then stops. He hates me."

"Emmett, give him a minute to digest it all. It's a lot, and I'm sure he's busy and hasn't gotten to finish his text or can't answer. Now, the car is gonna be here in a few minutes, and as much as

I hate to say it, I really need you to change out of that robe and get dressed, baby."

Somehow, I manage to throw myself together while shoving all my toiletries in their case. Then, I do a quick search running around the room like a crazy person. Looking under the bed, in the closet, and in every drawer in the room, making sure we didn't forget anything in our haste. As I check the last bedside table, there is a light knock on the door.

My heart stops, wondering who it could possibly be.

"Don't worry, it's the hotel manager. He's going to take us the back way."

"Oh, okay."

Wow, he really took care of a lot while I was asleep.

"Bonjour. Right this way, please."

Max and I follow an older gentleman, possibly in his late sixties—dressed superbly in his blue suit even at this time of the morning—who has taken our bags and put them on a cart. He leads us to a hidden staff-only elevator in a little alcove in the hallway that I had never even noticed.

Max holds my hand, and his thumb subconsciously moves back and forth over the back of it while we plunge deeper into the belly of the hotel. When the doors open, we exit into a beige concrete hallway where our luggage rack is passed to another hotel employee who heads off ahead of us. Ten feet later, we take a left into the hustle and bustle of the kitchen, where they're preparing for the breakfast rush. We maneuver around the confused yet discreet employees. None of them makes eye contact with us, and it feels like I'm living a scene out of a movie. Finally reaching the back door, the gentleman assisting us steps out into the alleyway for a few moments before returning.

"Sir. Madame. Your bags are in the vehicle, and the street is clear."

"Merci," Max says, shaking his hand that looked a little padded with a very special way of saying thank you for your help.

The driver has the door held open, and we only have to take three steps from the hotel's back door to the waiting car. Max is practically pressed against me as I climb in, trying to shelter me from any prying eyes.

He confirms with the driver that we're headed to the airport, and I check my phone yet again. Still no reply from Josh. I text him to let him know we're on our way to the airport.

Max sits back in his seat, and I can feel the tension radiating from him. "So, this was really last minute, and Sibby was able to make some calls and get us a plane, but because of the last notice, there may not be provisions."

"That's fine. I appreciate everything the two of you did to make this happen. I'm still just so sorry it ended this way. I had a great week."

Neither one of us took the time to put our seat belts on, so he pulls me onto his lap, wrapping his arms around me, and quietly speaks into my ear. "We'll have many more great weeks, baby. We just need to get through what lies ahead. But I promise there are endless great weeks to be had."

"Even with all of this, I'm so glad I met you."

"Me too."

Sinking deeper into him, I rest my head on his shoulder, remembering every touch, every word, every laugh, and every single moment of our time in Paris. Bottling it up in case I need it in the days, weeks, or very possibly months that follow.

About twenty minutes later, the airport is in sight when my phone vibrates, and I see Josh's name light up my screen.

"Oh, Josh. I'm so glad you called. We're just getting to the airport right now. I am so sorry about all of this, Josh. Just tell me what I can do to make it better."

"Not now, Emmett. The pilot has instructions to fly you home. I would call Miles or someone to pick you up."

"Miles? What do you mean?"

"Emmett, go back to Eastlyn. I'll send your things. I won't need you in LA anymore. I spoke to the pilot. You'll fly to New York and then from there to Pendleton. Like I said, you'll need a ride. I'm done. I'll contact the lawyers and deal with the contract. With the holiday, you more than likely won't hear anything from them until the 2nd."

"Josh, talk to me. Please."

"What's there to talk about? You've just made me look like a fool in front of the entire world. I never would have thought you could be so selfish, but I guess I was wrong. Apparently, getting laid was more important than our friendship."

"That's not true, and you know it!"

"Thanks a whole fucking lot."

The line goes dead, but I continue to sit with the phone to my ear in shock at Josh's reaction to the situation. What happened to the man who let us borrow the plane to fly to Paris? The man who was happy I had found love, who encouraged us to spend time together. I don't know who that was on the other end of the line, but it wasn't my best friend.

Moments later, Max takes the phone from my hand. "We're here."

"He's having me sent home to Eastlyn." I stare straight ahead, not believing the words coming out of my mouth. "He's contacting the lawyers, and he'll be sending me my things home from California. I've ruined our friendship."

"Give him time. He just needs to work through this. We all do."

Chapter Twenty-Six

Through the small rectangular window on the plane, I see Amelia and her Mini Cooper waiting for us on the tarmac. I feel relief and shame flood through me in a single moment, if that's even possible. Relief to see my friend. Shame that I have to face all of those I know and love and admit to them that I've been lying.

My first instinct was to call Miles because he's always been the go-to for all the Crew members. He always seems to know what to do, but he'll also keep it real and put you in your place, and I'm not ready for that. Not just yet.

So, I called Amelia. She's the only person outside of Josh's inner circle who knows what's going on, and I know she isn't going to lecture me, at least not yet. We'll get there, I'm sure.

As I step off the plane's stairs, Amelia gets out of her car, bundled up to fight the cold winter breeze biting at us like some sort of punishment. She hurries to the back of the mini to open it up for our bags. I rush to the car and embrace my friend.

"Hey, girl, you hanging in there?"

"Been better."

"It's gonna be okay, especially if we get in the car to talk about it."

She lets go of me and runs back to the warmth of the car. Blinded by my hair when the icy wind blows it into my face, I can barely see Max when I hear his voice in my ear. "Get in the car, baby. I got this."

The warmth of his voice momentarily calms me, but as soon as I take a step toward the car, it vanishes into the frigid air, and I can't tell if I'm shaking from the cold or my nerves. When I crawl into the back seat of the car, Amelia has the heat blasting, and I start to thaw instantly, but the shakes remain.

"Dang, Emmy. He's huge." I look out the front passenger window of her little car where he's standing, and it barely comes up to his waist.

I don't say anything because what is there to say? Yes, he is a big man, but he's also the man I love. I've spent the past week in his arms, experiencing the most romantic moments of my life, and now, I have no idea what's in store.

Will I have to choose between the man I love and my friend? If we do work this out, how do Max and I make it work if I'm in Eastlyn and he's in LA with Nick? Will my family ever look at me the same way? Will Josh and I ever be the same? Will he ever get to live a life where he can be his authentic self? Will I still have a job after this? The entire world thinks I'm a lying, cheating bitch. Not exactly corporate management material.

A wave of cold air fills the car when Max gets in the front passenger seat. The right side of the car leans ever so slightly from his weight.

"Thanks for picking us up, Amelia."

"It's no problem, Max. Glad to do it."

A heavy silence blankets us as Amelia navigates the car off the airport property. But I know my friend, and she has a lot to say. I'm not sure if she's just being nice or maybe she isn't comfortable around Max yet, but it's not like her to be so quiet.

Once she's on I-84, she pulls off her beanie and shakes her red locks free and the Melly I know and love lets loose but not quite how I expected.

"So, Max. What are your intentions with our sweet little Emmy?"

"Excuse me?" he says, looking at our driver with a raised eyebrow.

He finds the humor intended in her question if the smirk on his face is any indication.

Chiming in, I try to help him from the back seat. Leaning as close as I can to the front seat with my seat belt on, I don't hide the annoyance in my voice. "You don't have to answer that."

But Amelia is relentless and pushes her questioning to the next level. "Do you love her?"

"I do. With all my heart."

His honesty and lack of hesitancy take my breath away and have me falling in love with him all over again.

"Good. Because she's about to be put through the wringer, and she's gonna need you."

Her words ring true.

Things are about to go from bad to worse.

What I wouldn't give to be back in our hotel room in Paris right now.

"Emmett, I know you love Max, so I'm not even gonna ask." Max's enormous body moves just enough in his seat to give me a little smile and a look that says he knows I love him too. "I just hope you two know what you've gotten yourself into. The whole world is watching, and Em, I know you love Josh, we all do, but that doesn't mean you should sacrifice yourself. You deserve better than being the fall guy for him."

"It's not that simple."

"It would be if you hadn't signed that stupid contract. I'm still pissed he let you do that, by the way."

"Amelia, you aren't supposed to know about any of this. Please tell me you'll keep it between us. Josh and I will figure this out."

"The three of us will figure this out," Max says, sounding a little put off that he wasn't a part of my equation.

"That's what I like to hear," our driver says, smiling at me in the rearview mirror.

"Hopefully, Josh will actually speak to me about it, and I won't have to work this all out through his lawyers. It's just so confusing. He was one hundred percent supportive of Max and me. The pictures they took conveniently didn't show he and Max talking. And they sure as hell didn't print the part of him telling us how happy he was for us and how glad he was to hear what a romantic trip we were having. He was completely on board, but when he talked to me after the pictures came out, I didn't even recognize the person on the other end of the phone."

"Em, you've always only seen the good in Josh, and as much as we love him, the rest of us know just how selfish he can be. He loves you, and he'll come back around, but he's got to get over feeling sorry for himself first. It is all about him, after all. He'll get to worrying about you eventually, but for a bit, he's only going to see how this is affecting his life. Nobody else is going to register in his mind. You know that, right?"

I sigh, not wanting to acknowledge she's right. But her eyes meet mine in the mirror again, and no words are needed.

Lightening the mood, she changes the subject to Paris. Before I know it, we're taking the exit off the highway and entering our hometown. The town full of everyone I know and love who are thinking the absolute worst of me right now. When we pass the road that leads to my parents' house, my first tear falls, opening the floodgates.

I'm able to keep the tears to myself until Max turns in his seat, clearly about to ask me something, but when he sees my tear-stained face, his eyes soften. "Baby?"

"I'll be okay. Being home just makes it all so real. I've let so many people down. I have no idea how I'm going to face my parents."

"We'll do it together."

"I think I need to do it on my..."

My words stop, and my world begins to spin at the sight of the cars in my driveway. Miles's truck is front and center, and the rented SUV says Josh or maybe someone from his team is here as well.

"Shit," Amelia says under her breath.

Max doesn't say a word and is out of the car before it's in park. When it's just the two of us in the car, Amelia and I connect via the rearview mirror again. "It's gonna be okay, Emmy. Just promise me you're going to put yourself first this time. Promise me?"

Before I can make her any promises, I'm not sure I can keep, my door opens, and the large hand I've been holding openly for the last week reaches out to me. I take it but drop it as soon as we start walking toward the house. Instantly feeling like we're doing something wrong now that we're home.

Now, not only do I have guilt for all the lies I've told, but for not walking hand in hand with Max as we walk into the line of fire.

Amelia walks ahead of us, and before she gets to the front door, it opens with Miles on the other side. She walks past him, and when Max and I reach the threshold, he pulls it open wider, stepping out of our way. No welcome hug. Just a wide berth.

I break out into a cold sweat from his reaction and at the sight of Josh, Jace, and Reeves in my living room. The walls of my own home quickly begin to close in on me.

Josh is pacing the floor, knocking needles off my slowly dying Christmas tree every time he passes it. Jace is sitting on the loveseat next to the fireplace, and Reeves is hanging back by the sliding glass door in the kitchen nook where Max heads after giving me a kiss on my temple.

I shrug my coat off and go to hang it up in the hall closet when Miles finally speaks. "Why don't you give me that, and I'll take your bags to your room for you?"

He takes my bags, and Amelia takes my coat and scarf, hanging them up for me, while Reeves fades into the background in the kitchen.

Feeling like a stranger in my own house, I take a seat on the couch and wait. Wait to see if the man pacing my living room will be the man I heard on the phone before I left France or if it's going to be the person I grew up with who loves me.

Not stopping his back and forth path across my hardwoods, he finally speaks. "This is really fucked up, Emmy."

"I know it is, and I'm so sorry."

"How the fuck could you do this to me?" he yells. His voice growing louder.

Max leaves Reeves in the kitchen to stand behind me. I'm sure this is his way of saying take it down a notch before he has to step in.

Scooting to the edge of the couch, I hope he'll stop moving and look at me. I say I'm sorry once again.

"You're sorry? Is that all you have to say right now?"

He finally stops and looks at me, so I stand to meet his steely glare, reminding myself we're in my house and in this situation because I was trying to help him.

"What else do you want me to say, Josh? Do you think I enjoy the entire world thinking I'm a cheating whore? I can't wait to explain all of this to my family! Oh wait, I don't get to explain because I signed a contract that says I can never tell them the truth! I'm sorry I've embarrassed you, but you'll have everyone around the globe feeling sorry for you and women lining up to comfort you! But, I'll forever be the gold-digging slut who cheated on Josh West. So, yeah, sorry is about all I have to say right now."

"What contract, and what truth?" Miles says from the hallway.

But Josh ignores him and pulls me into his arms. "I'm such a selfish prick. I'm so sorry, Em."

I don't say anything because what is there to say?

I'm sorry.

He's sorry.

And yes, sometimes he can be a selfish prick.

"Would someone like to fill me in on what the hell is going on? What fucking contract?"

Miles is the only one in the room who doesn't know what's going on, and the silence is deafening until Jace's phone rings, and he nearly jumps out of his skin fumbling with his phone. When he finally catches it, he accidentally pushes the speaker button.

"Hey," he says, standing to leave the room, but the person on the other end of the phone cuts him off.

"Why hasn't the money hit my bank account yet, asshole? I flew all the way to fucking Paris to get those shots for you, and I haven't seen a damn dime."

Jace turns crimson red as I watch my best friend's heart break when he realizes the person he trusts with his career and his heart has betrayed him.

Jace reaches to hang up the phone, but Josh grabs it from his hand. "What pictures haven't you been paid for?"

Clearly not noticing a different person's voice speaking, the idiot on the other end of the phone sings like a canary.

"Don't play stupid, Jace, the ones you set up for me to get of

Josh West's slutty little fiancée. I did my part, so now it's time you did yours. Where the fuck is my money?"

"Ron, stop talking. You're on speaker—" Jace yells toward the phone from the other side of the room with a once again pacing Josh, but he cuts him off before he can finish his warning.

"Ron? As in Ron Benson the paparazzo?"

"Who's askin'?"

"This is Josh West, you asshole!"

"Well, shouldn't you be saying thank you then? Jace said this was all your idea. Busting your fiancée would be big news for you. Aren't you signing some new movie deal this week? You'll have all of America feeling sorry for you. I made that happen for you. Now where's my money?"

Josh presses the red button on the phone and throws it down on my coffee table.

"Tell me this is some kind of joke, Jace? Tell me it hasn't been you all along?"

His question is met with silence.

I move to stand next to Josh, but he holds his hand up to stop me. Max takes my hand in his a moment later, standing by my side.

"Why? Why did you do it when you knew what it would do to me?"

"Why, Josh? You really have to ask me why?"

"Of course I do! I have no idea what could have been going through your head to make you do something like this!"

"Of course, you couldn't because all you do is think about yourself! How do you think I felt when after years of hiding our relationship, you take it a step farther and get engaged? Not only am I hidden, but now the world sees the man I love pretending to be in love with someone else. I have to watch her on your arm for the entire fucking world to see when it should be me, Josh! Not her! Me!"

"But you've always known this was how it had to be. You're my manager, you've been involved in my image and have known all these years that this was the way it was, and you still chose to be with me."

Josh tries to calm himself. His fists flex, but he lowers his voice, closing the distance between himself and the man he loves.

"Well, maybe I got tired of being your dirty little secret. Watching the world fall in love with the two of you was too much." The venom in his voice stinging Josh and stopping him in his tracks.

"So, you thought it was okay to scare the shit out of Emmett and threaten her? To smear her name in the press by letting the world think the worst of her? If you were uncomfortable with all of this, why didn't you say something before she signed the contract? If you were pissed at me, why not take it out on me? Why do this to her?"

"What fucking contract?" Miles bellows from behind us.

"Later, Miles," Amelia whispers.

"Answer me! Why do this to her?"

"Because I loved you! I didn't want to hurt you. I thought the threats would scare her off, and she would come back home. I thought she'd be gone, and things would go back to normal, and nobody would ever get hurt. After I paid her ex to break into her house here in fucking Po-Dunk, Oregon, I figured that would be enough. It wasn't supposed to go this far."

"Well, turns out you were wrong mother-fucker," Miles says, charging the room, but Reeves stops him before he can get his hands on Jace. He puts his hands up, taking a step or two back.

"You disgust me," Josh says, barely audible.

Jace's demeanor changes. Reaching out to Josh with tears in his eyes. "Don't you see I did this for you? For us."

"No, I don't see that. But I do see you getting the fuck out of my life." He throws a glance in Reeves's direction, and his bodyguard takes instant action by grabbing Jace by the bicep.

He tries to pull out of Reeves's grasp, but he's no match for him, and when he can't escape, you can see the desperation take hold, and an entirely new and vicious side of him comes pouring out of him as he's dragged from the house.

"Don't do this, Josh! I will fucking destroy you. Do you really think the studio is going to sign you as their new action star when they find out you're a fucking fairy? Think about this because there's no going back."

It's Miles who steps in front of him once Reeves has dragged his fighting body to the front door. "Get the fuck out."

Miles goes to close the door in his face, but Jace pushes on it with his free arm.

"You know I have all the proof I'll ever need. I have videos you have no idea about, pictures. You'll never work again."

Amelia pushes her full weight against the door and shuts him out. We can hear him screaming all the way to the car, and I can only imagine what my neighbors must be thinking.

"I'll be right back," Max says, heading out the front door.

Taking Josh by the hand, I pull him down onto the couch, and he plops down next to me.

"How could he do this?"

"I'm so sorry, Josh."

"I'm finished."

Miles pulls the loveseat over until he's sitting in front of Josh. "Dude, a little fucker like Jace will not bring you down. However, I may take you down if you continue to keep things from me, and more importantly, don't start being yourself around the people who love you the most."

"Like you would have wanted a queer as a best friend?"

"Do you really think I didn't know?"

Both mine and Josh's eyes nearly fall out of our heads. But it's Josh who says what we're both thinking.

"What do you mean you knew?"

"C'mon, man. I've known you your entire life."

"Why didn't you ever say anything?"

"I figured you'd tell me when you were ready."

Amelia squeezes herself into the loveseat next to Miles with a sweet smile adorning her face.

"You knew too?"

"Of course, I knew," she replies, taking his hand in hers. "I also love you like a brother and couldn't care less. All I've ever wanted is for you to be happy."

"Why do you think I was so suspicious of the two of you getting engaged?" Miles says. "I love you and Emmy both, but I had a feeling something was up. I had a very strong hunch that somebody would end up getting hurt in the end. Sure wish I hadn't been right about that."

"You guys know I would never do anything to hurt Emmy. I never meant for any of this to happen."

"Let's talk about what exactly is happening." Miles sits back in the chair, and Amelia settles in next to him with his arm behind her, resting on the back of the loveseat. "Start at the beginning, and let's figure this shit out."

Chapter Twenty-Seven

"Josh. Brother. I know you feel like your life is over, but you're gonna figure this out. More importantly, I think you will be happily surprised how people react should you decide to share who you really are with the world. Either way, you got us, and we love you no matter what."

The energy in my cramped living room is palpable. Josh has just bared his soul to Miles and Amelia and was met with nothing but love. Miles and Amelia sat and listened except for a few expletives whispered in both of our directions when he got to the part about me offering to be his fake fiancée. All the while, Max worked at my kitchen table on his computer with earbuds in to give Josh privacy.

Eventually, Josh's story became mine, and all heads turned to me. I timidly told my best friends how it had gone from an innocent crush to falling head over heels in love with Max while he sat across the room listening intently. He did his best to remain neutral, but I knew he was listening because, try as he might, he couldn't hide the small smiles that snuck out during certain parts of my story.

Our story.

He stopped what he was doing and gave me his full attention when I talked about his hometown. His family. His friends. His son.

I laid it all out to them. My story may not be quite the same as Josh's, but I wanted everyone to know how I felt about Max. How serious our relationship was to me, but that I also had every intention of holding up my end of the bargain for Josh, whatever that may be after the calamity I had made of our situation.

"What do you think you're going to do, Josh?"

"Amelia, I have no idea." Turning in my direction. "Emmy, do you think I could hide out here with you for a while? The thought of going back to LA alone sounds too depressing." Now he looks at Max. "Would I be intruding?"

"Never. You're family. Of course, you can stay here," I say, not giving Max the chance to reply.

"I actually have to head home." Taking his glasses off, Max stands from the table, joining us in the living room. "My son has a lot of questions right now, and I would rather be there to discuss them with him in person."

My heart shatters into a million pieces when I think about what this could be doing to Nicholas. He worships his father, and now to the entire world, he's the bad guy. The man who betrayed one of his favorite action heroes.

There's no stopping the tears once they begin to fall, but Max crosses the room and takes a seat next to me on the couch, pulling me into his arms.

"Shh...it'll be okay."

"Max, I am so sorry." I sob into his chest.

"You don't have anything to be sorry about, Emmett. I knew the risk, and I took it. And you know what? I'd take it again."

Pulling away from him, I scoot to the edge of the couch, my head in my hands, talking to the ground.

"Max, Nick worships you. Because of me, he thinks you're cheating on one of his heroes. How could I have let you risk Nick? He'll never trust me. If we are ever able to be together and make a real go of this, he'll hate me."

"Em..."

"No, I don't want you to try to tell me this will be okay. This is so unfair to him. He's just a kid and doesn't deserve the undue attention he's now going to get because of the poor decision-making of three adults. What were we thinking?"

"Girl, you were thinking you were in love, and you wanted to be together," Miles says, taking my hand in his. I finally lift my gaze from the floor. "There's no way I could hide my feelings for Mason. Don't beat yourself up."

Max rubs my back but remains quiet while Josh sits dumbstruck on the other side of me. Miles is still holding my hand and doing what he does best. Taking care of everyone in the room, but even he can't say the right thing when it comes to Nick.

"Man, I'm really sorry this is affecting your kid. I wish I could offer some great advice, but it's gonna be tough. I wish you luck, I really do. Just know that while you're home taking care of business, we'll all be here with Emmett and Josh, and we'll make sure they're both okay. I know you've got my number. Don't be afraid to use it."

"Thanks, Miles. I appreciate it."

Amelia wiggles out from the tiny section of the chair she was squeezed into and stands up, grabbing my free hand and pulling me up with her. She opens her arms, and I lean down and accept her hug.

"Emmy, it's gonna be hard, but it's gonna be okay."

She pulls back, wiping some stray tears from my face, and then, after wiping her hand off on her jeans, she holds it out to Max, and he stands, accepting it.

"Welcome to the family. I hope things will be okay for your son, and I can't wait for you to bring him here so we can meet him one day. But I think it's time we give you guys some space to decompress. I mean you came home from Paris and walked into all of this. You must be exhausted."

"Thanks, I can't wait to bring him here too. I think he'd love it."

Amelia says goodbye to Josh, and Miles follows suit. Finally, the front door clicks closed, and it's just the three of us left in the house.

Drowning in the silence, I've never felt so awkward around either one of these two men. But, really, what is there to say at this point? We've said it all, and now we just have to figure out what to do with Jace, how Max is going to explain this to his son, and Josh has to decide if he's going to blow up his entire life. So, really. What is there to talk about?

Max cleans up his workspace on the kitchen table and lets out a heavy sigh before turning around.

"Babe, I have to get to the airport so I can catch my flight to Portland and my connection to LAX. I hate to ask you this, but I don't think Eastlyn has joined the world of ride-sharing yet, and I'm going to need a ride."

"Of course…"

Josh cuts me off before I can get my sentence out and steps in front of Max.

"Listen, I really don't know what to say except I'm sorry, Max. I helped you plan the trip to France with Jace, and he did what he did, and now here we are in this mess. And your little boy is caught up in the middle of it. I hope you know if I could make it all go away, I would."

Max doesn't break his eye connection with Josh for three full heartbeats before saying, "I know, Josh. I know."

The man who has my heart steps around my fake fiancé,

grabbing his bags. The tension hangs over us like a dark cloud about to open up and pour down on us.

As much as I hate for Max to leave, I follow him out of the house to avoid anything being said that one of us might regret. We both know that Josh could fix this if he wanted to, but I get it's not a simple ask. It would be a life-changing decision for him to do what needs to be done to right the situation.

The ride to the airport is quiet, but he holds my hand the entire way there, and I'm so glad I traded in my 5-speed for an automatic last year. Pulling up to the tiny regional airport terminal, I already miss him. And he's still in the car. After spending every moment with him over the last week, it's hard to imagine going through these next few days without him.

"Don't get out, it's cold."

"Oh, okay."

I know I sound put out, but he's really going to leave without me giving him a kiss outside the car?

"Emmett, none of that. It's freezing out there, and I would rather kiss you goodbye inside the car."

I slip off my seat belt so I can turn and face him. "I miss you already."

"Me too, baby. But I want you to know something. And I need to be sure you're listening. Are you listening?"

"Yes, Dad. I'm listening."

"Smart-ass."

He kisses the back of my hand.

"Things are about to be really hard. You're gonna feel like the world is coming down all around you. But I need you to know that no matter how hard it gets, no matter how many tabloids try to tear us apart, I will never wish you hadn't signed that contract. Never. It brought you to me, and I will always be grateful for that. So, when you're feeling low, I want you to remember that. Can you do that for me?"

I nod my head in reply.

"If you feel tempted to cry yourself to sleep, I want you to remember making love in front of the Eiffel Tower. Baths by candlelight. Holding hands as we strolled through magnificent ancient churches. Getting lost in the Louvre and chased by pigeons. And most importantly, remember I love you. We will get through this. We will figure this out."

"I love you, Max."

"I love you too."

He takes my face in his hands, kissing me long and hard. Then, pulling back, he rests his forehead against mine, and our heavy breaths mingle together for a few seconds before he gets out of the car, grabs his bag from the back, and disappears inside with a wave.

Chapter Twenty-Eight

"So, the truth of the matter is, Emmett Ford is my best friend. She has been since we were kids. In the sixth grade, we made each other one of those silly promises kids make. We vowed that if neither of us were married when we turned thirty, we would get married. Well, the thirty-year mark came and went for both of us, and no mention of the vow was made. Then one day, the two of us were talking about some issues I was having with my personal life. Issues I knew were sure to soon be affecting my work life, and she offered to help. Reminding me about our childhood promise. I should have said no."

He finds me off camera and speaks directly to me.

"Because I was too afraid to be my true authentic self, the person who I loved went to extremes and hurt my best friend, who is currently being torn apart in the press. She's fallen in love and had to hide that love. This should have been the happiest time of her life, but instead, the two of them had to sneak around because of me. Because of my career. After a lifetime of hiding who I was and who I love, I know how it feels, and I expected them to do the same for me. How could I ask that of them? Because my career was more important than their happiness?"

I mouth, I love you, through my tears, and Josh directs his attention back to Candy after giving me a barely noticeable smile. Max takes my hand in his, and my nerves settle, his presence grounding me. While my other hand is fisted over my heart as I watch my best friend tell his truth to the world.

"Listen, I don't need more money or fame or accolades, but I do deserve to be happy and for the first time in my life, true to myself. I may lose job opportunities, and that's a shame, but I've finally come to the conclusion that it's okay. I'd rather lose work than those who mean the most to me. And Emmett. Well, she's the best person I know, and I won't let the press continue to vilify her."

Max squeezes my hand because we know what's coming. We've all been together these past few days, and his journey feels like our journey.

The day after I got back to Eastlyn, I needed to get out of the house. So Reeves and I went to the grocery store since Max was in LA with Nicholas and putting out fires. My trip to the store was a disaster. One simple trip to the grocery store equated to glares from my neighbors, whispers as I passed by, and people I've known all my life pretending they didn't see me so they wouldn't have to talk to me.

I came back to the house in tears. Utterly devastated.

My parents had already expressed their disappointment, and my boss had called and politely asked me to take a leave of absence. My life was falling apart, and Josh couldn't help but blame himself.

After my trip to the store, I locked myself away in my room for an hour or so. When I finally gathered myself enough to join Josh and Reeves at my kitchen table, Josh had already called

Sibby. He told her to make the arrangements with Candy and Wake Up America.

Now, here we are back in Josh's LA living room, standing behind the lights and cameras of America's number one morning show.

Today, they've brought the show to him. They think they've got the exclusive about my cheating. They have no idea their exclusive is going to be one of the most life-changing moments in Josh's life.

He wanted to be sure that Max and Nicholas were here with me as well. He wanted Nicholas to hear this before the rest of the world. When I told Josh about the things the kids were saying to him at school it broke his heart.

Candy has always been kind to him over the years, so Josh went to her first with the exclusive. Of course, she jumped at the chance. But when Josh West asks for a one-on-one in his very own living room, any journalist in the entertainment business will jump at the chance.

"So, Josh, what is it you want to share with us today?"

"Well, Candy, my best friend reminded me about our childhood agreement because someone had been threatening to out me to the world. And she thought if she followed through on our promise and the world thought I was engaged, those threats would stop. And you know what? They did."

"Well, that's good, right?"

"It would be, except as long as I was in the closet, the fear of those threats never really went away. It was a momentary fix. As long as I was too afraid to admit to the world that I was a gay man, I would always be living in fear of being found out. I had gotten used to living in fear, but it was different when it was Emmett who was having to deal with that fear, when it was her safety in jeopardy. Now she's been demonized because the world things she cheated on me when that couldn't be further from the truth, I finally realized the lies had to stop."

"How does it feel?"

Josh exhales, smiling. "You know, it feels good. But only because I have the support of my friends and family. I wouldn't be anything without them."

"And you mentioned that you had someone in your life. Do you still?"

Josh looks down at the ground and doesn't answer for a few seconds. After everything he's just shared, losing someone he loved seems to still be the most challenging part of all.

"I did. But unfortunately, because of all of this, it has come to an end."

"I'm sorry to hear that."

"Thank you."

"So, what comes next for you, Josh?"

"That's a good question, Candy. I'm not sure. I hope to continue working on all the projects I already had on the calendar, but if not, I have other things I've always wanted to do, and maybe I'll find a new path."

"Well, thank you for trusting me and Wake Up America with your truth, Josh. We wish you nothing but success in your future, and I have a feeling we'll be seeing a lot more of you on the silver screen."

"Thanks, Candy. I sure hope so."

"Thank you to Josh West for joining us this morning, and we'll be right back after these messages."

"And that's a wrap," a man to my right says.

The thunk of the big LED lights turning off next to me makes me jump out of my skin. Besides Max's hand in mine, I had been oblivious to everything but Josh.

"Hey, you okay?"

Max pulls me into him, so my back is against his front, and

then he wraps his arms around me and kisses me on the top of my head.

"I'm just so proud of him."

"I know you are, babe."

"Miss Ford?" Nicholas asks shyly.

"Yes, Mr. Hopper?"

His adorable little head tilts to the side, and with a puzzled look on his face, he says, "You love my dad?"

Because I'm leaning against his chest, I feel his dad stop breathing for a beat, but it's the most straightforward question I've ever been asked.

"I do. I love your dad a whole lot."

"That's cool."

Max kisses the top of my head. "It sure is."

Epilogue

Max

There's a sweetness in the refreshing inhale of the summer pines that clears my head and feeds my soul. It's the scent of home.

I had no idea how much I had missed it until the first twinge of home hit me when she walked into my life. Emmett Ford made me want more out of my life, to be a better man, to make sure those most important to me knew I loved them, and to right what were wrongs in my life.

But watching the two loves of my life lying on their backs in the middle of my dad's acreage counting fireflies? Now that feeds my soul. More than anything, it feels like home.

As West Coasters, neither of them had ever seen a Firefly before. As an East Coaster, I never really gave them a second thought. These days, I think if I could catch every single lightning bug in Phillipsburg for them, I would do just that.

I would give them the world if it were possible. Because that's what they are to me. My world.

However, the two who make up my world need to call it a night. So, I meet them out in the grass.

"Hey, you two, we have to get up early to get to the airport. So it's time we go in."

"Aw, come on, Dad. Just a little longer?" Nick half-heartedly pleads through a yawn.

"Sorry, buddy, but Grandma and Grandpa want to say good night before you hit the hay."

"He's right. We do have to get up pretty early. We should probably head in and say good night."

They've known each other for about eight months now, and they are two peas in a pod. She never tries to be his mom, and he has never acted like she was trying to move in and steal me away from her. In fact, he wants to include her in everything we do. It's me who has to make sure we get time to ourselves, just father and son. If anything, I'm the one getting replaced.

Emmett holds her hand up so I can pull her to her feet. Once she's up, she plants a peck on my lips, and just as they have since the first time they touched mine, my heart races. Against my lips, she whispers, "I'm with him. I wish we could stay just a little bit longer."

Spinning around, she offers her hand to Nick, so all three of us are standing amongst the fireflies.

"Dad, this was the best summer vacation ever! Can we come back every year?"

I pull him into me and squeeze him tight. "I'd love that, little man. I think Grandma and Grandpa would like it too."

"Can Emmett come with us again next summer?"

Her eyes grow big, surprised by his question.

"Buddy, if we're lucky, Emmett will be here every summer for the rest of our summers."

"Cool," is his simple reply.

With my arm around my sweet eleven-year-old boy, I lock

my gaze on hers. It may be dark, but I can see the happy pools of tears glistening in her eyes, and there's no time like the present.

"So, Emmett, what do you think? Got any summer plans in the coming years?"

I release Nick, stepping closer to take her face in my hands, using my thumbs to wipe away her tears. She holds on to my wrists and lets my question sink in, and I can feel her smile against my hands once she's sure she understands what I've asked.

Pulling one of my hands from her face, she looks up at me through her lashes, leaving me breathless as she places a gentle kiss on the middle of my palm before placing it over her heart when she finally replies.

"As a matter of fact, I believe I'm booked every summer for the rest of my summers."

Bottle It Up Playlist

Beautiful People ∼ Ed Sheeran (feat. Khalid)
Superposition ∼ Young the Giant
I See You ∼ MISSIO
The Long Way ∼ Brett Eldredge
Break Up in a Small Town ∼ Sam Hunt
Look What God Gave her ∼ Thomas Rhett
Speakers ∼ Sam Hunt
Love Lies ∼ Khalid & Normani
Bottle It Up ∼ Sam Hunt
Saturday Night ∼ San Hunt
So Right ∼ Eric Dodd
Hostage ∼ Billie Ellish
Obsession ∼ Vice (feat. Jon Bellion)
Lost My Mind ∼ FINNEAS
Beyond ∼ Leon Bridges
All To Myself ∼ Dan + Shay
Love Me Less ∼ Max & Quinn XCII
Stay Bullets ∼ Joshua Speers
Belong ∼ X Ambassadors
Lauryn Hill ∼ Can't Take My Eyes Off of You

What To Read Next

Disregarded Heart

A Grumpy / Sunshine, single dad contemporary romance.

The Between the Pines Series

Meet *The Crew* from Eastlyn in this series of standalone contemporary romance novels about found family.

Raised On It

Bottle It Up

Want to read Reece and Rachel's story? Sign-up for my newsletter and get their novella for FREE! Click here for your copy of We Are Tonight!

Blackbird

Standalone second chance contemporary romance.

The Gorgeous Duet

A steamy, suspenseful romance about breaking the rules and following your heart.

Gorgeous: Book One

Gorgeous: Book Two

The You & Me Series

Read this three-book series of sweet and sexy standalone novels filled with love, loss, secrets, and sass.

<u>You & Me: Part One</u>

<u>You & Me: Part Two</u>

<u>More</u>

<u>Something Just Like This</u>

About the Author

Lisa Shelby is an international bestselling contemporary romance author, a self-proclaimed love geek and cake-pop addict. Born and raised in the Pacific Northwest, this is still where Lisa calls home with her husband and their dogs. When she isn't writing her next happily ever after, you can find Lisa with her husband traveling, listening to live music, and impatiently waiting for her next FaceTime call with her son, who is currently deployed with the United States Marine Corps.

Join Lisa's Reader Group: Lisa's Love Geeks
Newsletter Sign-up